# THE PROBABILITY OF MIRACLES

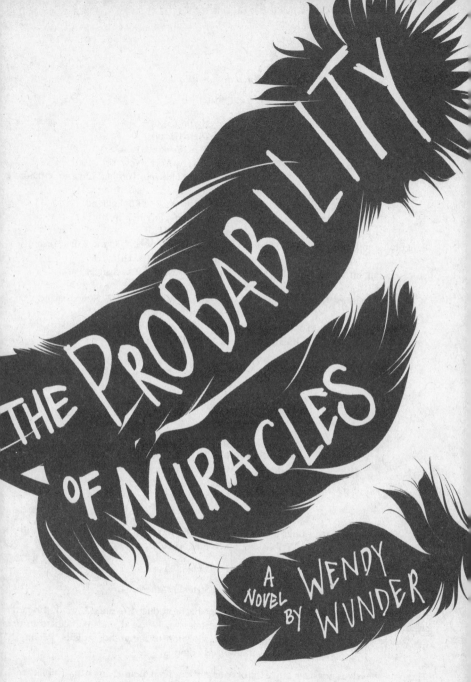

# THE PROBABILITY OF MIRACLES

### A NOVEL BY WENDY WUNDER

razOr
bill

An Imprint of Penguin Group (USA) Inc.

*The Probability of Miracles*

RAZORBILL

Published by the Penguin Group
Penguin Young Readers Group
345 Hudson Street, New York, New York 10014, U.S.A.
Penguin Group (USA) Inc., 375 Hudson Street, New York, New York 10014, U.S.A.
Penguin Group (Canada), 90 Eglinton Avenue East, Suite 700, Toronto, Ontario, Canada
M4P 2Y3 (a division of Pearson Penguin Canada Inc.)
Penguin Books Ltd, 80 Strand, London WC2R 0RL, England
Penguin Ireland, 25 St Stephen's Green, Dublin 2, Ireland
(a division of Penguin Books Ltd)
Penguin Group (Australia), 250 Camberwell Road, Camberwell, Victoria 3124, Australia
(a division of Pearson Australia Group Pty Ltd)
Penguin Books India Pvt Ltd, 11 Community Centre, Panchsheel Park,
New Delhi – 110 017, India
Penguin Group (NZ), 67 Apollo Drive, Rosedale, Auckland 0632, New Zealand
(a division of Pearson New Zealand Ltd)
Penguin Books (South Africa) (Pty) Ltd, 24 Sturdee Avenue, Rosebank,
Johannesburg 2196, South Africa

Penguin Books Ltd, Registered Offices: 80 Strand, London WC2R 0RL, England

10 9 8 7 6 5 4 3 2 1

Copyright © 2011 Alloy Entertainment

**alloyentertainment**

Produced by Alloy Entertainment
151 West 26th Street
New York, NY 10001
Design by Liz Dresner

First published as a hardcover by Razorbill 2011
Published in this edition 2012

ISBN 978-1-59514-480-5

Printed in the United States of America

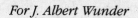

*For J. Albert Wunder*

*There are two ways to live your life:*
*One is as though nothing is a miracle.*
*The other is as though everything is a miracle.*

—ALBERT EINSTEIN

# ONE

WHEN CAMPBELL'S FATHER DIED, HE LEFT HER $1,262.56—AS MUCH AS he'd been able to sock away during his twenty-year gig as a fire dancer for the "Spirit of Aloha" show at Disney's Polynesian Hotel. *Coincidentally*, that was exactly how much her fat uncle Gus was asking for his 1998 Volkswagen Beetle in Vapor, the only color worth having if you wanted to have a VW Beetle. Cam had been coveting it since she was six, and it was worth every penny. It blended into the mist like an invisible car, and when she drove it, she felt invisible, invincible, and alone.

She hoped this was what it would feel like in heaven.

Not that she believed in heaven, or a god (especially a male god), or Adam and Eve, like half of the morons who lived in Florida. She believed in evolution: Fish got feet, frogs got lungs, lizards got fur, and the monkeys needed to walk upright to travel across the savannah. End of story.

She didn't believe in the Immaculate Conception, either, but it could get you into a buttload of trouble if you admitted to anyone that you thought the Virgin Mary probably just got herself knocked up like 20 percent of the teenage girls in Florida. That was an idea you kept to yourself.

Because other people needed their miracles. Other people believed in magic. Magic was for the people who could afford the seven-day Park Hopper and the eight-night stay at the Grand Floridian. Magic, Cam knew from a lifetime of working for the Mouse, was a privilege and not a right.

She inhaled the car's plumeria-oil air freshener. It was a powerful Hawaiian aphrodisiac, but since no one ever drove with her, it had only served to make her fall deeper in love with her automobile. Who was male. She called him Cumulus.

Right now Cumulus was parked on the Zebra level of the Children's Hospital parking structure. Cam typically parked on the Koala level; she preferred the eucalyptus tree mural and the soft, muted gray tones to the stark black-and-white stripes on Zebra. But when she arrived two hours ago, there were no spots available.

If she had been perceptive enough, she would have taken this for a sign. This appointment would not go well. They'd come to the point where things would be black and white. The good ol' gray times were over.

A family of four disembarked from the parking elevator.

The mother tried to hold the hand of a healthy four-year-old as he skipped wildly and gawkily in his Spider-Man sneakers with blinking red lights on the side. A sick, bald-headed two-year-old in a pink dress slept on the shoulder of her father, who walked in a daze toward the family's SUV, probably wondering how this had possibly become his life.

Cam knew the feeling. She needed to do *something*—binge and purge, get drunk, smoke a cigarette, *something*—to get rid of this feeling. Her hands shook as she opened the glove compartment and rustled around to see if her mom had hidden any cigarettes in there. Her fingers felt the sharp corner of something.

*What's this?* She pulled the tiny square of notebook paper out of the glove box. It crackled as she unfolded it. The handwriting didn't seem like hers at first. The pencil had pressed these letters forcefully into the paper. The *o*'s were round and full and the consonants stood proud and upright as if the writer knew she had all the time in the world. (In the past few months, Cam's handwriting had become the faint and falling-down mess of an old woman's.)

FLAMINGO LIST
* *Lose my virginity at a keg party.*
* *Have my heart broken by an asshole.*
* *Wallow in misery, mope, pout, and sleep through*

*Saturday.*

* *Have an awkward moment with my best friend's boyfriend.*
* *Get fired from a summer job.*
* *Go cow-tipping.*
* *Kill my little sister's dreams.*
* *Dabble in some innocent stalking behavior.*
* *Drink beer.*
* *Stay out all night.*
* *Experiment with petty shoplifting.*

Cam stared at the sheet of notebook paper. She hadn't seen the list in almost a year, since she wrote it last summer from the top bunk in cabin 12 of Shady Hill Empowerment Camp for Girls. The camp brochure had promised to "help girls access their inner strength and help wallflowers blossom into the life of the party!" which made Cam shudder at first. But she had wanted to spend time with her best friend, Lily, outside a hospital and it was better than becoming counselors at "sick camp," where the sea of bald heads, the meds cart making its rounds with the pill bottles clicking together, and the occasional pity visit from a popular celebrity were constant, depressing reminders of their condition. At Shady Hill they were just regular campers—the Flamingos. Each cabin had to choose a bird, and they decided to choose one that you'd least likely find in the woods. One that would not blend in with its surroundings. Like them.

Cam closed her eyes and leaned her head against Cumulus's headrest. She could practically hear Lily's voice thinking out loud from her adjacent top bunk in cabin 12:

". . . Then you put the list away and stop thinking about it, and slowly . . . eventually, the simple act of writing things down will bring them about."

Over the summer, Lily had become obsessed with making fun of the self-help books she found in the self-esteem section of the camp "library." While the other girls were sneaking their way through the yellowing pages of *After-School Action* and *Graduating to Passion* that someone's cousin had hidden beneath one of the library's floorboards, Lily read about "affirmations." They'd spent one afternoon in front of the cabin's cracked and patinaed bathroom mirror jokingly informing their reflections that they were beautiful and powerful and deserving. Lily read about "visualizations," and they giggled as they closed their eyes and imagined a rainbow of light purifying their diseased organs. Then it was this *list*.

"Lil," Cam had said, but Lily was on a roll, twisting a strand of the green part of her hair around her finger as she summarized out loud.

"You can't type it or text it. It has to be handwritten on paper, old-school like. And you can't show it to anyone else, or it won't come true."

"Come on, Lily—you don't believe in that, do you? Write it, and it will happen?"

"Of course not. But we should do it. Just for laughs. Here," she said, and she threw Cam the oversize three-foot-long orange pencil she bought at the Davis Caverns gift shop on the last all-camp field trip. "Get writing. A list of everything you want to do before you die."

Cam doodled in the top margin of her notebook. "What should we call it?" she asked Lily, who was already scribbling furiously. "'Bucket list' is so grandpa."

"What's another phrase like 'kick the bucket'? 'Pushing up daisies'? We'll call it the Daisy List," Lily said without looking up.

"No way," said Cam.

"I don't know, Campbell," sighed Lily. "Just call it the Flamingo List then."

"Isn't that sort of irrelev—"

"Just write it."

Cam sighed, wrote *Flamingo List* in big block letters, and then thought about what to include. It should be realistic, she decided. What she really missed since becoming sick was normalcy. That's why she came to Shady Hill instead of cancer camp, even though the cabins smelled like mildew. Maybe *because* they smelled like mildew. Cam wanted a life that was mildewed. Metaphorically speaking. So she began making a list of all the regular stuff she might miss out on if she didn't make it through her teens. Like *Lose my virginity at a keg party*, she wrote. Or *Wallow in misery, mope, pout, and sleep through Saturday* . . .

"What do you think it's going to be like?" Lily interrupted. She had finished her list and sat tentatively on her bunk, chewing the end of her pen.

"What is *what* going to be like, Lily?" Cam asked. Lily could jump right into the middle of a conversation, forgetting that Cam did not necessarily inhabit her brain to experience the beginning of it. "Senior year? The Winter Olympics? The prom? Sex? Tonight's dinner?"

"Death," Lily answered.

"Death." Cam paused. "Well, I guess there'll be the tunnel and the white light and the looking down at your own body. . . ."

"I didn't think you believed in an afterlife," Lily said.

"I don't," Cam answered. "The so-called 'near-death experience' is a neurological event. A big dream set off by massive amounts of hormones released by the pituitary gland. It's all caused by dimethyltryptamine. Not God."

"Oh," said Lily, disappointed. She looked out the window. "Well, what do you think it'll be like?"

"I think it's going to be dark at first. There has to be darkness when your body shuts down. Then a bright rainbow bridge will arch through the blackness, and stars will blink on around it, lighting your path to the Spirit World."

Cam smirked. "Spirit World? Wait, let me consult my dreamcatcher. . . ."

"Heaven," Lily said. "I believe there's a heaven."

Cam opened her eyes, staring out at the bleak underground parking lot. *Maybe it's time I start crossing some of these off,* she thought, running her eyes down the list again. Since the last item seemed to be the only quest fully within her power right now, she would start with that one first.

She called Lily. "What should I steal, Chemosabe?"

"What?" Lily's voice was raspy and slow, as if she had just woken up.

"It's on the list."

"What list?" Cam could hear sheets rustling and the bed squeaking as Lily pulled herself into an upright position.

"Remember that list from summer camp?"

"Why is shoplifting on your Flamingo List?" Lily asked, exasperated. "You're not supposed to force it, anyway, Campbell. You're just supposed to let things happen."

"I'm feeling the need to hurry things along a bit," Cam said. She let her forehead fall to the steering wheel and rolled her head along the upper arc of it.

"Get some Burt's Bees lip balm, then. I just ran out," Lily said, conceding. Cam could practically see her squinting as she inspected her dry lips in the mirror.

"And what else?" Cam asked.

"A plastic flamingo from the dollar store," Lily threw out. "Like one of those lawn ornament things."

"That will be a challenge."

Cam lifted her head from the steering wheel and patted her car.

"To Whole Foods, Cumulus," she said, and they were off.

# TWO

CAM LOVED THE SMELL OF WHOLE FOODS: A BLEND OF SANDALWOOD, patchouli, lavender, dirt, garlic, and B.O. Whole Foods was one of the few places in Florida where Cam did not appear suspect in her tight black hoodie and the torn-to-shreds, faded black skinny jeans that she could wear only because the big C had wasted her half-Samoan body to a size zero.

Whole Foods embraced people like her. Oddballs with a touch of the native to them. This was where people tried to get in touch with the native. The authentic. And where they pretended to be more tolerant. So Cam sniffed an aluminum-free deodorant stick while she stuck some Burt's Bees lip balm into her green canvas biker bag shellacked with a collage of ripped bumper stickers. The top one read, IMAGINE . . . and the rest bore such slogans as A FREE TIBET, MARRIAGE FOR ALL, NO HUMAN BEING IS ILLEGAL, PEACE IN THE MIDDLE EAST, THE

GOLDEN RULE, HEALTH CARE IS A HUMAN RIGHT, and WHERE'S MY VOTE? (in solidarity with the Iranian people who had had their election stolen by an evil dictator).

She was the only person in Osceola County, Florida, who cared about things like stolen elections, freedom, human rights. . . . The rest were too busy procreating, which started early down here. Three couples had gotten engaged at her senior prom.

Cam hadn't gone to senior prom because they probably had rules about dating your car, but if she'd been there, she would have wished the happy couples *pomaika'i*, "good luck" in Hawaiian. They would need good luck. A miracle, really. Without a miracle, each of the couples would end up divorced and trying to raise three kids on twelve dollars an hour, increasing the population of trailer-park-livin', broke-down-car-drivin', dollar-store-shoppin', processed-food-eatin' diabetics that populated the happy Sunshine State.

But maybe it would work out for them. Cam hoped so. Maybe they were different.

She stuck some calendula root into her sweatshirt pocket. She didn't even know what it was, but she loved the sound of it, *cal-en-du-la root*. She'd swallow some on the way out the door.

"Excuse me?" chirped a voice behind her.

Cam jumped. Was she busted already?

She turned to find the typical Whole Foods shopper: fifty, gray hair tied back in a loose bun, blue eyes, no makeup, baggy pants, Clarks, organic cotton shopping bag. More and more ex–college professors and social workers were making their way to these parts because this was all they could afford in retirement.

"Yes?" said Cam, fiddling with the bottle of calendula root in her pocket.

"Who does your hair?"

"Um. My hair?"

"Yes, it's such a great cut."

Cam's thick black hair was short. She buzzed it with her dad's old electric clippers on the one-inch setting. "I do it myself," she said.

"Well, it really suits you. You have such a beautiful face," Typical Whole Foods Shopper said as she put some fiber capsules in the front basket of her cart.

"Thank you," said Cam, and she waited for the lady to turn the corner before sticking a tiny box of chlorine-free, all-natural tampons into the cuff of her jeans.

She'd heard that before. "Such a pretty face." God, she hated that. Pre-C, that was code for, "What a shame. She's so fat." Now it was code for, "What a waste. Such a pretty lesbian."

It *killed* Cam's mother that she wouldn't let her hair grow back after the chemo. Her mom thought long hair was powerful. Plus, without long hair, Cam would never get to dance in "Aloha." Without long hair, she was relegated to the kitchen in the back of the hotel, where she spent hours as a prep cook, carving out pineapple boats for the Polynesian rice.

"There's always Perry," Cam would say to her mom. "She could dance with you someday."

"Agh!" Cam's mom would throw up her hands in disgust. As a hula dancer (who was really an Italian-American woman from New Jersey), her hands were very expressive. Alicia had met Cam's dad in New York when they were in their twenties, dancing in clubs and the occasional Broadway chorus. She took Polynesian dance class just to spend more time with him and then eventually made a career out of it.

Perry, Cam's eleven-year-old half sister, could never dance in "Aloha." She was the result of a post-divorce one-night stand their mom had had with a cast member from "Norway" in Epcot. Perry had white-blonde hair and moved with heavy steps, like a Viking.

"Perry is a lot of things," her mom would say, "but she is no dancer."

Cam's mom wanted her to dance not simply because she wanted a legacy but more because the dance had healing powers. At least for the spirit. And Cam did dance—it was in her blood—but she did it alone, at home, in front of her Spikork mirror from IKEA.

TYLER, A WHOLE FOODS TEAM MEMBER scanned the bar code on the breath mints she'd decided to pay for.

"You're a cashier," Cam mumbled, staring at the green name tag with the cheap white letters.

"What?"

"You can see through their bullshit, right? You're not a team member. They don't really care about you as a person."

"Okay. Whatever."

"Disney was the first to use that trick. They call their employees 'cast members' so the poor guy twisting balloon animals thinks he's a star at Disney."

TYLER just grunted.

"If you have to wear a name tag, you're an employee," she went on.

"I know you took the lip stuff," he said, handing the breath mints to Cam. He had strong, knuckly fingers, messy black hair, and brown eyes with one adorable golden fleck in the left one.

"But you don't know about the calendula root. Or the tampons," she said. Or the natural sea sponge she'd stuck in her bra. "Have a nice day."

And as she slowly made her way to the door, she imagined a Rolf moment from *The Sound of Music*—the one where Rolf finds the whole family behind the tombstone in the abbey and hesitates, deciding whether or not he loves Liesl, before blowing that pansy-ass Nazi whistle. Did TYLER,

A WHOLE FOODS TEAM MEMBER, love her, or would he blow the whistle?

He loved her.

She was free, walking across the Alps of the parking lot to the neutral, loving Switzerland of her car. She let out a sigh and wished for a second that she were in the Alps. Living in Florida was like living on the sun. She could actually see the gaseous heat rising from the asphalt.

Cam arranged her Whole Foods booty into a still life on the dashboard and sent a photo of it to Lily. She crossed *Experiment with petty shoplifting* off of her Flamingo List and stuck it back in the glove box. Then her phone rang with the Lily ringtone, "I Believe in Miracles," by the Ramones. She'd picked it because she suspected that perhaps Lily did believe in miracles. In a small, somewhat sarcastic kind of way.

"Good job, Cueball, I didn't think you had it in you," she said when Cam picked up.

"What's that supposed to mean?"

"Nothing. You know how you are."

"How am I?" Cam asked, opening the little pot of Burt's Bees and sliding the goop across her pursed lips.

"You know, that thing where you're brutally honest and truthful and always right even when you're sick and tired of always being right because you know it makes you seem obnoxious. I thought that would get in your way."

"I heard some bad news today, Lil."

"We've heard bad news before."

Cam was silent. She unstuck the suction cup of her dashboard hula doll and waved her back and forth so that her eyelids opened and shut.

"It doesn't matter," Lily went on. There was a pause. No one said anything. And then: "Nothing matters but getting that flamingo."

"'Kay," said Cam, and she hung up. She sucked in some breath, which buoyed her for a moment. But after she exhaled she felt everything inside her—her stomach, her solar plexus, her throat—getting wrung out by an imaginary pair of cruel and strangling fists.

Cam drove past the pink and aquamarine–canopied strip malls until she found the one with the Family Dollar. No one dressed in black shopped in Family Dollar. That was pretty much a rule. She would not blend.

Cam donned her grandmother's old straw beach hat with the yellow ribbon for a splash of color. She put on her big red sunglasses. And, luckily, while she was crossing the parking lot, she was able to catch a Family Dollar plastic bag that was swirling away in a miniature tornado.

She walked up to the sidewalk sale and pretended to peruse the plastic, lead-painted offerings made in China. The flamingos were stuck pole-first into a big cardboard box, where they butted up against one another and stared with their black spray-painted eyes at the tiki torches, kiddie pools, water wings, and plastic margarita glasses that were all half-price for summer.

Cam examined one closely, as if one needed to inspect the quality of one's plastic flamingo. Then she dumped it headfirst into her Family Dollar bag, suffocating it, and made it all the way back to her car. She was searching for her key when someone tapped her on the shoulder.

"You going to pay for that flamingo?"

*Rats*, thought Cam, but before she could say, "What flamingo?" she felt it happening. It felt like fear, only stronger. She could feel a cold breeze; her left arm began shaking. Her head seemed to fill up with air like a head balloon. An electric shock shot through her spine, and then she got dizzy and lost her balance. It was like being struck by lightning.

And then it was black.

# THREE

WHEN SHE CAME TO, DRENCHED IN SWEAT AND WITH A POUNDING headache, she struggled to remember where she was and who in God's name this mustachioed man, staring at her through inch-thick glasses could be. His name tag read HELLO, MY NAME IS DARREN.

"Hello. My name is Cam," said Cam. "Where am I?"

"Dollar store parking lot. You stole a flamingo."

"I don't think we formally established that," she said, still fully reclined on the blacktop. It was so hot that the asphalt beneath her was beginning to melt. She felt a little tar bubble beneath her fingers and pierced it with her fingernail.

"Well, it's in the bag, and you don't have a receipt."

"Did you call 911?"

"Yes. They're on their way."

"All righty, then, cowboy, I'll need to motor on out of here." Cam could hear the siren approaching in the distance,

and she winced in pain as she slowly lifted herself from the pavement. These would be city paramedics and not the pretend Disney ones that she could shoo away with a doctor's note.

"Wait," said the Family Dollar manager. "You can't just leave. You can't drive like this. You were flipping around like a fish, foaming at the mouth."

"Yup. That happens. Next time you see that, grab a tongue depressor so a person doesn't swallow her tongue. Mind if I take the flamingo?"

"It's $2.89."

"Whoa, Darren, you drive a hard bargain. How about I'm just going to take it?"

Cam grabbed the flamingo and threw it into the backseat, started the Beetle, and peeled out of the parking lot. She was slowly regaining control of her limbs, but they felt heavy. Darren was right; she probably shouldn't be driving.

Cam looked into her rearview mirror. Darren was still in too much shock to really do anything about her getaway. Hopefully he hadn't taken down her license plate number.

Before she drove home, she decided on a perfect home for the flamingo, whom she'd named after Darren. She would take a picture of Darren the flamingo in front of Celebration, Disney's planned community. Most of Disney's top executives lived in Celebration, where they had rules about what you could wear and what you could drive and how many kids you should have (three) and whether you could have a pet.

"Performers" like Cam and pink flamingos like Darren were definitely not part of the plan. Cam took a photo of Darren in front of the Celebration gates. Then she drove through the community, where everything looked eerily telegenic. It was like living on the soundstage for *Leave It to Beaver*. She found Alexa Stanton's house in the federalist section of the town, where each home was designed to look like the abode of a founding father, complete with yellow paint, black shutters, and stately white columns.

Alexa was the head cheerleader; she used to hate Cam because Cam was smart and could talk to Alexa's brainiac boyfriend about politics. She used to tease Cam about her weight.

Cam threw the flamingo onto Alexa's perfectly manicured lawn, just to let her puzzle over that. A plastic flamingo. Was it a sign? Like the horse's head in *The Godfather*? Was someone after her? Alexa would never think this way, Cam knew. She would just ignore Darren and let the gardener deal with him. She would never think of the *Godfather* reference. Not everyone was a film buff like Cam. A consequence of sitting for hours with platinum dripping into the shunt in your chest. There was nothing else to do during chemo but watch films.

Darren hated it here, she could tell. He looked scared and

alone lying on his side in the perfect square of green sod. His black eye seemed to widen and plead, "Don't leave me!"

*He should be frightened*, thought Cam. He had good instincts. This land of make-believe wanted nothing to do with him and what he represented: beer in cans; bad teeth; immigrants; minimum wage; the uninsured; blood, sweat, and tears; hard rock; the real world; death.

It all came back to that, didn't it? People were afraid to die. So they lived in Celebration.

On second thought, Cam would keep Darren.

Cam lived far away from Celebration, on Ronald Reagan Drive in a crumbling three-bedroom ranch with beige shag carpet from the seventies, spackled ceilings, and walls so thin that Cam had to sleep with headphones on so she could drown out the sounds of her mom's lovemaking.

Cam understood that in most people's universes the words *mom* and *lovemaking* never appeared in the same sentence. But unfortunately Cam had to live in reality, with a real mother who brought home real men from the fake countries of Epcot. Her current and yearlong conquest was Izanagi, a chef from the Benihana-style grill in "Japan."

He was the last person Cam wanted to see when she walked through the door, exhausted from her doctor's appointment and having had a seizure in the dollar store parking lot. He wore a pink kimono as he chopped vegetables for an omelet, juggling his knife before flipping a piece of red pepper into Perry's mouth. Perry applauded like a trained seal.

Cam tried to sneak right into her bedroom for a nap, which should have been easy in their cave of a home. The stalactites of the spackle and the stalagmites of the shag carpet should have muffled the sounds of her entrance, but the funny thing about her mother was that she had supersonic bat hearing, appropriate for their cavelike existence. People adapt. Natural selection. Darwin. Evolution.

"Campbell!" her mom screamed from the bedroom. "Eat something. Izanagi is making an omelet."

"Really? I hadn't noticed. He's so subtle about it."

"What?"

"Nothing. I'm not hungry."

"Cam. Please."

She was turning into a little bit of a cancerexic. A small part of her enjoyed the fact that she could now wear skinny clothes, and she was a little afraid to eat. Another part of her couldn't believe that healthy girls would starve themselves to look like her—a size zero, a nothing, a sick person. At least her old fleshy self would have lived to see eighteen.

Cam heard *chop, chop, scrape*, and then she used her fire-juggling reflexes to catch the shrimp that was flying toward her face.

"You need protein," said Izanagi.

"*Domo arigato*, Mr. Roboto."

Cam bit a tiny piece of the shrimp, and it actually didn't make her gag. Maybe if she covered her omelet with ketchup, she could eat. "I'll take mine by the pool," she said, and she wasn't joking. They really did have a pool. It was the only reason their mom stayed in this house, and the only thing she seemed able to maintain. The rest of the house was crumbling and mildewed, but the kidney-shaped pool sparkled. When Cam's mother was twenty-five, she had vowed never to live in a house without a pool, and so Cam's dad had bought her this one.

He'd enjoyed it, too, inviting the whole cast of "Aloha" over for parties when the weather dropped below fifty degrees. That was the only time Disney would cancel the outdoor show.

Cam missed that, and so many other things about her dad.

"Hi, sweetie," said her mom, her wavy, waist-length hair glistening in the sun as she came out to the deck to deliver Cam's omelet. Alicia was a stomach sleeper, which says a lot about a person. Only 7 percent of people on the planet sleep on their stomachs, and stomach sleepers are vain, gregarious, and overly sensitive. Also small-breasted, apparently, because that position couldn't be comfortable with big boobs.

When she was pregnant with Cam, she'd had trouble sleeping on her side, so Cam's dad had driven Alicia all the way to Clearwater, where he could dig a hole in the sand for her belly. Alicia would flop down like a beached whale and finally get to nap. Cam began her life like a baby turtle, buried in the beach. Her dad had called her Turtle sometimes, though it hadn't really stuck.

He was thoughtful, her dad, and yet after all that—the driving to the beach, the digging of the hole, the buying of the pool, the fathering of the child—her mom still hadn't even cried at his funeral. It was the final proof for Cam, as if she needed it, that true love did not exist. Connections between people were temporary. Selfish. Opportunistic. Designed to perpetuate the species. "Love"—romantic love, anyway—was a fantasy people indulged in because otherwise, life was just too boring to tolerate.

"Will you cry at my funeral, I wonder?" Cam asked as she sliced through her omelet with the side of her fork. The neat pillow of egg leaked its juices into the ketchup, creating a pink watery puddle on her plate. So much for her appetite.

"What? Campbell, I'll be dead at your funeral. This thing will kill you over my dead body. I told you. Which is why I need you to apply to those schools. You need a plan for September." Alicia had been collecting community-college brochures filled with bright photos of happy multicultural coeds, and they had been sliding around on top of one another, dry humping on the kitchen counter for months. Stomach sleepers are also prone to passive-aggressive tactics, like secretly hoarding college brochures and finding ways to beat around the bush when they really just wanted to ask how their daughter's doctor's appointment went.

"I'm not going to any of those schools, Mom."

"Yes, you are. And if you hadn't spent that money on that car, you could have had more money for books. I'm going to kill that Gus for taking your money. I swear to God."

"Why don't you get someone from Jersey to do it?"

"I could, you know." Her mom took a sip of coffee and got a mischievous, nostalgic look in her eye. *Old people always exaggerate the danger and lawlessness of their youth*, thought Cam, *because their adult lives have become so boring.*

"You don't really know anyone in the mob, do you?"

"Just a friend of a friend's cousin."

Her mom often glorified her Jersey roots. People from New Jersey were tough; they were cool. Jersey had the best bagels and the best pizza and the best corn and the best tomatoes, and on and on. Cam thought they should open a section of Disney called JerseyLand for all those hopeless Jersey romantics who wanted to simplify themselves. Because that was what Disney did. It provided a simulacrum of your life that looked better than the murky one you lived in and convinced you that your life was okay. Baudrillard described this concept, and Cam had written about it in her essay to Harvard. And she'd gotten accepted. Which she would never tell anyone. It was her final secret triumph, but she wasn't stupid enough to get her hopes up.

Plus they'd only accepted her because of her extraordinary story. Being almost dead made her special, like the Olympic athletes, movie stars, eighteen-year-old venture capitalists, published authors, and children-who-were-raised-on-a-sailboat that made up the rest of the freshman roster.

"So," her mom finally said.

"So what?"

"The PET scan, Cam. What did they say about the PET scan?"

"You're supposed to call them. They're not supposed to tell me anything. I'm a minor." This was true, but Cam still would not let her mom come with her to the Children's Hospital anymore. It was already torture to sit in a waiting room with a bunch of bald, sick three-year-olds. She wasn't going to sit there with her mother.

"But I know you got it out of them."

"I did," Cam admitted.

"So."

"Sew buttons." That phrase always made Cam laugh. Her grandmother was the only one who still used it because she was probably the only person who still actually sewed buttons.

"Campbell."

Cam pushed a piece of her omelet through the ketchup on her plate and then just covered the whole thing with a napkin. "So the cancer is everywhere. Pretty much. Nothing's changed. Oh, except for some new growth around the kidneys."

The PET scan had showed Cam's skeleton shimmering like a Christmas tree with glowing nodules of cancer draped around her center like a garland of lights. The cross-section view of her torso looked otherworldly, like a view from the Hubble telescope or from a place deep underwater, aqueous and murky, except, again, for the bright glowing ember of cancer, which Dr. Handsome did not like to see.

Dr. Handsome—that was really his name, and it led to endless jokes about whether he was a doctor or just played one on TV—held his silver pen above the computer screen and used it as a pointer to trace an imaginary circle around the bright orange glow surrounding her kidneys. He used the same silver pen every visit. *Which says a lot about him*, Cam thought. The pen was probably a gift, which meant he had people who loved him and were proud of his doctor-dom. And he was sentimental if he cared enough not to lose it. It was either that or he was a little obsessive. Detail-oriented. *Which is a good trait for doctors to have*, Cam thought. You didn't want them slipping up. The longest Cam had ever kept a pen was probably five days, max. She and Dr. Handsome were very different.

"This is not what we were hoping to see," he said as he swirled the pen in a little loop-de-loop and then just let it droop between his finger and thumb. He dropped his head into his free hand and combed his fingers through his black hair and sighed.

This was the first time Cam had seen him show any negativity. He had always been so positive. His posture today seemed so defeated.

"Maybe that"—Cam took the pen from his hand and traced it around the orange—"is my second chakra, you know? I think that's about where it's supposed to be. The second chakra is the orange chakra. The seat of power and change. Can that machine pick up chakras and auras and whatnot?"

Dr. Handsome tried to speak, and then something caught in the back of his throat. *Is he about to cry?* Cam wondered. He was.

"Cam . . ." He composed himself. "I'm sorry. I'm just very, very tired. . . . Cam, there is nothing we can do."

Cam had been coming here for five years, and she thought she'd seen all of his moods. He could be goofy and giddy when he was tired, and he was great with the little ones. He had a rubber blow-up punching clown in his office, so the kids could blow off some steam before their appointments. Cam gave the clown a little jab now and he rocked back and forth. "But you're Dr. Handsome," she said. She knew what really centered him was when he focused on the medicine. "Put away those emotions and pull out some of that doctor-speak. You need to talk cold, hard science. Say 'malignancy' or 'subcutaneous' or something. It'll make you feel better."

"Science is just not enough this time, Campbell Soup. What you need is a miracle."

Cam's mom sat on her favorite deck chair and leafed through an *InStyle* magazine. She put her coffee down on the glass patio table and without looking up asked, "And so is there a new trial we can get into?" She was pretending to be non-chalant, but Cam could see that telltale crease between her eyebrows change from fine line to deep-set wrinkle.

"There's nothing left."

"There's always something left," she said, turning another page of her magazine, to an article that showed you how to wear the latest trend (black lace) in your twenties (stockings), thirties (little black dress), forties and beyond (never!).

"They've run out of trials, Mom. Anything else they try will kill me before the cancer does. My counts were not good."

"I'll call them today, Cam. I'll get you into something. They can at least give you some more cisplatin," she said, finally looking Cam straight in the eye.

"Mom. You're not listening. There's nothing left."

"We'll just go to St. Jude's or Hopkins or something."

"We've been there, Mom. St. Jude's twice. They've done everything they can do." Cam was tired. She didn't want to think about this anymore. She just wanted to sleep and forget for a few hours. The new, rubbery, custom patio cushions in parakeet green hissed a little as Cam let her head fall back. The Florida sun felt good on her face for a couple of seconds, but soon it started to feel less like warmth and more like radiation. "Dr. Handsome said I need a miracle."

"Well then, Cam," her mom said, sighing and then snapping a stale piece of Nicorette, "we'll find you a goddamn miracle."

"That's not exactly a good way to start." Cam opened her eyes and looked at the cloudless blue sky overhead. "You don't *damn* God before you ask for a mira—"

"I'm not giving up, Campbell. I will never give up on you." The last four syllables built to a crescendo, followed by Alicia's hand slamming onto the glass table.

"Cancer's not in my ears," Cam mumbled. "Yet."

"Dammit!" Alicia yelled and threw her coffee mug onto the cement pool deck. It shattered with an empty pop.

"You're going to regret that. That was the Santa mug," said Cam, unfazed. Her mom's favorite coffee mug was printed with a faded, barely perceptible picture of Cam and Perry sitting on Santa's lap taken ten years ago.

Cam was used to her mom's outbursts. She had been

living with them for years. Something had happened to Alicia in midlife, where every emotion—sadness, fear, joy, confusion, helplessness—could only find an outlet through her anger. It was especially prominent after her first cup of coffee in the morning. Her mom said it was hormonal. Cam thought it was just Alicia!.

"Campbell, you have to believe me," Alicia said, composing herself. "I am not going to let you die."

"That's reassuring. Really. I believe you. Now I need to take a nap."

As Cam hugged her mother and walked back to her room, she realized she'd be spending the rest of her short life making other people feel better about the prospect of losing her.

# FOUR

CAM HELD HER BREATH AND DUNKED HER HEAD BENEATH THE SURFACE of the water. She needed to drown out the sounds of her neighbors cheering as they caravanned to school for graduation.

It was too hot for a ceremony on the field, so each graduate could only invite two people to watch from the air-conditioned seats of the auditorium. Cam had stuck her tickets to the "Commencement Excercise"—with the word *Exercise* misspelled in expensive golden ink—between pages 218 and 219 of *Anna Karenina*.

Cam blinked her eyes open in the bright turquoise pool. It was harder to tell that you were crying when your head was underwater. Plus the cold water felt good on the lovely blue-spotted rash that she was developing all over her forearms, called "blueberry spots." What a cute little name for a cancerous lesion.

The buzzing of the pool's robo-vacuum vibrated up through her spine, and she let herself sink until she sat on the slippery pool bottom. Cam had decided to skip graduation today. She had missed so much school because of her chemo and trials that she had lost touch with most people there. And she didn't want to hear about her classmates' plans for the future, most of which involved working at Disney, at least for the summer. Alexa and her sidekick Ashley were waiting anxiously to see if they had gotten cast as one of the Cinderellas. Cam was a little jealous that people had futures at all, if she had to be honest. She didn't want to think about the future.

The final straw may have been that no one on the faculty could spell *exercise*.

Cam sprang to the pool's surface, taking a gasping breath. Then she climbed out and dabbed at the mysterious rivulets of tears that had merged with the streaming drops of chlorinated water dripping from the ends of her hair. She blotted them away rather than swiping because her nana had told her years ago that wiping your face causes wrinkles. *As if.* She laughed.

Luckily she had signed up for a shift at work. That would be a welcome distraction.

Cam loved mornings in the kitchen. A restaurant kitchen in the morning was like a gentle, yawning beast. Blinking, stretching, clicking, opening, closing. You could still hear distinct, individual sounds before things got going full steam and the beast recovered his fiery breath amid the cacophony of the cooking.

Joe, the cook, was always the first one on the job, and he and Cam had a system that worked. No one talked until noon. Joe needed his coffee to kick in, and they both enjoyed the silence before the chaos.

But this morning, Joe could not shut up.

"So maybe I'll put some tarragon in the sauce," he said. "What do you think, Cam? A little mustardy bite to the sweet and sour?" He was stirring a stainless-steel vat of the stuff with a big wooden paddle. Joe's hoarse and staticky boom-box choked out his favorite Zeppelin track. He had figured out years ago how to disconnect the magical mood music piped in through the infinite sound web that reached every corner of the park.

"You need to stick to the recipe, Joe. It's only a temporary move, remember? So you can have some health insurance for the kids," said Cam without lifting her gaze from the cutting board. She sliced through another pineapple, halving it perfectly with one swing of her mouse-ke-cleaver.

"Right," he said. "No tarragon." Joe was a brilliant chef who hoped to move quickly up the ranks to one of the Disney restaurants that actually had a menu. The Polynesian Hotel served meals banquet-style, which was boring—the

She didn't generally demur. Demurring was not in her bag of tricks, but Jackson was being so sweet, acting as her date, she didn't want to do anything to crush his ego.

Even as she was juggling fire, she couldn't help noticing that Jackson was filling out, the muscles of his thighs bulky and defined beneath his cargo shorts. He would look great in his *lava-lava* in a few years.

The music began to die down, and people drifted to their posts to prepare for the real show at five thirty. After it was over, each family stopped by Cam's table and gave her a gift wrapped in *siapo*, sacred Samoan cloth made out of bark and painted with a special pattern that was unique to each family. The cloth was said to be life-giving (legend had it that if you wrapped someone's dead bones in it, the person could come back to life) and to provide miracle cures, which was sort of a joke to Cam, but she accepted them politely and promised people that she'd sleep with them. The *siapo* reminded her of her dad. He couldn't remember what the family pattern of his *siapo* looked like, so he had one made with the face of Mickey Mouse on it.

"Ready to go?" asked Jackson. He was back in his Tigger costume, holding the head under his right arm.

"You're wearing that?" asked Cam.

"I have to return it to wardrobe, and I can't just carry it on the monorail in a bag. Kids would be devastated."

"God," said Cam. "All right. Let's go, then." Every Disney

employee's family got a passport good for free entrance to the park at any time. It was like having the golden ticket in *Willy Wonka & the Chocolate Factory*, and it was, Cam had to admit, a pretty fun way to grow up.

They walked across the lush, tropical rain forest of the lobby, complete with its own waterfall, and upstairs to the sleek, cement monorail track that passed through the hotel. The track and the futuristic train provided a stark contrast to the natural wood and foliage and traditional arts and crafts that made up the heart of the Polynesian. It was Disney's plan to create a world where past and future were slammed together in disjunctive harmony, and nowhere in the park was that more evident than the monorail track at the Polynesian.

Cam stood on the platform with Jackson, watching him get mobbed by sunburned kids who wanted their picture taken with Tigger. Her phone buzzed.

**Lily:** Happy graduation! Where R U?

**Cam:** On a date.

**Lily:** ☺!!! If you don't at least get to second base I'm going to kill you.

**Cam:** Second base? What are you, 11? Who sez 2nd base anymore?

**Lily:** Just do it.

Cam clicked her phone off and Jackson shooed some children away playfully. He grabbed Cam in his soft furry arms, dipped her, and pretended to plant a slobbery Tigger kiss right on her lips. This spurred a wild, tinkly wind chime of giggles from the kids. Cam loved how assertive Jackson could be when in disguise.

He posed for a few more shots with the children, and Cam made sure to sneak at least one of her body parts into each of the pictures, putting her fingers in a *V* over Tigger's head. But when the last camera flashed, Cam felt herself getting dizzy and nauseated. She fought to stay conscious. Her vision tunneled, the green of the rain forest closing in on her. She looked at the mahogany and teak carved ceiling tiles above her. Their patterns moved in and out and back and forth in her field of vision.

"Hey Jackson," she said weakly, but Jackson was busy with his Tigger-lovin' public.

"Jackson," she said, more loudly this time. "I need to go home. Can you drive me home?" she managed to say before doubling over with a horrible, stabbing stomach pain.

Jackson got Cam to the parking lot, where he de-costumed and threw the Tigger head into the backseat. He sped home in Cumulus, and by the time they got there, whatever it was that gripped her had subsided. Enough for her to speak at least.

"I'm sorry," Cam said. They sat in her driveway, dusk falling around them. Heat lightning flashed and lit up the inside of the car like a slow, intermittent strobe. Cam loved heat lightning. It reminded her that she lived on a *planet*. With each flash she caught the Tigger head in her peripheral vision—that famous underbite and the beady eyes locked in a constant state of surprise. Would he ever know anything? Cam wished she could be like Tigger—in a perpetual state of ignorance.

"Love means never having to say you're sorry," Jackson mumbled. At least that's what Cam thought he said. He fiddled with Cam's Scooby-Doo keychain before handing it to her. His rough, calloused fingertips grazed hers. She loved his hands. There was nothing worse than soft man-hands.

"What did you say?" she asked.

"Never mind," he said. "It's a bad quote from a bad movie. I'm not very good at this."

"*Love Story*. Nineteen seventy. Starring Ali McGraw and Ryan O'Neal," Cam said robotically.

"It's pretty bad," Jackson admitted.

"Yeah, but in a good way."

"So do you want to go out some time?" he finally asked.

"God, Jackson, is your mother putting you up to this?" Cam could see the light blue collar of his Dunder Mifflin T-shirt sticking out of the stripy fur of his Tigger costume.

"No. I mean, not really."

"Please. You don't have to be the nice boy who dates the dying girl. Don't make that part of your identity. It will be hard to shake off. Believe me. It will stick, and you'll never get the hot blonde."

"I like you, Cam."

*Well, it's a little late for that*, Cam thought. She couldn't even look at him; he was just so well intentioned, it was heartbreaking. *Sometimes*, Cam thought, *men really are the fairer sex.* The more gallant and pure and innocent and upstanding. Perhaps because they didn't have to fight so hard.

Luckily, Izanagi was walking out of the house as Cam and Jackson were getting out of the car.

"Perfect timing," said Cam. "Drive him home, will you, Izanagi?"

"Sure," he said. "Let's go, kid."

Cam gave Jackson a little wave. "TTFN," she said, which was Tigger's favoritest thing to say.

"Oooh," said Perry when Cam came in the door. Perry wore a tight Hello Kitty T-shirt, short-shorts, and pink Uggs as she walked through the house texting someone on her hot pink phone. Two low, looped ponytails at the nape of her neck made her look like a Swiss Miss. "How was your date? Did you get any lip-lock or what?" she said, without looking up from her phone.

"What do you know about lip-lock?"

"More than you do, probably."

"I hope not, you little tramp."

"Mom! Cam called me a tramp."

"If the shoe fits, honey," sang Alicia, sweeping in, wink-
ing, and giving Cam a hug. She was in a good mood for
some reason.

"Mom!" screamed Perry.

"Stop boo-hooing, Perry. You know she was joking. Go
hug one of your unicorns."

Perry was eleven and still had unicorn posters plastered
all over her room, glass unicorns, porcelain unicorns, unicorn stuffed animals. Cam hated that stage in girls' bedrooms
when posters of rock bands coexisted with piles of stuffed
animals. But who was Cam to judge? She'd just gone on a
date with freaking Tigger.

"You know, a unicorn could heal you, Campbell," Perry
said, finally looking up from her texting. She stared at Cam
as if she'd just come up with a brilliant idea.

"There are no such things as unicorns, genius," Cam told
her. "Those are just freakish one-horned goat mutants."

"They're just rare and extremely wild and can only be
tamed by a virgin. So that's perfect. You could tame it. Easily.
Because. Of. Your. Virginitude," said Perry, punctuating each
word with a wag of her finger, before running away down
the hall.

"Shut up, Perry," said Cam as she made her way to her
room. She shuffled down the hallway, dragging her feet
through the browning shag carpet. She was too tired to

agonize over the fact that her eleven-year-old sister knew the status of her sex life. And really too tired to feel grateful about how at least her antagonistic relationship with her sister was still in the range of normal. It was probably the only thing in her life that was in the range of normal. Everything else, like the extreme fatigue she felt at that moment, was way, way out of the range of normal. She was even too tired to call Lily. She could not wait to flop onto her bed and fall into a deep, deep sleep, but then she turned the corner and gasped.

Everything was gone.

# FIVE

## "WHERE IS MY STUFF?" YELLED CAM.

She slid open her drawers and found them empty. Naked hangers swung back and forth in her closet. Cam's down comforter had been replaced with an old electric blanket. The Lite Brite Mondrian she had created with four screens taped together was unplugged. The solar system replica she'd made in second grade hung from the ceiling. Her Wonder Woman action figure, dressed in a grass skirt, stood traumatized on Cam's desk next to the Magic 8-Ball. Constellations of blue putty spotted the walls where Cam's posters used to be. "What did you do with the Ramones?" she asked. "And my *Citizen Kane* poster? Where is Tweety, goddammit?"

"We packed it," said Perry, appearing in the doorway behind Alicia. She kept her mom's body strategically between hers and Cam's.

"You packed Tweety?" The one dorky thing about Cam

was that she had a canary named Tweety. Everyone else in the family was allergic to cats and dogs, so she had to love a bird. He sat on her shoulder and ate from her hands. "Where's Tweety?"

"Tweety's in the kitchen, Campbell. We were just cleaning his cage. Getting him ready for the trip," Alicia told her.

"Yeah, I guess that's the missing piece of information here. What *trip*?" Cam demanded.

"To Maine."

"Maine?"

"Maine." Alicia picked up a pillow from the floor and tossed it on the bed. "You remember Tom. The guy I met at yoga?"

"Tom. Acid-trip Tom. Tom, who doesn't even know what day it is and hasn't showered in weeks, Tom? We're placing all our bets on writing-a-rock-opera Tom, who owns five iguanas—*Tom*?" Cam leaned woozily on her desk.

"Tom knows about a mystical town in Maine that has been known to have healing powers. He said we should leave right away. Something about Saturn being in retrograde." Alicia shrugged.

"This is what it's come to?"

"Well, you won't go to Tijuana," Alicia told her.

This is what it had come to. "Shall we check the Magic 8-Ball then? Just to get a definitive answer?" Cam grabbed it and silently asked, *Is Maine going to help us?* The dice bobbled for a while inside the cloudy purple liquid before turning to "Ask Again Later."

"What could possibly be in Maine, Mom? It's not like there's anything in the water. There are no magical springs. It's the Atlantic Ocean. The same Atlantic Ocean we have in Florida. Only it's cold. Freezing cold."

"It will be good to just get away, Cam," Perry said.

Cam paused. She couldn't argue with that.

Before he died, her father made her promise that she would get out of Florida. It was his dream that she go to an Ivy League school. They dreamed that together. He would have been proud of her for getting into Harvard.

And it was because she'd promised him she'd get out that she was almost ready to agree with her mom and sister. It might not hurt to get out of Florida for a while. Especially in this heat.

"For how long?" Cam asked.

"At least for the summer," Alicia said. "For as long as it takes."

"Fine," Cam conceded. "Let's go." She shook up the 8-Ball and put it back on her bookshelf.

"Great!" Alicia jumped up and down a little. She gave Cam a hug and said, "The U-Haul is all packed. We just have to hitch it to your car in the morning."

"My car is not being hitched to a U-freaking-Haul."

"You want to bring your car, don't you?"

"Oh, God, fine! Did you guys pack my movies?" Cam asked.

"We're not going there to watch movies," said Alicia.

"I'm bringing them." She rifled under her bed to find her DVD collection and the notes she and Lily were taking for their screenplay (or was it a comic book? They hadn't decided) *Chemosabe and Cueball Take Manhattan*, about two superhero girls with neuroblastoma. She stacked the DVDs and pages on the floor beside her bed and went under for a final search.

"And we're stopping in North Carolina to see Lily!" she said when she emerged. "And Nana's in Hoboken. And at every tourist trap along the way."

"Oh-em-gee," said Perry. Izanagi had their mom pressed up against the car as he kissed her with way too much tongue. "We are your children," she whined. "Just get your sayonaras over with already."

Perry gamboled to the driveway, her road-trip essentials overflowing from her backpack: two packs Sour Patch Kids, one pack Cheetos, three Twixes, some Altoids, her pink-encased iPhone and a large-print word search book.

Cumulus looked proud of himself, hitched to the rig and ready to pull them and their belongings all the way up the East Coast. His front fender puffed out a little bit with pride.

Tweety's cage was strapped to the backseat with a seat belt. Their dashboard hula doll winked from her perch on the passenger side. Cam walked around to the back of the U-Haul and duct-taped Darren to the right rear corner of the trailer. *Perfect*, she thought, and she felt something . . . excitement? Hope? Not hope exactly. But she thought maybe Alicia was right. Moving was better than waiting around.

"Mom, get in the car," she said as she walked around the U-Haul. Cam was getting used to the U-Haul idea, too. It was nice to be able to travel with all of your stuff. It was comforting. Liberating. It was a traveling garage. A modern-day covered wagon.

U-Haul branded each trailer with a "fun fact" from a different state. They'd gotten Utah. And their fun fact was about the canyons of the Escalante, which was apropos of nothing except that the four-foot-square image of the canyon was strangely O'Keeffian and vaginal. They were branded with a four-foot vagina.

"Oh, God, Cam. Only you would think that," their mother had said when Cam had objected to it yesterday.

"That makes me feel really good about myself, Mom, when you imply that my thoughts are crazy. Good parenting."

"Okay, Cam, I'm sorry," Alicia had said, exasperated. "Do you want me to ask for a different one? Without a vagina?"

"No. That's fine," she had acquiesced, and when she'd woken up this morning it didn't bother her that much.

"Come on, Mom, it's time to go," Cam said insistently as she tapped her mom on the shoulder.

"Okay, okay," Alicia said as she peeled herself off of Izanagi.

Izanagi took a deep breath and composed himself and then walked in his paint-splattered, turned-up jeans to his rusting Honda Accord. He reached into the open window and retrieved two rectangular gifts, impeccably wrapped in brown paper and tied with raffia bows. Izanagi was a stereo-typically neat and meticulous minimalist when it came to his artistic pursuits. When he wasn't working at the restaurant, he wrote spare poems and made paintings that were quiet and clean, like whispers.

He handed the gifts to the girls, and Perry tore into hers hungrily. Inside was a simple brown notebook and a brown paper–wrapped pencil.

"To record your trip," said Izanagi.

"To record the miracles!" said Perry, launching herself at Izanagi and hugging him around the waist.

"Thanks," said Cam, keeping her distance. "I'll open mine when we get there." She was resistant these days to writing anything down. She didn't want anyone reading her imper-manent thoughts after she had permanently left the planet.

"God, I love that man," Alicia said as she climbed into the car and blew him a final kiss. He slunk away with his hands in his pockets. He was staying in their house to keep an eye on things.

"You have a strange concept of love."

"What do you know about it?"

"Nothing, obviously. Which way?" Cam was driving the first leg of the trip.

"Take a left."

"South? From what I learned in geography—and granted, I missed a lot of school—Maine is to the north."

"We need to stop by Tom's."

"Oh God. Really?" Cam just wanted to get on the road before she lost her resolve.

"He needs to give us specific directions. This place is almost impossible to find, even with a GPS. And you know that phrase, *You can't get there from here?* People from Maine are really like that. No one will help us once we get up there."

Tom lived in an overgrown jungle of mangroves, vines, and palm trees. You practically needed a machete to hack your way to the front door. The inside—and it was difficult to distinguish between the inside and outside—was crawling with mice and salamanders and the five famous iguanas, who roamed freely around the place. The TV was usually blaring something like *Judge Judy* or *Divorce Court,* and the only way to determine that this was a place of business at all was a tiny gold plaque next to the doorbell that read THOMAS LANE: HERBALIST, HEALER, SHAMAN, CHIEF.

"Ladies," he said as he greeted them at the door wearing a green and blue tie-dyed shirt and smoking a joint. "Contact buzz?" he asked, about to exhale into Alicia's face.

"No." She shook her head. "I have to drive later."

"Suit yourself," he said. His shoulder-length gray hair was washed today, surprisingly, and his jeans were stain-free. His face was relaxed and his pale blue eyes were less bloodshot than usual. Maybe there was a new person in his life—*or a new herb*, thought Cam. "What can I do for you today?" he asked. "Campbell, you look great. Have you been taking the apricot seed like I told you?"

"Um, that would be a no," she said as she stepped over the motionless iguana basking in a patch of sunlight.

"Cam, you need to open your heart to the possibilities of the universe. We can't help you until you help yourself."

"Whatever," said Cam. "Can you just get us the directions?" A strange smell wafted her way from whatever potion was boiling in the dirty pot on the stove.

"To Promise?" Tom asked.

"Um, Promise?" This was the first Cam had heard of the town's hokey name.

"Yes. To Promise," said Alicia.

"Oh, Cam. I'm so proud of you for taking this step. Contact buzz?" he asked, leaning his face into hers.

"No. God. Blow it over there."

Tom had weird sour breath because he ate mostly Gerber

baby meat sticks. He claimed they were easier on the digestive system, so he ate jars and jars of them and used the empties, which were stacked neatly on shelves that ran floor to ceiling in perfect Gerber-meat-stick-jar increments, to house herbs. The jars were filled with powders, leaves, roots, teas, and other magical potions, and none of them were labeled. They were just laid out like a bizarre map of Tom's mind. He knew where everything herbal was. Finding the directions would be another story.

"Let me see," mused Tom, "Directions, directions. Where would those be?" He rifled through some of the books stacked all over the living room floor and on the dining room table and chairs.

"Promise is really a magical place, Campbell. It's so beautiful."

"Really. Have you been there, Tom?"

"Um, no. But legend has it that it's just Shangri-La."

"In Maine?"

"A-yuh. That's how they say 'yes' in Maine. Okay. Here it is." Tom unearthed an old, wrinkled-up Dunkin' Donuts bag with writing scribbled all over it. "So here's the map. The main road leading to Promise is behind the Dunkin' Donuts off of Route 3, and you can only see it from the drive-through squawk box. People say it's good luck to order a whoopie pie and some chocolate milk before driving into town. The number for the hotel is on the back."

"What in God's name is a 'whoopie pie'?" asked Cam. "This is such a joke."

"No, Campbell," said Tom, getting really solemn all of a sudden. His normally turned-up mouth flatlined across his face, and his wild and wiry eyebrows sank. "This is no joke. If you can find the town—and most people can't—magical things can happen. Amazing things, like tiny fish raining from the sky and miracle cures for diseases, which I think you are in the market for, young lady. So here," he said, handing over the crumpled bag.

"Thank you," said Cam.

Fish raining from the sky reminded her of that *Cloudy with a Chance of Meatballs* book her dad used to read to her. It was a story about a magical town where the day's food would rain down from the sky at every meal and people would catch it on their plates. Then things got out of hand and the townspeople had to sail to the real world on boats made of giant toast.

"Do they have sailboats made of giant toast?" asked Cam.

"What?" asked Tom.

"Never mind."

"Now go, and don't forget to send me a postcard," said Tom.

Cam looked at the map drawn with the unsteady palsied hand of some recovering drug addict. She caught the tears in her throat before letting them pool in the corners of her eyes. It was so pathetic that they were trying this. Part of her wished she could just stay ensconced in her thin-walled bedroom, wrapped in her down comforter, and have her mother bring her chicken soup until this was all over. But when she looked at her mom and Perry staring at her from the doorway, already wide-eyed and ecstatic in their altered road-trip reality, she knew this wasn't just about her.

"Let's go, bitches," she said in jest as she held up the crumpled bag. Alicia snatched it from her hand, and Cam said, "Maineward ho."

"Who's Maineward, and why is she a ho?" asked Perry as they made the treacherous walk through the mangroves back to the car.

# SIX

"WE CAN READ THEM, PERRY. YOU DON'T HAVE TO READ THEM OUT loud," said Cam.

Perry had been sucked into her first roadside attraction— that friendly euphemism for "tourist trap." They had been on the road for six long hours, and they were getting a little *loca.* Alicia had become obsessed with redialing the number for the ghost hotel in Promise, Maine—no one ever picked up—and Perry could not stop reading road signs. The South of the Border billboards had started in Georgia at about ten miles apart, and now, halfway into South Carolina, they were practically every ten yards. Cam's personal favorite—SOUTH OF THE BORDER: YOU NEVER SAUSAGE A PLACE!—had a three-dimensional, fifteen-foot-long hot dog hanging from the top of it in the shape of a smile.

Cam was actually grateful for the billboards. They gave her something to look at aside from the bleak landscape of America the beautiful. Beauty didn't seem to be a priority for people anymore. If you had to judge from I-95, America had become cancerous clusters of cheap houses, replicating out of control. They were dropped into empty, treeless soybean fields and connected by strip mall after superstore after strip mall. People just needed places to collect their stuff. Each house had a swing set and a green lawn littered with plastic toys. No one even built a fence to hide the plastic toy habit. People were shameless about their consumption of plastic.

It was no wonder the polar bears were drowning.

They were getting close. Cam could see the lights of the sombrero tower blinking above the pine trees like a UFO. And when they rounded the next bend and Alicia drove Cumulus between the legs of an enormous neon Pedro—South of the Border's offensive Mexican-guy mascot—all Cam could think was, *Por qué?*

South of the Border was empty. (Hadn't people seen the signs?) It was dusty, dry, and desolate. Just a few warehouses filled with schlock dropped in the middle of nowhere. Scattered throughout the compound were plaster-of-paris statues of animals from Africa. An orange giraffe; a huge, T-shirt-wearing gorilla. What these had to do with Mexico, Cam could not imagine. It cost a dollar to take the elevator to the top of the sombrero tower, where you could look at nothing for miles around.

"Wow, this place has really gone downhill," said Alicia. She finally stopped dialing the Promise Breakers Hotel, took the phone away from her ear, and looked around.

"Right. I'm sure it was very classy once."

"It wasn't this bad."

Cam was glad she got to see it at night, though, where the neon gave the place its special cache. South of the Border at night was quite a wonder. Sleazy, cheap, gaudy, garish, and filthy, except for the absence of any visible prostitutes, it almost compared to the real Tijuana. She put Tweety back in his cage and covered it up so he didn't have to witness the vulgarity.

"Okay, everyone gather round the stereotype," said Cam. Her dad used to say that when Disney tourists asked to have their picture taken with him. Cam took out her camera and snapped a shot of Perry and her mom pinching the cheeks of a huge plaster-of-paris Pedro.

Then she headed toward Gift Shop West, the city block–size store filled with, in Cam's estimation, much better stuff than Gift Shop East on the opposite side of the compound.

"The unicorn section is in Gift Shop East," said Perry.

"Then I'll meet you guys at the arcade."

Inside GSW were acres of shot glasses, snow globes, wind chimes, toothpick holders, keychains, bumper stickers, bobbleheads, and assorted novelties. It was rest stop heaven. Cam got to work. She could have paid for things with her check from Disney, but she had unfortunately become a little addicted to the thrill of shoplifting.

"This will be the last time," she told herself. She knew that was what addicts said, but this really would be the last time.

She found the perfect gift for Perry right away. She was standing in front of a rotating rack of plastic, personalized coffee mugs, and they actually had a "Perry." It was for a boy Perry—blue, with a big soccer ball bulging out from the side of it—but that was perfect. Perry hated that her name was "gender-neutral," and when she wrote it herself, she spelled it "Peri" and dotted the *I* with a big daisy. She had changed herself into a prefix.

The mug would piss her off for a second, but then it would make her laugh. Cam slipped it into the front pocket of her hoodie, and then for her mom she stole a googly-eyed frog made out of seashells. Her mother detested seashell arts and crafts. She vowed that she'd never have seashells as part of her décor. Especially in her bathroom. Cam would insist that this frog live in their bathroom in Maine.

Not that they'd come close to securing a room in Maine. Cam was pretty sure this hotel did not even exist. She slid a flamingo-shaped backscratcher down her pants. She was wearing her multipocketed cargo pants that tied at the knees so she could really pull in a good haul. And then she got a text from Lily:

YMSYCTAI [Your Mission Should You Choose to Accept It]: Btl rckts
from Rckt City + Roman candle.


They were stopping at Lily's in about an hour, and Cam
couldn't wait. If Lily wanted bottle rockets, then Cam would
get bottle rockets.

South Carolina was one of the few states left that didn't
have laws against letting your kids blow their fingers off
with M-80s. Cam pretended to browse her way out of the
gift shop and made it across the road to the fireworks store
Rocket City. It was next to the gas station, which seemed to
Cam like some bad planning. Who would put an explosives
shop next to the gas station? Anyway, it was an easy mission
to complete because the toothless woman at the counter was
busy watching a monster truck pull on TV.

The long fuses from the bottle rockets scraped Cam's legs
as she walked past the defunct, decrepit, and broken-down
Sombrero Ride, the train, and the roller coaster, which would
be fixed next month, according to Carlos, who stood guard
at the empty gate.

Cam found her mom and Perry at the arcade. Perry, a
white unicorn galloping across her left cheek, was pleading
with her mom to get her biorhythm chart from an old faux
wood–paneled machine from the seventies.

Alicia was still on the phone, listening once again to the
busy signal of the only hotel in Promise, Maine.

Perry eventually won her negotiation. Alicia fed a dollar into the machine, yellow lights flashed around a blinking swami's head, and Perry put her finger in a clamp that looked like the one Cam had to use in the hospital to measure her oxygen levels. The lights blinked again, and then the machine spit out a card that said Perry would be lucky in love.

*No shit*, thought Cam. *She's a blonde Scandinavian goddess.* Did they have someone sitting inside this machine?

"You try it, Cam. Go ahead."

"Right. And if it says I'm lucky in love, we know it's a sham."

Cam placed her finger in the clamp, the lights blinked, the swami's head blinked off entirely. The machine spit out Cam's card halfway and stopped.

She could already tell that her card was different than Perry's. There was no pretty red border around it, and when she tried to pull it out, it was as if the swami were pulling it back. He wouldn't let go of it. Cam tugged harder, using two hands, but it wouldn't budge. She put one foot up onto the machine and yanked one last time. When the card finally unstuck, she fell backward. She looked down. In her hands was a blank piece of paper.

She turned it over to see if something was printed on the other side. She looked back into the slot, but there was no other ticket. The swami's wax face seemed to smirk at her.

"It's blank," Cam said, disappointed in spite of herself.

"See," said Perry. "You have to believe in it, or it won't know you exist."

Cam crumpled the card in her palm. Maybe her oxygen levels were just really low. She'd been feeling weak since Atlanta, and she should probably go to the hospital. But she knew if she could get a good night's sleep, she'd be fine in the morning.

Or maybe not. Maybe her future was blank, after all.

# SEVEN

LILY'S DRIVEWAY, LITTERED WITH PINE NEEDLES, WOUND INTO THE tall, piney woods and opened up on to a newfangled log cabin–style home. The way Log Cabin syrup is "maple-style," it was an enormous, diluted, imitation of the real thing. The severe horizontal lines of the architecture were broken up by beautiful arched windows and softened by a completely chaotic English-style garden growing out of control in the front yard. The wet grass of the backyard sloped down to the lake.

It was only eight o'clock, but Cam was tired. It had taken them less than an hour to get to Lily's from South of the Border, and during the ride, Cam hadn't been sure she would make it. Her head throbbed and everything ached. She almost had to resort to the little dropper of morphine she kept in the secret knee-pocket of her cargo pants for emergencies, but she didn't want to be crabby and irritated when she saw Lily, so she drank a ton of water instead and

took some of her stolen calendula root from Whole Foods. But the sight of Lily's house eased some of Cam's pain. She'd only been there once before, but the house felt instantly familiar and comforting. People here knew what it was like.

Cam stepped out of the car and stretched her arms in the air. Before she could even put her shoes on, Lily bolted out the front door, grabbed her wrist, and pulled her down the hill toward the water.

"Ouch, ouch, ouch," Cam chanted as she tried unsuccessfully to dodge the pine cones that kept ending up under her feet.

"Watch out for those," said Lily, who whisked ethereally around them in a white, flowing dress like a tiny wood fairy.

They tiptoed out to the end of the dock, where Lily had set up two Cokes, a box of cigarettes, and a big abalone shell she was using as an ashtray. The fiberglass of the motor-boat squeaked as it occasionally rubbed up against the tires nailed to the side of the dock. The only other sounds were the chorus of the crickets and the lip-smacking noise of the water as it lapped up against the boat. The moon cast a glimmering yellow path on the water, as if inviting you to walk on it.

"So, I did it," said Lily as she lit a bottle rocket and sent it screaming off the dock. It exploded with a pop that echoed over the lake. Turned out Lily was quite the pyrotechnics expert—or pyromaniac, Cam wasn't sure. "What else did you bring me?" she asked, hungrily digging through Cam's bag for another explosive.

"Wait! Back up. You did what?" asked Cam. From the looks of it, Lily had done a lot of things differently since she and Cam had bunked together at their last clinical trial in Memphis. Her hair, normally spiked in a punk pixie and highlighted with green, was back to its natural dirty blonde. It was now tamed, shoulder-length, and held back with a thin, unadorned headband. She had stopped using her bold, liquid eyeliner and instead wore some soft blue (blue!) eye shadow that matched the crystalline of her eyes. "What did you do, Alice, jump down the rabbit hole?"

"I guess you could put it that way." Lily smirked. She sat next to Cam at the end of the dock and put her feet in the water.

"You did *it*, it?" asked Cam, seeing how far she could splash and then watching the water settle in concentric ripples.

"Affirmative." Lily kicked out her foot, sending a few drops of water about two feet farther than Cam's latest splash.

"With whom?"

"Ryan," said Lily, and she couldn't stop herself from smiling.

"Who is Ryan?" Cam asked. She was shocked that this was the first time she was hearing about this. They talked to each other every day. How had Lily failed to mention that she had a "lover"?

"I met him at church."

"You go to church now?" The surprises just kept on coming.

"And youth group," said Lily as she pulled her foot out of the water. She shivered a bit, grabbed her bright orange beach towel, and wrapped it around her. She snuggled up next to Cam, shoulder to shoulder.

"Aren't you youth group people against premarital sex?" Cam asked, wondering how Lily could possibly be cold. It was still eighty degrees and humid in spite of the slight breeze wafting in over the lake.

"Publicly."

"And privately?"

"Like rabbits."

"Ahh. Thank you for finally solving for me the mysterious allure of youth group," said Cam. "So do you go to Christian rock concerts now?"

"No. I had to draw the line somewhere," Lily explained. She still listened to Rancid, Propagandhi, Anti-Flag, and the Dead Kennedys, but she was straying away from Crucifux and Christ on a Crutch, for Ryan's sake. Lord's name in vain, and all that.

"What does he look like? I'm getting a gangly, freckly, pimply vibe."

"Cam."

"In a good way. I mean pimply in a good way."

"How can you be pimply in a good way?"

"I don't know." Cam felt something. Was it jealousy? Was she jealous of gangly, pimply Ryan? Or envious that Lily was having this experience? Or furious that Lily had never told her about it? She was suddenly embarrassed that she had sloppily confessed her every private thought and desire to Lily, while Lily was up here leading a secret life. She watched a firefly hovering over the lake blink five times before asking, "So is Ryan, like, your boyfriend?"

"Once he breaks up with Kaitlin."

"Right." *There's a catch,* thought Cam. *There's always a catch.*

"No. I know he loves me. He's just been with Kaitlin for a long time, so it's difficult for him to extricate himself," Lily said as she shook an American Spirit out of the box.

"Let me guess. Kaitlin does not believe in premarital sex."

"Cam. He loves me. A woman knows," she said through clenched teeth as she lit the cigarette with the South of the Border lighter Cam had stolen from Rocket City.

"Woman?" asked Cam. "He's made a woman out of you?"

"Entirely," Lily said, jutting her bottom lip out so she could exhale toward the sky and away from Cam's face.

"Don't smoke," said Cam.

"Don't nag," said Lily, flicking the cigarette into the lake.

"But how do you *know* he loves you? Like, how are you so certain?"

"There are signs, Campbell."

"Like in Bugs Bunny when his eyes bulge out and his head is encircled with a wreath of hearts and chirping birds, and his heart springs visibly out of his chest?"

Lily turned to her. "How'd you guess?"

"No, really."

"I don't know," said Lily, fiddling with her pack of cigarettes and letting another one loose. She clamped it between her lips and lit it. "When he touches me," she said, squinting one eye from the smoke, "there's a vibration. An energy that shoots through my body. A visceral wisdom. I get goose bumps. All of my hair stands on end. Every time he touches me. And only when he touches me. That's how I know."

"Visceral wisdom," Cam muttered. "Doesn't that just mean you want him?"

"God, Campbell. Enough! I know what I know, okay?"

"Okay, well, good for you. Congratulations about Ryan," said Cam. She tried to be happy for Lily, but she was skeptical. There was nothing hornier-sounding than a seventeen-year-old boy named Ryan.

"I have another confession to make," said Lily, turning toward Cam. For the first time since she'd arrived, Cam noticed how thin Lily had become. Her skin was silvery gray and diaphanous, her fingers spindly, and her facial features— her nose and cheekbones—sharp.

"There's more? I don't think I can take any more," said

Cam. "You're taking the cancerexia a little too far, by the way. Are you eating?"

"Yes, I'm eating, Cam, and I wrote a letter to Make-A-Wish," Lily said. Cam and Lily had vowed never to do that. They weren't going to join the cancer establishment or exploit their illness for free stuff. "I want to go to Italy with Ryan," she said.

"What does Kaitlin have to say about that?" Cam asked.

"Shut up. You should do it too. Write to them."

Aside from *Dear Make-A-Wish, I wish I did not have cancer,* Cam had no idea what she'd write. *Dear Make-A-Wish, Can you please get me laid before I die?* Come on. She'd trained herself for so long not to want or to hope or to wish, that she had a hard time pinning down something to ask for. And she was content. She had her car. She had her bird, and she was on the road, running. If she kept running, maybe the cancer would never catch up with her.

"I don't have a wish," she said.

"Yes, you do." Lily leaned against her.

"Stop it. I don't." She leaned away.

"You do," Lily said, flicking yet another cigarette into the lake.

"What's with the littering? Dear Make-A-Wish, I wish my friend Lily would stop smoking and flicking her cigarettes into the lake," said Cam.

"I'm going to write a letter for you then."

"Great. They'll probably send me to Disney World."

The chirping soprano crickets and a few croaking baritone frogs filled the awkward silence. With the new Ryan development, Lily had ventured to a place Cam would probably never go herself. It was like Cam was suddenly playing Sandra Dee to Lily's Rizzo from *Grease*, and Cam couldn't get that stupid phrase "lousy with virginity" out of her head. She felt a rift deepening and widening between them. A crack straight through her heart.

"By the way, Kaitlin has strep throat, so Ryan's going to take us on a picnic tomorrow. You'll get to meet him," said Lily.

"Terrific. And what am I going to do while you two are off sneaking into the woods?"

"Well, Ryan has a friend. Andrew."

"Oh, God, Lily, no."

"Oh my *goodness*, Campbell, yes."

"You know I can play the sick card, right? I really feel like crap."

"Trust me," Lily said.

"Okay, fine," Cam said. She wished she'd thought to put *disastrous blind date* on her Flamingo list because she felt certain she would accomplish that now.

"There's something I want to do," said Lily. She got up and moved behind Cam. Cam thought she was searching for some more fireworks or something, but before she could turn around, Lily muttered, "InthenameoftheFatherSonand-HolySpiritIbaptizeyouCampbellMariaCooper." And then she pushed Cam off the dock.

It took Cam a few moments to make sense of what had just happened. To make whole the pieces of synaptic experience, connect the dots, and understand: pushing, falling, fear, wet, cold, splash, muffled sounds, underwater, lake! She let herself hang suspended for a second in the underwater quiet. She felt some soft seaweed tickle her foot and then kicked to the surface.

The water felt so clean that Cam dunked herself under again and then grabbed onto the white plastic ladder at the end of the dock and pulled herself up face-first.

Lily peeked over the edge of the dock with an impish look on her face. That fabulous glint in her eye that meant she was up to some harmless no-good. Like the time in the hospital when she raided the supply closet, stole huge white garbage bags, tied toilet paper around their heads, and made Cam march with her in the Halloween parade as "white trash."

"Excuse me," said Cam, spitting some water, "but did you just freaking baptize me?" Cam's parents were agnostics and didn't believe in religious rituals that tried to set some people apart from others. How could dumping water on someone's head help them gain access to heaven?

"Sort of," said Lily.

"Lily! You can't do that to a person against her will."

"We do it to babies all the time."

"I'm not a baby. Here, help me up." Lily reached a hand out for Cam's. Cam pulled on it, hurling Lily into the water headfirst.

"I can't believe you fell for that," said Cam when Lily resurfaced. "That's the oldest one in the book."

"I deserved it," Lily said, trying to tread water. Their wet clothes weighed their skinny bodies down, so staying afloat was difficult. Cam held a hand out to Lily and dragged her to the ladder. She was so light.

"Yeah. How do I get unbaptized?"

"Sin. A lot."

"You seem to be better at that than I am. I'm the pure one."

"Except for the 'thou shalt not steal' thing."

"Yeah, that's getting to be a bad habit."

The moon threw its light right onto Lily as if it were her personal spotlight. It danced behind her on the ripples of the lake.

"You don't believe it makes a difference, do you?"

"I don't know. Did you find Jesus?" Lily asked.

"Why? Is he under there?" joked Cam, ducking under the dock.

"Very funny. I thought it was better to be safe than sorry."

"Um, thanks? I guess?" Cam tried to be angry, then figured

that if it hadn't mattered to her that she wasn't, it shouldn't matter to her that she was. Baptized, that is. Her Catholic grandmother would be thrilled. And it was sweet of Lily. It was her way of bringing Cam into the fold, into her new, Christian-y, Ryan-y life.

Cam climbed out of the water and wrapped herself in the huge orange towel. The two of them shivered as they picked up the Coke cans and the ashtray and the cigarettes. The house seemed to smile at them through a face of yellow-lit windows.

"Anyway, now you're saved," Lily said. She linked her bony arm with Cam's as they hiked up the sloping lawn together and made their way into the house.

# EIGHT

McMANSION LIVING WASN'T ALL BAD. THE NEXT DAY, AFTER SLEEPING with seven down pillows of different shapes and sizes beneath matching sheets in a room to herself that was perfectly climate-controlled to seventy-two degrees, Cam awoke feeling energized. Ready to face what Lily had in store.

She made her way groggily down the staircase made of shellacked split logs covered in the center with chartreuse carpeting. Lily's mom, Kathy, greeted Cam in the kitchen. She was southern. Like *Gone with the Wind* southern. She had a fake blonde bob, fake boobs, and fake fingernails.

"Good mawnin', Cayum," Kathy said. She wasn't as dumb as she sounded with the accent. Weird how an accent could make you seem dumb. Cam didn't have one because her mom's Jersey accent was tempered by the Florida one, and it all sort of morphed into a nonaccent. "What kin we git you for breakfast?"

Cam looked around the kitchen, with its requisite cherry cabinets, stainless-steel appliances, granite countertops, and huge center island for prep work. The window behind the sink looked out onto the morning lake, which was steaming with foggy wisps like a hot cup of tea. They probably had every breakfast food imaginable, except for what Cam really wanted: Lucky Charms.

*As long as breakfast doesn't involve pineapple*, thought Cam. Last night Lily's mom had set out a Polynesian (as interpreted by a North Carolina caterer) spread, heavy on the pineapple.

"Is this authentic?" Kathy had asked.

"I wouldn't know," said Alicia. "I'm from a big Italian family in New Jersey."

Everyone laughed. Their families were close, but they had only ever talked about the cancer. It had consumed their lives and their interactions. Blood counts, new trials, breakthroughs, symptoms, and ways to get more energy, more life.

Neuroblastoma was a baby cancer. Something happened to the baby nerve cells before they became mature nerve cells and they started growing out of control, creating tumors around the liver and then spreading to the bones or kidneys or anywhere, really. Ninety-nine percent of cases happened in babies. And most people, when they got it as babies, could survive it. With babies, it had even been known to spontaneously, miraculously, disappear. It was a different story if you got it when you were older. Chances of survival were pretty slim.

"Cayum. I wanted to talk to you for a minute, honey," said Kathy, pouring herself another cup of coffee.

*More cancer talk*, thought Cam. "Do you have any Lucky Charms?" she interrupted, trying to cut Kathy off at the pass. "I could go for some Lucky Charms."

"We might, honey. Check the pantry."

The walk-in pantry was almost as big as the one at the restaurant, with shelves and shelves of cans and dried goods organized by sundry. Cam looked at "cereal row," and as she'd expected, everything was organic and fibrous. No wonder Lily was getting so skinny. She grabbed a green box of Enviro-Pops from the shelf and reentered the kitchen. "You could feed a village with that pantry," she said.

"Yes, I guess we should take some of that to the food bank. Listen, Cam—"

"You didn't have any Lucky Charms," Cam interrupted, "but I found these," she said, shaking the box. "Forty percent less sugar and no trans fat."

"Great. Cayum. Listen, there's a new study we found out about, and Malcolm pulled some strings, and we got Lily into it. It's pretty expensive, but we'd be happy to foot the bill if you wanted to try it with Lily. It's in Chicago, and we got in because we know someone who knows someone."

Cam let herself be distracted for a second by the red dart

of a cardinal flying past the kitchen windows behind Kathy. "My mom knew Madonna once," she said. She settled on a stool at the center island and pressed her bony elbows into the granite.

"Um. Really, sugar?"

It wasn't that giving up on western medicine didn't frighten Cam. Western medicine was her life. Her whole identity had become wrapped up in leukocytes and lymphocytes and neuroblasts and metastasis, chemo, radiation, surgery, procedures. And none of it mattered. The entire trillion-dollar cancer industry and all of its machinery, Cam now realized, was for naught. All the pain it caused. All the bone-marrow transplants. For naught. The war on cancer, like any war, was useless except for its ability to stimulate the economy. Drugs were being sold. Doctors were getting paid. Pharmaceutical companies were getting rich. Cam had become collateral damage in the war on cancer. And she was done with all of it. She was throwing in *la toalla*.

"Don't think Madonna could pull any strings, though," Cam concluded.

"So, what do you think, sugar?"

"Kathy, I think that is very nice of you. Really. But I don't think that's my path."

"Since when do you have a 'path'?" Alicia asked, appearing in the doorway of the kitchen. She leaned against the doorjamb in her pajamas and kimono and held her cup of coffee in both hands. Her face was chiseled into the stern, serious, and yet slightly amused countenance of a disappointed mother that Cam rarely saw because she rarely did anything wrong.

"Since now. We're going to Crazy Town in Maine, remember? That's our strategy, since we don't *know* someone who *knows* someone."

"Don't you think we should at least try it?" Alicia said. "It's medicine, Campbell." She swept a long curly strand of hair out of her red-rimmed morning eyes.

Cam wavered for a second. Trying was usually better than not trying. But not in this case. The road trip was changing her a bit. Now that they'd gotten the momentum going, she wanted to finish what they'd started.

"*A'ohe I pau ka 'ike I ka halau ho'okahi,*" she said. It was a popular hula adage that meant: *All knowledge is not contained in only one school.* "No more trials, Mom."

All the last trial had done was diminish her immune system to the point where she got shingles (a seventy-year-old-man disease) and yeast infections all over her body, including her tongue. She couldn't close her mouth for three days. The "science" of these trials just didn't add up. You didn't demolish someone's immune system to make her healthy. Promise, Maine, made just as much sense. Cam grabbed a banana and made her way out of the kitchen.

Lily crashed into her. She was bounding into the kitchen

dressed in some child-size Daisy Dukes and a calico halter, asking her mom if she'd finished packing the picnic basket.

"You let your mom pack the picnic basket?" Cam asked.

"That's the last of it," said Kathy, as she put the Brie and apricots into the basket.

"Thanks, Mama." Lily gave her mom a squeeze. Lily was kind of a spoiled brat, but she somehow made it an endearing part of her personality. Finally she turned around to look at Cam. "You're wearing that?" she asked. Cam was still in the oversize, off-the-shoulder FRANKIE SAYS RELAX T-shirt that she wore to bed.

"I just woke up," said Cam. "It seems a little early for a picnic."

"Ryan has to be somewhere this afternoon. Come on! Get dressed."

Back in the guest room, Cam muttered to herself as she put her cargo pants back on and topped them with a plain black tank top. She combed her hand through her hair, and that was it. She was not going to try to impress anyone.

She was contemplating whether or not to even wear earrings when she heard a horn blaring from the driveway. She grabbed her biker bag, ran outside, and was mortified to find an idling yellow Hummer.

"Come on!" Lily said as she pulled Cam by the hand toward the enormous vehicle.

"God, Lily. Don't you think J. C. would drive a Prius?"

"Don't be such a buzzkill."

"I'm sorry I'm so reluctant to destroy the planet with my Humvee. I should be more of a sport."

"Campbell!" Lily dismissed her friend and then literally skipped toward the truck, the picnic basket banging against her legs. Cam had to help her open the monstrous door.

"Where's Andrew?" Lily asked as she glanced at the empty backseat.

"Lacrosse," said Ryan.

"Is he coming?" Lily persisted.

"Nope."

"Ry-an. Why didn't you tell me?"

"It's not a big deal, Lil. Come on," Ryan said.

"At least let me go get a book or something to entertain myself," Cam begged. She tried to turn back toward the house, but Lily pushed Cam's skinny butt into the backseat.

Ryan had curly red hair, ivory skin, and freckles. He was, in fact, a tiny bit pimply, but nothing too repulsive. Everything about him seemed new, nascent, hairless, like he'd just hatched from some alien egg and arrived onto planet Adulthood. Everything except his voice. He had a deep, booming actor's voice, and when he said, "Cam, it's nice to finally meet you," Cam could see how Lily could let herself get sucked in. Even so, she wished she had just stayed home and gone to the movies with her mom and Perry.

At the park they climbed to one of eastern North Carolina's

few hills. Cam mourned the loss of her quadricep muscles with each tiring step, but the air was cool and just refreshing enough to fuel her and to bring some color to Lily's cheeks. They got to the overlook, a cliff with a view of the entire "lake," which was mostly a man-made reservoir of sorts, an Army Corps of Engineers marvel, a flooded soybean field. Still, it was beautiful with the sun sparkling off of it and the clear voices of the loons and boaters echoing all the way up to them at the top of the hill.

Ryan spread out the checkered blanket and insisted on a little prayer before helping Lily set out the food. He made sure she ate something before he would touch a morsel.

"You have to eat, Lily. Come on," he said, creating for her a perfect bite of cracker with pimento cheese and a slice of pickle, Lily's favorite snack.

He had been chivalrous and entertaining during the entire hike, lugging all of their stuff and starting friendly, small-talk conversations. He must have taken the same southern etiquette classes at the "club" that Lily had growing up, which made them a good couple, Cam guessed.

Lily took one bite and then covered her nose and mouth with a napkin. In seconds the napkin was bright with Lily's blood. A nosebleed. "Shit!" said Lily.

"Squeeze it." Cam reached over to hand Lily a cloth napkin and searched through the cooler for an ice pack. She helped Lily tilt her head back and pressed the ice pack to the bridge of Lily's nose. Even Lily's front teeth were red with blood. "Is this happening a lot?" Cam asked. Aside from Lily's frail appearance, this was the first sign Cam had seen that Lily was not totally in remission.

"Yeah. It's my new thing."

"Nice. Well, I had a seizure in the dollar store parking lot, if that makes you feel any better."

"Awesome," said Lily. "I'll be right back." She made her way to the cabin of outhouses that was about a hundred yards behind them in the woods. "You two get to know each other," she said, still holding her nose.

Cam sat down on the blanket and washed the blood off of her hands with some water from the water bottle. She and Ryan stared out at the lake. "So." Cam was still feeling a little fidgety. "I'm to get to know you," she said as if she were in a Jane Austen novel.

"What do you want to know?" Ryan asked.

"Honestly?"

"I'm an open book," he said.

"I want to know your intentions," Cam said, keeping with the Jane Austen vocabulary.

"Intentions?"

A sibilant breeze whispered its way through the pine needles overhead, and in the distance Cam could hear the knocking of a woodpecker.

"Yeah. Like with Lily. She thinks you love her," said Cam.

Ryan sat up straight and crossed his legs. Probably feeling shifty at the mention of the word *love*.

"I intend to enjoy whatever time we have left," he said, grabbing a nectarine from the basket.

"What about the other chick?" Cam asked.

"What about her?"

"Are you breaking up with her?"

Ryan stared out at the lake, threw the nectarine up into the air, caught it, and took a sloppy bite. With his mouth still full of nectarine—*What happened to the etiquette*, thought Cam—he turned to Cam with a steely-eyed stare and said, "Now what would be the point of that?"

"Of what?" Lily startled them. A tiny smear of dried blood still tattooed her forearm, but there was otherwise no sign of the nosebleed.

Ryan got up and walked away.

"What's with him?" Lily asked.

"No idea," said Cam.

At dinner that night, after Cam made the mistake of eating off of her "charger plate," Perry read out loud the embarrassing list of miracles she'd recorded so far in her notebook from Izanagi. Only Perry could find miracles on I-95.

Arguments could be made for some of the more elusive

items on the list, like *#3 Alicia hasn't lost her patience since Atlanta*, or *#7 McDonald's French fries*. But when she started listing things like gas engines and cranes under *The Miracle of Transportation*, Cam had to draw the line.

"That's *technology*, Perry, not a miracle. Anything that can be studied under the guise of an *-ology* is disqualified as a miracle."

"What about angelology or unicornology?" Perry asked.

"Or theology." Lily's dad, Malcolm, smirked. He had a broad, handsome, clean-shaven face that was just on the verge of being jowly.

"I give up," Cam said.

"So Cam, how was your date with Andrew?" Kathy winked. In this family, everything awkward was laid out in the open at the dinner table, like the poor chicken carcass that sat cold, naked, and ashamed as the wind whistled through its bones.

"He stood me up, actually," Cam said, taking a huge bite of corn on the cob so that people would stop asking her questions.

"He had lacrosse," Lily threw out quickly, meeting her mother's accusatory stare with her own.

"Well, what did you think of Ryan, then?" Kathy continued.

Cam knew she was cooked. "He's really nice," she said carefully.

It was difficult for her to quell the compulsion to tell the truth, and when she did manage to tamp it down, it was obvious to everyone that she was lying. *That's what they must teach in those etiquette classes*, thought Cam. *Etiquette is really just politely lying to people's faces.* She wished she could do it now.

"Uh-oh," said Malcolm. His face was rosy, and Cam suspected he'd had too many chardonnays. "If she says he was 'interesting,' we know she hated him."

"He *was* interesting, though," Cam insisted, knowing she was fighting a losing battle. "And polite."

"Ohhh, Lily," Malcolm joked, shaking his big head back and forth. "She doesn't like him one bit."

"I never said that," Cam insisted. "I like him, Lily. He has a great voice."

"Okay," Kathy interrupted. "Who wants peach pie?"

Everyone was silent for a moment. Alicia stood up, clearing some plates. "I'll help you with dessert."

As the moms swept into the kitchen, Lily gestured at Cam with a stern look on her face. *Upstairs*, she seemed to be saying.

"But I like peach pie," Cam said out loud.

"Then take yours in my bedroom."

Cam followed Lily up the stairs, balancing her triangle of pie on a saucer and dreading the inquiry she knew was coming.

"Why don't you like him, Cam?"

"I do like him! I said he was great," Cam insisted.

"No, you said he was nice and interesting and had a good voice—which, coming from you, means that you hate his guts."

"Lily, I only talked to him for ten minutes. How could I possibly hate his guts?"

Lily stared into Cam's eyes, trying to ferret out the truth. Finally, she gave up and let her face relax into a smile. "I just want you two to like each other."

"Okay," Cam said. "Want to work on the graphic-novel-slash-screenplay? I brought it with me." Cam rose excitedly and pulled it out of her suitcase.

"Sure," said Lily. "Let me just say good night to Ryan. Five minutes. I promise." She slipped out the door and headed down the hall.

But as five minutes stretched into half an hour, Cam slid their project back into its envelope, suddenly painfully aware of how immature it seemed. Writing a comic book. It seemed like the geekiest thing in the universe. Only an extreme social outcast or a ten-year-old would ever dream of attempting it.

Cam was alone except for Lily's bright-haired troll doll collection. They kept staring at her, and she cringed in embarrassment. She covered her head with her pillow and willed herself to sleep.

The next morning, Cam went to wake Lily up to say good-bye. Lily's bedroom was white. Lily white. All white except for one huge magenta painting of an abstract gladiola on the far wall. The white was intended to ease tension, according to Lily's therapist, who made her paint over the black walls previously spray-painted with the purple names of Lily's favorite bands. The white stressed Cam out, though. What if you accidentally spilled something? It was too much pressure.

Lily was buried under her puffy white cloud of a comforter. She was so tiny, the lumps of her body under the blanket were barely perceptible. Cam jumped on the bed to say good-bye.

"I'm leaving," she said.

Lily just giggled beneath the covers.

"Why is that funny?"

"Hold on," said Lily, and when she popped her head out from under the comforter, Cam realized that Lily was on the phone. "I'll be with you in a minute, Cam," she said, and she swept the back of her hand at Cam like a little broom before sinking under the covers to resume giggling.

That sounded so cold. *With you in a minute*. And the hand broom? Cam was tired of being swept away. She was leaving and had no idea when she'd see Lily again. They never used to speak that way to each other. *With you in a minute*.

On her way out the door, Cam noticed an oxygen tank standing next to Lily's clear plastic desk. Two white picture frames sat on the desk staring at each other. One was of Lily and Cam, sitting on a hospital bed at St. Jude's with their arms around each other. Their bald heads knocked together as they smiled for the camera. Before she knew what she was doing, Cam grabbed it and stuck it inside her hoodie. Then she went out and closed the door.

"You ready?" Alicia asked from downstairs in the great room.

"Yeah," said Cam. "I'm ready."

As they were starting up the rig, Cam put some extra-reinforcement duct tape around Darren. Lily's parents waved good-bye from the front stoop. They were about to pull out when Lily came running out the front door.

"How dare you leave without saying good-bye!" she said, trying to catch her breath. She stopped in the middle of the driveway.

"I tried," said Cam, meeting her halfway between the house and the car.

"Oh, Cam, don't pout." Lily placed her hands on her hips. The drawstring of her light blue hospital scrubs was cinched as tight as it could go around her waist. And yet the hem of the pants dropped over her Ugg slippers and onto the drive-way, sucking up the morning dew like the roots of a flower.

"I'm not pouting. I'm happy for you. Good luck with Ryan, and I hope you get your wish," Cam added coldly.

"Cam," Lily said.

Cam took a moment to watch a ladybug crawl up and over a blade of grass. "He's just using you, you know," she blurted.

"How could you possibly know that?" Lily's icy blue gaze shifted from concern to dismissal. Her eyes hardened.

"I asked him, Lil. And he was strangely honest about it, actually. I was right about him," Cam said, and she immediately regretted it. She felt numb inside. As if she had no organs. She was a shell. A carapace. An empty carcass alone and adrift.

"Oh, God, Campbell, you are not right for once." Lily's voice went up an octave on the word *right*. "You're just so obviously jealous." She sighed and ran her hand through her hair. She turned around and began to walk away but then stopped. "You can't stand seeing me happy, can you? You just need to pull me back into your misery. But I need to enjoy my life. Let my guard down a little. Maybe you should try it."

Cam knew that letting her guard down would be the end of her. Her guard was all she had left. "I guess I'm just not that desperate," she said.

It took Lily a moment to absorb that blow. She looked down, kicked a few pine needles, took a deep breath, and said, "That's funny because you are the most desperate person I know, Campbell Cooper." She looked up with a final, watery stare. "And I have no more room in my life for your negativity. I need to be surrounded by positive energy. I need you to leave me alone."

"You sound like one of those stupid self-help books," Cam said.

"I'm serious, Campbell. Good luck with everything." Lily backed away toward her pretend–log cabin house and politely waved to Alicia and Perry.

"Lily—" Cam started. But Lily was gone.

Back in the car, Cam took the screenplay that they had started together out from her biker bag. As Lily's house disappeared into the distance, she tore it right down the middle.

# NINE

### "MARIA! LYDIA!"

Their nana came screaming out of her three-story house in Hoboken, which had a view of the Manhattan skyline if you stuck your head out the attic window and looked to the left. Nana was wearing a bright blue matching tracksuit. She was very matchy.

"Mom. Call them by their first names," Alicia said.

"I don't even remember them anymore. What are they again? Harry and Jonathan?"

"Mom."

"I'm kidding. Girls, just promise me you'll give my great-granddaughters girls' names, would you? That's my dying wish. What about Rose? Name one of your kids after me."

"Sure, Nana," said Perry, giving her grandmother a hug.

"That's a good girl," said Nana, kissing her on top of her pert blonde head.

Cam couldn't yet speak. Something about seeing her nana really choked her up. She didn't realize how much she'd missed her.

"Campbell," said her nana, opening her flabby arms wide as Campbell let herself melt into them.

"See, you remember my name," said Cam.

"You, I never forget, my love. My firstborn grandchild . . . you are my heart," she whispered so Perry wouldn't hear. "Now come," she said, secretly wiping away a tear. "Let's eat. You must be hungry. Look at you, all skin and bones. You look like an Olsen twin."

"Which one?" joked Campbell.

"The one who's dating Justin Bartha."

"Who is Justin Bartha? You need to stop reading *People* magazine."

"What? I read it at the beauty parlor. I don't have a subscription or anything." She fiddled with some containers in the fridge. "Here. Eat this. It's Miracle Lasagna. Tony Spinelli ate it last month, and his gallstones completely disappeared."

"Do you believe in miracles, Nan?" Cam asked.

"It doesn't matter what I believe, does it? Right now, Campbell, it only matters what you believe," she said as she poured herself another cup of coffee from her seventies stainless-steel percolator.

That was what Cam loved about her grandmother's house: the way that, aside from a gradual yellowing or fading, nothing ever changed. Her nana still had her coffeepot from the seventies, the same NANA'S KITCHEN needlepoint in a frame, the same cast-iron trivets, the same crocheted pot holders, and the same yellow, ruffled cotton valence in the kitchen window that she'd take down three times a year to wash and iron. The kitchen had the same checkerboard, black and white linoleum tile, the same chrome-plated Formica kitchen table with four red vinyl seats. Everything was the same.

"She doesn't believe in anything," said Perry matter-of-factly.

"I believe in you, Nana," said Cam.

"You better find something more powerful than me, kiddo."

There was a time when Cam would have Believed, with a capital *B*, in all of this miracle business. In fact, there was a time when she'd thought she was special. Things had happened to her. Subtle yet amazing things that made her believe that someone, a higher power, was watching over her.

When she was six, she thought a lot about the hands of God. God, to six-year-old Cam, was a bearded old man on a cloud with enormous hands that would hurt if you got spanked. She was never spanked by the hands of God. But once, when she was trudging up her street on a hot day in the swamps of Florida, wishing she had a bicycle so she could get more quickly to her friend Jessica's house to play Barbies, she was swept off the ground by . . . a mysterious vortex? The hands of God? . . . and delivered right to Jessica's doorstep. One minute she was in front of Mark VanHouten's house—the one with the scary Rottweiler tied to a chain—and the next, she was a quarter mile down the road at Jessica's, holding her Barbies with the shorn blonde hair, a consequence of living with a baby sister who got her hands on some safety scissors.

Anyway, there was a time when Cam would have believed in miracles. A time when she was lifted up by some mysterious force and placed gently back down onto Jessica's doorstep. But that was before divorces and before cancer and before her father died right smack-dab in the middle of his life. Way before Cam knew she'd never see her eighteenth birthday.

After nightfall, when Cam and Perry were drooling in front of some reality TV, and their mom was visiting some old friends, Nana walked into the living room dressed in black. She wore her black leotard and tights from Jazzercise underneath some black Bermuda shorts and a black baseball cap. She had black eyeliner smudged beneath her eyes.

"You ready, Campbell?" she asked.

"Oh, my God, Nana. For what?"

"Our mission. We're going over the wall."

According to church history, on a Sunday morning in 1999,

the Virgin Mary appeared to housewife Joan Caruso while she was teaching Sunday school to preschoolers at Our Lady of Ascension Church on Church Street. She was out in the churchyard, letting the little ones burn off some of their pent-up Catholic steam, and she was staring at a knot in a tree. Slowly, according to Joan Caruso, who'd had five kids in five years and probably hadn't slept in as much time, the knot in the tree morphed into the visage of the Virgin. And the Virgin told her, "Build for me here a shrine and let all who come here be healed. Hoboken will become the Lourdes of America."

Anyone who heard that sentence would know it had to be a joke. It sounded to Cam like this Joan chick was watching the Pocahontas movie on acid. The one with the talking tree. But people believed this woman instead of putting her on some antipsychotics. And those who knew the story made pilgrimages to the tree in Hoboken to be healed by its mystic maple leaves.

"Come on," said Nana. "Here's a flashlight."

"Why can't we do this in daylight again?" asked Cam, flicking the light on and off to check the batteries.

"I told you. Because of Rita." Nana's ex-friend Rita was the volunteer in charge of leaf administration and had denied Nana's application to visit the tree and take away a leaf for Cam three times. "There's bad blood between us."

"What'd you do to her?" Cam asked as she stood up from the recliner.

"I accidentally slept with her husband once. Or twice. Maybe it was twice," Nana said distractedly as she opened and closed the attachments of her Swiss Army knife, and then placed it into her black fanny pack.

"What do you mean, 'accidentally,' Nana? How can that happen by accident?" Cam asked.

But Nana just shrugged her shoulders. She was all business. "You coming, Perry?" she asked.

"No, thanks. I'm too tired."

"Feed Tweety for me, would you?" said Cam. "But don't let him out of his cage. He gets nervous in a new environment."

Cam was already dressed in black, as usual, so she walked with her grandmother two houses down to Our Lady of Ascension Church. They turned the corner and walked to the back, where the courtyard was enclosed by a ten-foot-high sand-colored brick wall.

Cam did not believe any leaf could cure her, of course. She didn't even believe the Virgin was a virgin. She imagined Mary after getting knocked up, powwowing with her girlfriends, gathering round the well, trying to figure out what to do.

"I know," one of them said. "Tell them that God did it."

"Perfect," Mary's girls chimed in.

And then the publicity of the thing must have just gotten way out of hand.

So Cam did not believe in any Mary miracles, but she

loved the prospect of a caper with her grandmother, and the idea of helping her get revenge.

"There it is," she said, pointing to the tree at the very center of the church courtyard. Someone, a nun probably, had taken very good care of this space. It was lush, verdant, fecund—words one didn't usually associate with Hoboken. It looked a little like the Polynesian Hotel, but with different flora. Rosebushes surrounded the perimeter just inside the wall. There was soft green grass, some other flowering plants, miscellaneous Mary statuary, and a soothing angel fountain trickling in the far corner. At the center stood the maple tree.

"Can't we just take a leaf from one of these?" asked Cam, pointing to the leaves growing conveniently out and over the wall.

"No. That's the one. In the center. It has to be that one," she whispered and covered her head with the hood of her sweatshirt. The baker and his wife had just stepped out of the Italian bakery across the street, closed the door, and locked it. They gave Cam a suspicious look before turning and walking home with their box of cannoli tied up with red string.

"Okay. You stay. I'll go. I don't want you breaking a hip," Cam said. The traffic light at the corner turned from red to green, but there were no cars to take advantage of it. It was a quiet night in Hoboken.

"But I'm going to look suspicious out here," Nana said, shifting from one foot to the other.

"Then why did you dress like that?" Cam asked.

"I don't know. I got caught up in the heat of the moment."

"There seems to be a lot of that going on in your life. You need to work on impulse contr—"

"Just go. Up and over," Nana said, bending over and cupping her hands to make a human step for Cam.

"I'm not exactly 100 percent, you know. Feeling a little weak these days," Cam said as she stepped into her grandmother's hand-stirrup and then placed her own hands on her Nana's increasingly stooping shoulders.

"You want me to do it, honey?" Nana asked. Cam was close enough to smell her breath, which was always licorice-y, like anisette.

"No. I'll do it."

"Okay. Up and over. Wait, what is our code word? In case of an emergency or something," Nana asked.

"Banana," Cam said as she took a quick step, grabbed the top of the wall, and then hoisted herself over it. She slid her stomach down the other side and clung with her fingers for just a second, trying to avoid dropping into a rosebush. As soon as she let go, she heard, "Oh, God. Banana. Banana. Banana."

"What is it?" Cam whispered. "Police?"

"No. Rita. I'm going home. Good luck."

"Nana?" said Cam. But her grandmother was already gone. Cam turned her attention to the tree, which was gated off with a white fence and bottom-lit with blue and white spotlights implanted in the ground. She snuck up to it and reached for a low-hanging leaf when suddenly she heard the unmistakable, ding-dong, doorbell chirp of Tweety.

"Tweety?!" Cam could just make out his tiny little yellow belly perched behind a flapping leaf at the very top of the tree. She knew she shouldn't have trusted Perry with him.

"Tweety, get down here!" Cam whispered insistently, but he wouldn't budge. Adrenaline must have taken over because Cam's usual fear of heights disappeared. She felt weightless and nimble enough to scamper to one of the highest branches, where she held onto a branch above her and sidestepped herself along the one she was standing on. She reached for Tweety and called to him again.

"Come here, silly boy. This is Jersey, Tweety. You can't handle these mean streets. Come back here, Tweets."

She whistled the little call that he liked. "Here, Tweety." She almost had him. Her fingertips grazed the sharp claws on his left foot, when she felt her own foot begin to slip. The peeling bark beneath her sneakers began to give way and fall in chips to the ground until both of her feet were dangling. Cam hung by her armpits from a high branch of some crazy tree in Hoboken.

And then a door slammed. A bald-headed priest,

struggling with his big black-framed glasses, came storming out of the rectory in his bathrobe.

"Get down from there this instant! You must get out of that tree!"

Tweety chirped a last ding-dong chirp. Everything started to move in slow motion. Tweety looked Cam straight in the eye as if to apologize for something. Then he flapped his wings. He didn't take off. He just flapped. As if to say, *Come with me. Let's get out of here, Cam. Why can't you come with me?* He let out a tiny sigh and then flew away in the moonlight toward the blinking stegosaural skyline of Manhattan.

"You asshole!" Cam screamed down to the priest, who, even in New Jersey, was not used to being called an asshole. "You scared away my bird. You asshole," she said in a barely audible gasp because for the first time since her dad's funeral, she couldn't stop herself from crying. She tried to. She stiffened and tried to swallow the aching lump in her throat. But once the tears started, she couldn't stop them.

The priest, Father John, actually turned out to be a pretty cool guy. He literally talked Cam out of her tree and walked her home. He told her he would pray for Tweety's safe return, which he really didn't have to do after being called an asshole. Twice.

"Cam," said Perry as she came up the stairs and into the living room.

Cam held up her hand, catching a glimpse of Tweety's empty cage in her peripheral vision. "Don't even speak to me, Perry. Just leave me alone."

She turned to her nana. "I don't know which of your lost causes is most lost, Nana: reforming the Catholic Church, curing stage-four cancer, or finding a canary set loose in Hoboken. But if you could at least pray to St. Jude for the last one, that would be good." Cam flopped into her grandfather's old vinyl chair, which was covered with dishtowels and lace doilies in strategic places to prevent stickage.

"Did you get the leaf?" Her grandmother couldn't help herself.

"Here," said Cam, opening her clenched fist. There she held a crumpled green leaf. When unfurled, it seemed to be veined in almost exactly the same pattern as the creases in her palm.

Good-byes with Nana were difficult. Because in order for her to get through it without crying for ten days straight, she had to pretend to be angry with you.

Cam and Perry sat at the breakfast table. Their mom was packing the car, and they were supposed to leave in ten minutes. They had stayed in Hoboken for three extra days, combing the neighborhood for Tweety without any luck.

"Who used all the syrup?" Nana sighed as she hung her head into the refrigerator, and then she slammed the door shut.

"Ca—" Perry began, but Cam shot her a look like *Don't you* dare *throw me under the bus, child,* and because Perry was still trying to repent for losing Tweety, she said, "I did, Nana. I'm sorry." And then she ducked her head and covered it with her forearms to protect herself from the dishtowel Nana threw at her.

"You people eat me out of house and home," Nana said, sitting indignantly at the kitchen table without looking at either of them. "I guess I'll just drink this small glass of grapefruit juice, since that's all that you've left me."

"Cheers," Cam said, and she held up her glass to clink with her grandmother's. Nana just looked out the window above the kitchen sink, ignoring her.

"Where's your mother?" she finally said. "Don't tell me you two lazy bums let her pack the car by herself."

"She likes to do it herself," Perry said, and Cam smirked a little because Perry still hadn't learned when to keep her mouth shut. Cam waited for her grandmother to erupt. *Three . . . two . . . one . . .*

"Your mother does *everything* by herself. The least you can do is help her pack *your* suitcases into the trunk. She does everything for you and this is how you repay her?

Ingrates. That's what you are, a couple of ingrates. Don't have kids because this is how they treat you."

"Wait, Nana," Perry said, "she really does like to do it herself."

*Oh, Perry*, thought Cam, *shut up!*

It was true, of course. Alicia had a sick, neurotic blueprint for packing the trunk in the most efficient way, and she needed to be in complete control of it. But that was beside the point. When Nana was on the rampage, you just needed to stand clear.

Cam watched her grandmother swallow a sip of grapefruit juice and then watched her rheumy eyes narrow as she stared at Perry and contemplated her next move. Cam saw it coming, but before she could warn Perry to get out of the way, Nana tilted her little juice glass and threw its contents toward Perry's face.

The pinkish blob of liquid flew through the air in slow motion before it landed with a splat on Perry's forehead. Perry sat midgasp with her mouth half open and her bangs dripping and stuck to her head. She was deciding whether to laugh or cry, and since she'd had a bad week with everyone blaming her for Tweety's escape and all, she cried first. But she looked so ridiculous that Cam started laughing, and then Nana started laughing, until they were all laughing and crying at the same time and the ice was officially broken.

Cam reached over the table to pass Perry a napkin, her sleeves riding up. She tried hastily to pull them back down, but it was too late.

"What's that?" Nana asked. In the last three days, the blueberry spots had gotten worse. Cam's right forearm was pocked with ugly, raised purple bubbles the size of dimes that marked the plodding progress of the disease and its ambitious plot to take over her entire body.

"What?" Cam said, sneaking her thumb back into the hole she'd created in the wristband of her sweatshirt to keep her sleeves down.

"Don't say 'what.' You know what I'm talking about. That. On your arm."

"Bug bites," Cam said.

"We don't have those kinds of bugs in Hoboken."

"Ah, but you haven't been to the Magic Tree," said Cam.

"Campbell. Should you go get that checked out?"

Campbell just shrugged. "Let's go," she said. "I'm sure Mom's finished packing."

The three of them walked down the narrow, wood-paneled staircase to the front hall. Cam first, then Nana, and Perry trailed behind, jotting something down into her brown notebook from Izanagi. "Miracle number thirteen," she said as she wrote, "Nana is walking us to the door."

"Yeah, what are you doing, seeing us to the door?" asked Cam. Normally after pretending to be angry and then throwing a faux tantrum, Nana retreated to her bedroom without even saying good-bye.

"Just making sure you get the heck out of here," Nana joked.

Outside, it was a glorious day. Their ridiculous rig took up two metered spots on Church Street. Alicia wiped some sweat from her brow with the back of her hand, looking pleased with herself. Everything was packed up and ready to go.

"Let's go," she said. "Bye, Ma." She gave her mother a hug without even realizing how strange it was that Nana had actually made it outside to see them off.

Perry hugged her grandmother. Nana apologized for the juice.

"I guess it's our turn," Nana said. Cam and Nana circled around each other like wrestlers in a ring.

"Yeah."

"You want to just do one of those exploding fist-bump things?" Nana asked, holding out her fist.

"You can hug me if you want," Cam said.

Nana wrapped her arms around Cam and Cam choked back her tears. "I'm going to be okay, Nan."

"I already know that about you. You asked me what I believe. I believe that you are going to be okay," Nana said, and she squeezed Cam one more time. "Now go. I have my ten days of crying to do."

# TEN

THEY WERE BACK IN THE VAGINA TRAIN AND HEADING NORTH. CAM missed Lily. It had been days since they'd left North Carolina, and still Cam could not get the words *he's using you* out of her head. That was probably a little harsh, as was the word *desperate*. She wished she could take it all back.

They passed blue sign after blue sign advertising the fast-food options at each exit. Cam still got a little excited, a vestigial feeling from her overeating days, when she saw a good sign—one with four or more restaurants at one exit. But the thought of eating any of that garbage now turned her stomach. She had a metallic taste in her mouth, and she felt nauseous, with a strange pain shooting from her jaw down into the sides of her neck. She wished she could just throw up and maybe feel better.

After they had gotten through New Jersey and Connecticut, the strip-mall landscape on the side of the road had slowly and thankfully disintegrated until they were flanked on both sides by forest. Aside from her time at summer camp, Cam had never really been flanked by forest before. She peered through the trees, taking snapshots with her eyes of the ancient, falling-down rock walls and the ruins of an old chimney left standing after a cabin fire. Then the forest seemed to get darker and denser until she could barely see through the trees. It was all Hans Christian Andersen-y, and maybe, Cam had to admit, a little magical—as if there might be pixies and leprechauns hidden among the mushrooms or monsters lurking in caves. That was until she looked up and saw five beautiful semis piled with long, dead trees headed south toward the paper mill. *So much for magic*, she thought.

Their mom rolled over the perfect sine wave of the Maine Turnpike. It was as if they were driving up and down along the humped back of a giant sea serpent.

Perry bobbed her head back and forth as she mouthed the words to some tinkly Taylor Swift song. Their mom had gotten Perry a new phone when she got Cam one, just to be fair, which, if she hadn't been so sick, would have really pissed Cam off. But that was the thing about dying. It made you shrug off the truly petty concerns in your life. Let Perry enjoy her Taylor Swift. Even if she had lost Tweety.

"This must be it," Alicia called from the driver's seat. It was still daylight, but a street lamp shone on a bulbous pink and orange Dunkin' Donuts logo that sat right smack in the middle of the Exit 33 sign. Exit 33 had absolutely no other amenities, apparently. No gas. No lodging. No special attractions. Just a Dunkin' Donuts.

"I thought you said this was hard to find," she said, glancing up the exit ramp. One winding path led straight to a white brick Dunkin' Donuts at the top of the hill. The edifice itself was tiny, but it was lit up by the enormous three-story-high neon sign.

"It's a miracle!" Perry exclaimed, and she reached again for the notebook.

The Dunkin' Donuts driveway was not even paved. Tiny rocks popped beneath Cumulus's tires as they pulled in.

"You're supposed to go through the drive-through," Perry remembered.

Alicia steered the car toward the rusted squawk box in the back. It seemed to have been dented by some teenage vandal's baseball bat. The speaker scratched with a staticky crackle. They heard a woman's tired voice ask, "Ayuh?"

"Um," Alicia started. "Three whoopie cakes," she said.

Cam exploded in laughter, and Perry squealed.

"I think it's whoopie *pie*," Cam corrected.

"What difference does it make?" Alicia asked, beginning to giggle herself. They were all punchy from having been too long in the car. "Whoopie pies," she said into the squawk box. "And three chocolate milks."

"Whoopie cake just sounds so wrong." Cam laughed as they pulled around to the pay window.

"Whoopie pie. Whoopie cake. It's all just very wrong," Alicia agreed.

A large woman with greasy black hair tied back in a bun must have heard them laughing because she scowled at them as she took their money and handed them their whoopie pies, which were basically big flat Devil Dogs, and chocolate milks.

"Apologize, Mom. You made fun of their cuisine," Perry whispered.

"Thank you," Alicia said out the window. "We're just very tired."

"Ayuh," said the lady.

Before pulling out of the parking lot, they idled for a second. "When in Maine," Alicia said before the three of them took simultaneous bites from their whoopie pies.

"Cheers," giggled Perry. She held up her chocolate milk carton, and they clonked them together. A sudden breeze blew, rocking their little car and parting the underbrush to reveal a gravelly path.

"That must be it," said Alicia. She maneuvered the car around the Dunkin' Dumpster and plunged Cumulus in through the bushes. After about a quarter mile, the trees opened up to reveal the most beautiful (as even Cam had to admit) hidden cove of Penobscot Bay.

The sheer authenticity of it blew Cam away. She had never been to a place that was not trying to be someplace else. It wasn't pretending to be Maine. It wasn't Maine-like or Maine-ish. It wasn't McMaine, or MaineWorld, or MaineLand. There wasn't even a giant lobster billboard welcoming them to town. It was just Maine.

The gray wooden shanty buildings near the docks provided a splintery buffer against the wavy blue harbor. As buildings moved up the slope away from the water, they became sturdier and more permanent. The brick buildings of Main Street housed a fire station, complete with a jumpy Dalmatian pacing back and forth in front of it; a hardware store; and some art galleries in what used to be the gristmill. The big waterwheel, still in operation, provided entertainment for the toddlers who watched it from behind a fence while they ate their ice cream cones from the parlor across the street. At the end of the street the sharp white needle of the church's steeple poked into the sky as if heaven were a big balloon that needed to be popped.

Cam rolled down her window and pulled the earbuds from her ears. The sound of the buoys clanging in the distance harmonized with the sloshing of the waves against the dock and the squawking of the gulls. The bright light of the setting sun was tempered just enough by the mist so that you didn't need to squint. The air was not too cold or too hot, not too dry and not too wet. It was perfect, and it felt like climbing into a bed with fresh, clean sheets.

"I forgive you," she told her sister, still focusing on the

view. And because they were sisters, Perry understood exactly what she was talking about.

"I won't feel better until you're in a good mood."

"That's going to take a while."

"Maybe we should have gotten rid of his cage," said Perry, and they both looked at it, still strapped to the back seat with a seat belt. Tweety's little swing creaked back and forth with the swaying of the car.

"No. I want to keep it," said Cam.

"Keep your eyes peeled for a hotel or something," said Alicia as they drove down the main street past a bookstore, café, post office, and lobster pound.

Every time they turned off the main road, they seemed to get lost and have a hard time getting back to it. And when they did get back to the main road, each time it looked a little different. The bookstore seemed to have morphed into a pub with a hand-painted, golden beer mug sign swinging on its hinges. The post office seemed to have become the bakery. It seemed to Cam like the barbershop pole she had seen on the far corner had now become an upside-down blue tuna fish sign advertising the fishmonger's. On their third pass, Cam finally saw a real estate office, but it was closed for the evening. They tried to find the gravel path that brought them into town from the Dunkin' Donuts, but it seemed to have completely disappeared. There was no place in town to stay and no way to get out.

Alicia was starting to sweat a bit. She sat slumped over the steering wheel as she drove, and she couldn't stop cracking her gum. Cam could tell she was having one of those single-mother moments where she felt totally alone with no one to turn to. She was doubting herself, wondering what she had gotten them into. It reminded Cam of the time she took them to Sanibel Island with every penny of her savings, and it rained the entire time.

Cam hated how she could feel her mother's emotions, her desperation, as if she were still symbiotically connected to her with some kind of tortuous emotional umbilical cord, while Perry sat happily in the back seat licking the cream out of her whoopie pie. Cam hated being the oldest.

"It's okay, Mom," she said. "We'll figure something out."

"Thanks, hon," said her mom. "Why don't we take a break at the lobster pound?" It was the only building that seemed to stay put.

Cam didn't get why it was called a lobster "pound" except for the fact that this was where lobsters went to die. Like a dog pound. Were they bad, vagrant, stray lobsters? Or just law-abiding crustaceans minding their own business at the bottom of the ocean? "Lobster pound" was just a misnomer and an unappetizing name for a place to eat.

It was a gray-shingled shack on pilings jutting out over the ocean. Someone had nail-gunned plastic lobsters to the outside wall and then trapped them cruelly in an old fishing net. It had a red roof and a little cupola topped with a brass lobster weathervane. Inside were a bunch of picnic tables with red-and-white checkered tablecloths.

The door slammed behind them, jingling the leather strap of sleigh bells tied to the handle.

"We're about to close up," said a handsome boy with broad shoulders. He had wavy shoulder-length hair that started out brown, but got more and more golden toward the ends that haphazardly looped in all directions as if they were trying to grow toward the sun.

"I'm Asher," he said. "You guys new to town?"

"What gave it away?" asked Cam. "The U-Haul?"

Asher looked up and seemed confused. She was trying to be funny, but she realized how abrupt it sounded.

"I mean, yes, we are new to town, and we have a U-Haul because it has all of our stuff from the old place and we wanted to take it with us to this place. A town . . . to which . . . we are new," Cam said, her cheeks reddening with every bumbling syllable.

Asher grinned. He must have thought she was autistic or something and looked as if he felt sorry for her. He kindly held out his hand and said, "Welcome to Promise."

"Thank you," said Cam. "I'd like to adopt a lobster." That probably did nothing to dissuade him from his autism diagnosis, but she was determined to rescue one. Especially when she saw the crowded conditions in their tank.

"Adopt?" Asher wore a faded blue Red Sox cap to hold down the hair and a gray sweatshirt with three little holes in the elbow. Cam liked that. She didn't trust men who were too neat and put together. His five o'clock shadow caught the sunlight and glinted with golden specks. He wore a leather apron and white terrycloth wristbands. *Wrangling lobsters must be hard work*, thought Cam. *Like shoeing horses or wrestling gators.*

"Yes. Is this a lobster pound?" she asked.

"It is. Yes," he said, taking off his cap and scratching his head. *A little serious for my taste*, she thought.

"Well, I'd like a lobster for a pet. Can I rescue one of them, please?"

Asher smiled a little, revealing a dimple in his left cheek. "Sure. I guess. They're ten bucks a pound."

"We've had a long trip," Alicia said, ignoring them. "Is it really too late to get dinner?"

"Let me check in the back and see what we can do," he said, and he went into the kitchen, where, after a moment, Cam heard someone angrily tossing about some pots and pans.

"Have a seat," said Asher as he came back to the front with some bendy laminated menus.

"Are you sure?" Alicia asked. They heard some more clanging from the kitchen.

"He'll get over it," said Asher with a smirk. "Let me know

when you're ready to order."

Cam, Alicia, and Perry settled into a booth and ordered from the menu. They had been in town for almost an hour, and the sun was still setting. Stripes of orangey peach and purple hung like a backdrop behind the lighthouse, which stood on its own little island about ten feet away from the peninsula that shouldered the bay. Seagulls and pelicans dive-bombed for their dinner and pecked at the mussels glued to the sharp black rocks silhouetted by the waning half-light. The scene evoked in Cam some words she had never actually used in conversation. Words like *craggy*, *shoal*, and *cockles*. It was a barnacly, salty place. An entirely new ecosystem.

"Is it weird to anyone that the sun has been setting for like two hours now?" Cam asked after Asher had delivered their piles of fried shellfish in paper boats. *Vespertine*, she thought, *of or related to twilight: gloaming*. Another SAT word she had never used in conversation. Then she noticed the white dot of the evening star slowly materialize above the lighthouse. Normally she wouldn't think of making a wish, but tonight she actually had one. *I wish Lily would call*, she said to the star. She couldn't imagine going through the end of this disease without her.

"It's a miracle!" Perry exclaimed. She opened up the damn notebook and wrote *Everlasting sunsets* with a flour-ish of her pencil.

Alicia was finished with her fried clams, and she talked to Izanagi, the phone in one ear and her fingers covering the other. "We're okay," she said. "Everything will be okay. Here, say hello to the girls."

Her mom held the phone out to Cam, who curled her lip, stuck out her tongue, and swept it away with Lily's hand-broom trick.

"Cam!" her mom insisted, covering up the phone. "He just wants to know you're all right." Cam had never been expected to talk to any of the other creeps her mom had dragged home from Epcot. This was a first.

Cam grabbed the phone and made scratching inter-ference noises with her throat. "Hi," she said, then made some more noises. "I think we're breaking up. Here, talk to Perry."

"Oh, Cam," Alicia said with a sigh.

Cam handed the phone to Perry, who gladly recounted for Izanagi the highlights of the trip. When she was done with her long, meandering account, it was still sunset.

Asher arrived at their table with a live lobster in a box. It scratched at the sides a little as he set it down on the floor.

"Cam," said Alicia, "where are we going to put a lobster? We don't even know where we're staying tonight."

"You don't actually have to take him," Asher offered.

"Sorry," Alicia apologized. "It's just we've driven all the

way from Florida. We tried to call the hotel, but no one ever answered."

"They're renovating it," he explained.

Cam kept her gaze focused on his feet. He even had holes in the toes of his construction boots. Weren't those things impossible to destroy?

"They could have said that on their voicemail. Does Maine not have voicemail?" she asked.

"We have it." The banging from the kitchen started up again, and it seemed like their cue to hurry up and leave. "Sorry about him. Hey, you could stay with me if you like."

"Really?" asked Alicia.

"Mom!" Cam glared at Alicia. She envisioned a beer-drenched bachelor pad with gray, sheetless futons on the floor. "Stranger Danger," she said.

She and Perry had spent a few years as latchkey kids. There was no money for babysitting, and Alicia worked nights. So she had drilled them with rules about stranger danger, showing them scary videos and even signing them up for a class about how to protect themselves from being kidnapped. Stranger-danger class frightened Perry so much that when she was six, she refused to talk to anyone who wasn't a blood relative.

"He's not a stranger," Alicia said. "He's Asher."

"Mom, he's just being nice, and he's trying to get us out of here so he doesn't get fired. He doesn't really want us to stay with him."

"Really. It's okay. You wouldn't be staying *with me*, with me," Asher clarified. "I stay in the carriage house. But the main house is my grandfather's, and it's empty for the summer. I'm trying to fix it up. You can stay if you don't mind me rattling around in there a bit."

Cam turned to her mother. "We came here for a lobster. We can't leave with this guy's house."

A pot slammed to the floor. "Shit!" someone yelled.

"We have to get out of here soon before Smitty turns the hose on us. I've seen him do it before," Asher warned. "So what do you think?"

Alicia put a hand on Cam's shoulder, squeezing firmly, painfully, which was her signal for Cam to keep quiet. "Thank you. That would be wonderful."

"You both realize he could be a serial killer," said Cam as they piled back into Cumulus.

"Nope," said Perry. "Way too cute for that."

"Relax," Alicia said to Cam. "We came here expecting miracles. Maybe this is our first one."

"This is number twenty-seven, by my count," Perry said as she recorded *Cute boy offers us a free house* in her notebook.

"Please," said Cam, rolling her eyes. Getting offered an abandoned house did not qualify as a miracle in her book.

Asher drove a Jeep, of course, and he had them follow him straight up a hill away from the ocean to the top of a bluff.

"What the . . ." Cam muttered as Alicia parked. A very square, very white home stood stacked on top of itself in square layers like a wedding cake. The house had a sloping lawn and a beautiful view of the ocean. It had an enclosed porch all the way around the bottom level, black shutters, and a black front door with a brass knocker in the shape of a dragonfly. A sign tacked to the mailbox read AVALON BY THE SEA.

They all stared at the house with their mouths open. "Are you kidding me?" asked Cam. The house was bigger than Lily's.

"Make yourselves at home," Asher called from the window of his Jeep. "I'll come back to check on you guys later." Then he drove toward a smaller cottage farther down the hill.

Even Cam felt euphoric and giddy as they clambered out of the car, giggling, and took off their shoes so they could feel the cool grass under their feet. Alicia turned up the radio and left Cumulus's doors open so they could hear the music and dance the sacred volcano-goddess hula, to the tune of Pink's "Please Don't Leave Me." Even Perry tried.

"Better, Perry!" Alicia exclaimed, as she was rolling through her own steps. "Right arm first, Cam."

Of course Cam knew that. It was the first dance she'd ever learned when she was three, but she was trying to hide the blueberry spots. When she turned her wrist and fingers in the right posture toward the everlasting sunset, though, she noticed that two of the biggest ones had disappeared. There was no trace of them—not even a scab or a scar or the faded outline of a ring. Just the smooth, taut, brownish skin of her forearm. *Must be the salt air,* she concluded, because she was suddenly able to breathe a bit easier, too, that little wheeze on her exhale becoming less and less distinct.

The song ended, and Cam felt tired. She wanted to put her new lobster in the bathtub, so she walked up the porch steps with his box tucked under her arm while Alicia and Perry kept dancing. Cam listened to the waves crash in the distance as she thought of possible names for her new pet. Pinchy, Red, Scuttle . . . She was about to wipe her feet on the welcome mat when she looked down.

She got closer, sat down on the front stoop, and gasped.

"Mom! Mom! Perry! Come here quick!" she screamed.

They must have thought Cam was going to have a seizure because they sprinted to the front porch.

"Are you okay?" Alicia asked. She put her hands on her knees and tried to catch her breath. "What's wrong?"

Cam pointed to the ground.

It was Tweety.

He was just sitting there, blinking innocently up at Cam, from the black, rubber welcome mat of Avalon by the Sea.

# ELEVEN

"HEY, TWEETY, CAN YOU SAY FAIR-WEATHER FRIENDS?" ASKED CAM.

Her mom sat at the kitchen counter, cutting up bits of papaya and feeding them to Tweety. Alicia and Perry were convinced that his presence here was a miraculous sign that they'd come to the right place. For the last week, ever since they moved into the Maine house, they had been showering Tweety with attention, and Cam was sick of it. They hardly knew he existed when they lived in Florida. They never even called him by his name. It was always "that bird."

Cam rummaged through the pantry for something to eat. They had gotten more and more comfortable in the house. At first they tiptoed around, making sure to cover their tracks, trying not to leave any evidence of their inhabitance. They stayed in just two or three rooms because they were not used to so much space. But slowly Asher, who seemed to find some excuse to fix something every day, assured them

that no one was coming back. They eventually began to relax, spread out, leave a dish or two in the sink.

Cam grabbed the peanut butter and a spoon and dove in. "And did you have to pimp his cage?" she murmured before washing the peanut butter down with some milk. Alicia had bought him a new deluxe cage from the town's pet store. It was black with white zebra stripes and decorated with a tiny purple couch and an orange shag area rug the size of a panty liner. "His old one was perfectly fine." The cage sat at the end of the kitchen's center island. The bright colors of Tweety's décor clashed with the muted, mustardy brown–painted kitchen.

Alicia held another piece of papaya out for Tweety. "The entire twenty-two years I lived in New Jersey, I never even saw a papaya," she said. "The fruit stand in town is a miracle. You would know about it if you ever left the house."

"Finding a *papaya* at the *fruit* stand is not a miracle," said Cam as she tried to open a cabinet that seemed painted shut. *They should have just left the natural woodwork*, she thought. Finally the cabinet unstuck with a smacking sound and swung open with an empty vibrating thud.

The house was nice enough on the inside, but it needed a woman's touch. No woman would tolerate the painted-over cabinetry or the lamps made of anchors, the musty smell of wet wool, the tartan plaid bedding, or the ancient maps and star charts that hung on the wall beside the shellacked dead fish and deer-antler trophies.

"It's a miracle in Maine, isn't it, Tweety bird?" said her mom, puckering up next to the cage to give Tweety a kiss.

"Give me that. You're not allowed to feed him anymore," said Cam. "I don't want you confusing him with your false allegiance."

"He's a miracle, Campbell."

Tweety finding them in Maine was no miracle. Pets found their way home all the time. It was an instinct. The homing instinct. Hadn't anyone heard of the homing instinct? Cam was thrilled that Tweety *had* a homing instinct, but she wasn't giddy enough to call it a miracle. Even if it wasn't *their* home that Tweety flew to. Even if he knew exactly where to find her. It was still an instinct. A migratory response.

Cam held out a piece of papaya for Tweety, and he turned his head, snubbing her. "Not you, too, Tweety bird, geez."

She left Tweety downstairs with his new friend and climbed the spiral staircase back up to her room on the widow's walk.

"Campbell, why don't you hang out with us?" asked her mom. "What are you doing up there all alone all the time?"

"I just feel like being alone," Cam said as she twisted up the stairs with her jar of peanut butter and a huge, two-foot stalk of celery from the "miracle" fruit stand.

Unlike most widow's walks in Maine, which were just splintery railings on the roof, this one had a glass room—a cupola—in which the proprietor's widow could sit for hours and pine for her husband unperturbed by the elements.

Cam had turned it into her bedroom. She loved it up here, suspended between the clouds and sea, between life and death, removed from anything close to reality.

It had just enough room for a mattress, a small wooden chair on which she set her laptop, and her suitcase, which she lived out of because there was no closet. Her suitcase was an actual case, not one of the sloppy nylon and plastic sacks of today that people have trouble recognizing on the baggage carousel. It was a proper forties crocodile bag that she had inherited from her grandmother. It still had stickers on it from when her great-grandparents took an ocean liner "overseas." A faded orange one read, LISBON. A round green one said, BARCELONA.

She rummaged through it now, looking for something that would keep her warm. Dressing for warmth was such an alien concept to her. She now understood why people would deign to wear that shapeless utilitarian garb from Patagonia. What she wouldn't give right now for a fleece jacket. She was even sort of fantasizing about a turtleneck. Or a down vest. She layered on what she had—a black scarf, a ripped gray cardigan, and her thin faux leather motorcycle jacket. Then she reached her hand into the suitcase's yellow silk "unmentionables" pouch. Instead of the pair of wool socks she was hoping for, she pulled out the magical maple leaf from New Jersey and then her Flamingo List.

The paper was wrinkled and soft after having been crumpled up and flattened back out a few times since Cam's fight with Lily in North Carolina. Cam had almost thrown it away, but something wouldn't let her.

"*Lose my virginity at a keg party,*" she read at the top and wondered what she had really meant by that. She got a bad visual of some creepy jock slyly locking his parents' master bedroom door as the music blared from the crowded living room. But that wasn't what she'd meant.

When she wrote it, she had imagined a consensual, playful encounter underneath a pile of coats with some old friend like Jackson who would not take it too seriously and yet not completely ignore her when it was over. It would be something they could wink about in math class.

It frightened her a little, but she respected the idea of getting it over with and moving on. People didn't get married at seventeen, and they didn't wait until thirty to have sex. So it could make sense to do it quickly, like removing a Band-Aid. You could tear it off and be done with it, rather than picking and pulling at it for years, wondering about "where" and "when" and "with whom."

She looked down the list and stopped at *Have an awkward moment with my best friend's boyfriend.* When she wrote that one, she had imagined a flirtatious transgression. A onetime kiss. Not the weird moment with Ryan at the picnic. *But that definitely counted*, she thought. She crossed it off proudly, as if it were an actual accomplishment.

She opened the glass French doors of the cupola and walked outside. She listened to the sounds of Maine, which rather disappointingly and un-idyllically included the screeching giggles of her sister and the bikini-clad, tweeny-bopper friends Perry had already made in her one short week in Promise. The girls played on the public beach about a quarter mile away from the house, and yet Cam could hear them above the waves, above the wind, above the truck making its way down Main Street. She could hear them above just about everything else. She watched through the telescope that someone had left on the porch as they scrambled among the rocks like a colorful swarm of insects playing some game that included stealing and hiding the handsome lifeguard's binoculars.

Not surprisingly, it had only taken Perry two days to infiltrate Promise's sparkly pink tween underground. Once on the inside, she quickly rose to the top of its ranks, organizing a small Ugg-clad army of giggling attendants to do her bidding and make things right in Perryville. In just one week, Avalon by the Sea had been the host to two slumber parties in the basement, where poor Tweety had to be subjected to off-key, high-pitched karaoke girl-pop long into the night.

Cam shifted the telescope to take in the figures on Avalon by the Sea's front lawn. Alicia's Hula 101 class was fully enrolled, with ten lumpy retired women now filing in the front door wearing bright muumuus. Each carried a foil-wrapped loaf of something to enjoy after class with their tea. Cam's mom had asked her to assist in teaching, but Cam had been dancing for so long, she wouldn't know how to break it into its parts.

She focused the scope on the jolliest of her mom's students, a dark-haired woman whose eyes squinted when she smiled. She let out a big belly laugh that Cam could hear all the way on top of the house. *It's been way too long since I've done that*, thought Cam. *Belly-laughed.*

When the last of the hula dancers was in the house, Cam was about to walk away from the telescope. She knew she should. She tried. She looked up for a second and began to forcefully take a step back toward her room. But she had to do one more thing. She turned around, bent her head toward the eyepiece, and scanned the town's brick storefronts, looking for Asher.

She found him sitting on a wooden bench in front of the lobster pound, taking a break from his shift and drinking a vanilla milkshake. He had placed the football he carried around with him underneath the bench and was reading something. Cam couldn't catch the title of the book. *A jock and a braniac*, she thought. "A person can be too perfect, you know," she said out loud.

She secretly loved how his calves, covered in soft, curly

blond hair, dead-ended into his perpetually untied construction boots. She moved the scope up to view his face. He had a little beauty mark to the side of his right eye and a chicken pox scar in the middle of his forehead. It was his only imperfection.

Perhaps she'd meet up with *him* one day at a keg party, she joked to herself. He seemed sweet enough to help her take care of item number one on the List.

"Uh-oh," Cam said. "Incoming . . ." A girl, leggy and blonde, like a Barbie doll in short white shorts, slid next to Asher on the bench and tossed her gleaming hair. She giggled and stroked his hand with her finger. She laughed and grabbed his shoulder. She guffawed and took hold of his knee.

Tossing the hair. Excessive touching. These are the top two *Cosmo* Signs that She's Into You, and yet Asher, a seemingly healthy eighteen-year-old boy, was having none of it. He wasn't outright rude or anything. He just sat there and politely answered her questions until she got up and strutted away without realizing that the dusty bench had left a huge gray splotch on the back of her shorts.

Asher turned back to his book, which Cam could see now was *A Portrait of the Artist as a Young Man*. He took one last slurp of his milkshake, took the straw out of his mouth, squinted for a second, and then seemed to look directly into Cam's scope. He winked. Then waved.

Cam hit the deck. She turned her head to the side and pressed her cheek into the scorching wooden planks, trying to disappear beneath the treeline.

A half-inch splinter lodged itself right into the meat of her pinky finger, but she was too mortified to feel anything. Had he really seen her?

If her mom thought she was isolating herself before, she hadn't seen anything yet. Cam would never leave her room again.

At least she could cross off *Dabble in some innocent stalking behavior* from her Flamingo List.

# TWELVE

## HOMER NEEDED SOME FRESH SALTWATER.

Cam's pet lobster lived alone in the basement of the house, where Cam had found an unused twenty-gallon tank built into the brick wall. She'd filled the bottom with sand and rocks, thrown in some faux coral and seaweed, and then added a big upside-down SpongeBob pineapple for Homer to hide in.

She tapped on the glass, and Homer climbed up the side of the tank to greet her. Then he swam around, performing big, loop-de-loop figure-eights that seemed more ice skaterly than lobsterly. *He's happy here*, Cam thought. Or else he was trying to get out. She couldn't really tell.

Cam had done some research on lobsters and found out that their genus and species name was *Homerus americanus*. Another fun fact about lobsters was that they were once, like Samoans, rumored to be cannibals. They got a bum rap because someone found lobster shell in the stomachs of some dead ones. But they didn't actually eat each other. They just ate some of their own personal molted shells so that they'd have enough calcium to grow new ones. It was nutritional genius, not cannibalism. They were misunderstood creatures, and Cam immediately identified with Homer.

She grabbed her big yellow saltwater bucket with one hand and then tugged at the handle of the basement's sliding glass door with the other. It wouldn't budge. She yanked again without looking up and then gasped. The door flew open a couple feet, nearly tossing her onto the ground. Asher stood on the other side of the glass with his hand on the door handle. "Sorry," he said. "I didn't mean to startle you."

He helped her heave the heavy door open the rest of the way as it scraped on the rust and pebbles of the track. "I need to grease that," he said, combing a hand through his wavy hair. He had caramel-colored skin and eyes that were amber and brown. His nose was the round triangular shape of one of those plastic noses that hang from the gag disguise glasses you get in the joke shop. But smaller and in perfect proportion with the rest of his face.

"How do you do that?" asked Cam.

"Just some WD-40. Not a big deal."

"No. I mean, how do you appear in moments of need like a brave knight for a damsel in distress?"

Asher shrugged and stuffed his hands into the pockets of his jeans, revealing a perfectly flat, tan stripe of belly between his too-short T-shirt and the waistband of his underwear. Cam found herself wanting to slide her finger across it, which was not like her at all. She was a realist and did not engage in fantasy. Asher would never want anything to do with her. From what she'd been able to piece together from snippets of overheard conversations between him and the fawning Perry during their daily chess game, he was the town's humble football star. And he was, as the saying goes, seriously out of her league.

On their drive in, signs at business after business congratulated the regional high school's win in the state football championship. Cam couldn't get over how pathetic that was. A whole county glorifying a little boys' game. Girls never got the chance to be celebrated like that. To be made into demigods. First they made girls go to church to learn how to worship a male god, and then they made mere boys into mini-gods for girls to worship here on Earth. She vowed that one night, she would drive out in Cumulus and change all the signs to read CONGRATULATIONS, LADY LOBSTERS FIELD HOCKEY: THIRD PLACE!

"Do you need help with that?" Asher asked, pointing to the bucket.

"What? Um, no. No, I can handle it," she said, finally looking away from Asher's stomach. She blushed.

Asher went back to the carriage house, and Cam walked across the lawn and down the steep rocky path to the house's own private beach. The beach was so rocky you couldn't walk on it with bare feet. Cam plodded along in her black Chuck Taylors and waded into the water with them still on. The water was so cold, she swore it had to be part of the Arctic Ocean. She could actually feel the blood vessels in her legs start to constrict and throb like a big bruise. She didn't know how Perry and all her newfound friends could scamper around in it all day long. She squatted for a moment on a rock and watched the waves wash in, suck up rocks, and then spit them back onto the regurgitated shore.

Her new skinny body, wracked as it was from disease, was so accessible to her sometimes. She could squat there for hours with her knees bent up beside her like the tiny poisonous frogs they saw at the National Aquarium in Baltimore on their way up the coast. She could never have done that when she was "heavy."

She looked down into a little tide pool and saw a starfish stuck to a rock. She had a window on an entire world. The starfish, the kelp waving back and forth, a snail, some sea worms, plankton, grains of sand, molecules of grains of sand, atoms in molecules of grains of sand, protons, neutrons, and spinning electrons.

Infinity fascinated her. How systems and universes could keep getting infinitely smaller in one direction and infinitely larger in another. How the shape of an atom so precisely mimicked the shape of the solar system. How there wasn't an end to anything. Except her own life, she guessed. That was going to end pretty soon, but everything else was going to keep spinning without her. It gave her a sense of vertigo to think about it, and she stood up so she wouldn't topple over.

"Crazy how nothing stops, isn't it?" Asher was standing about ten feet away, where the bluff slammed perpendicularly into the beach. There was nothing gradual about the topography of this place. No sloping hills or molded dunes. One thing just fell into another at steep angles.

"Would you please stop sneaking up on me? That's something that can stop right now."

"Shhh. Look!" Asher pointed out at the middle of the whitecapped waves.

"Did you just shush me?"

"Look," he insisted, lifting his chiseled, tan, and perfectly veined throwing arm. Cam's eyes caught on a yellow piece of plastic around his wrist. Was he wearing a rubber Livestrong bracelet? He was. *Please don't tell me it says Jesus on it*, thought Cam.

She looked out to sea. And that's when she saw it. She actually heard it first. A pregnant silence. And then *whoosh*. A mother orca and her baby leaped ten feet out of the bay at the exact same time.

"Holy Shamu, Batman," said Cam. The rest of the bay maintained its workaday bayness. A lobster boat chugged slowly back to the dock. A few dinghies remained moored to their buoys as they rocked back and forth. A seagull sat motionless on her nest atop some wooden pilings. And the sun began its everlasting gobstopper descent behind the lighthouse. No one even seemed to notice that two whales had just performed a circus trick that people paid top dollar to see in Orlando.

"Watch. They'll do it again."

"How do you know?"

"They do it every night at sunset. Animals are creatures of habit."

And sure enough, the whales circled around and leapt up into the air again, shiny and black, like a mismatched pair of patent leather shoes.

"Amazing."

"The sun rises and sets on this place," said Asher as he picked up a flat gray rock and skipped it seven times across the water.

"Well, I'm glad you don't take it for granted. You do *own* a piece of the ocean, which is pretty obnoxious," Cam said, even though Asher was anything but obnoxious. He owned a beach. Girls threw themselves at his feet. And yet he seemed so pensive and alone.

"No, I mean the sun literally rises and sets in the same

place," Asher explained. "Behind Archibald Light. The lighthouse. Haven't you noticed?"

"That's impossible," Cam replied automatically, but then she thought about it and realized that it seemed true. She was able to watch the sunrise and sunset from the same window of the widow's walk.

"It's probably caused by pollution," she reasoned. "My grandmother says that the sunsets off the New Jersey Turnpike are caused by gasses rising from the landfills. That's probably the deal here too. It looks like the sun setting, but it's just some extra methane wafting up from all those cows in Vermont."

"That's a lot of methane," Asher said as he skipped another rock. *Why must boys always throw things?* wondered Cam.

"Cows eat a lot of grass. And they're making a hole in the ozone."

"So you're saying our sunset is a big cow fart?"

"I am."

"That's a bold assertion." Asher smirked.

"There's an explanation for everything," said Cam.

"Right," said Asher. But from his tone, Cam could tell he didn't agree.

"It's past my bedtime," she said, and she walked with her big bucket sloshing behind her, back to the house. She was tired and cold and looking forward to snuggling up in the widow's walk and watching the movies she bribed Perry to get her from the town library. Maybe someday she would take Asher on an expedition and show him where the sun was really setting. In the woods behind the house. A place called *the west*.

Up in her glass roost, the pinks and purples of the sunset began to sink and bleed around her like watercolors into a paper sky. Cam layered every long-sleeved thing she owned on top of one another and put on two pairs of socks. She popped in *Disturbing Behavior*, a Katie Holmes classic about an impossibly perfect clique of teenagers who turned out to be zombie-alien-monster things, and waited for the familiar movie-watching calm to come over her as the opening credits began.

"Cam!"

Cam could hear Perry's big feet inadvertently stomping toward the stairs. Poor little bastard. Literally.

Cam was proud of how Perry handled her bastardy, actually. She took it in stride, never questioning her self-worth. She seemed to know it wasn't her fault that her parents were impulsive fools. Cam wondered, though, if the day would come when Perry would set off in search of her pale father in the dark hinterlands of Norwegia. (That's what Perry called it when she was three and they told her she was Norwegian). Cam pictured a determined twenty-year-old Perry trudging through the tundra in her snowshoes and rucksack, knocking on the doors of Norwegian villagers. Too bad Cam wouldn't be around to see that.

Perry's rosy cheeks popped up through the floor of the cupola where the staircase ended. The Maine cold was good for her arctic blood.

"Cam!" Perry was excited.

"What?!" Cam feigned sarcastic excitement back at her.

"There's a party!"

"So?" said Cam.

"So you have to go," said Perry.

"Why?"

"You need to meet people. It's a summer solstice party. On the island of the lighthouse. You have to take a zip line to get to it. Everyone will be there. There will be a bonfire and everything. You like fire."

"Who's 'everyone'?"

"Everyone. Asher will be there."

"So what?"

"Agh. Campbell, please?" Perry came all the way upstairs and sat on Cam's bed.

"Why do you care so much that I go to this party?" Cam grabbed one of Perry's silky ponytails and looped it around her finger.

"Because I want to go and I can't, and if I can't go, you should go. I'm sick of seeing you moping around up here.

It's depressing. This place is really amazing. You should start exploring. We came all this way."

"When's the party?" Cam asked, toying with her.

"Tonight."

"Nope, sorry. I have an appointment tonight with Katie Holmes and her Disturbing Behavior."

"Campbell, you are so lame. Are you ever going to leave the house?

"No."

"Pathetic." Cam heard Perry clomp down the stairs as she whipped out her phone and complained to some Hannah Montana on the other end.

Fine, so she was pathetic. Cam had agreed to come to Maine, but she hadn't agreed to parties. She felt safe and comfortable in her aloneness. Maybe it was a stage of dying.

When the movie ended, Cam could hear the sounds of gathering voices echoing off the bay, so she knew the party was starting. Could she really sit up here listening to it all night? She wondered if she were pulling some kind of passive-aggressive moping stunt just to get people's attention. She knew she wasn't, but just to prove it to herself, she might go.

At eleven o'clock, Cam snuck down the stairs. She didn't want to give Perry the satisfaction of knowing she was going, though, so she tiptoed through the living room. As she passed Tweety's cage, he started flitting around and chirping his head off, threatening to blow her cover. He was still mad at her for not giving him credit for his miracle.

"Shh. Tweets. Tweety," Cam whispered. "Calm down," she said, peeking underneath the canvas cage cover. "You of all creatures should know the deal, Tweets. I'm very proud of you, okay? But I can't believe in miracles."

"Chirp?" asked Tweety.

"Because. Just because, okay?"

Because she had to be prepared for the inevitable. The very real thing that was happening to her. It made no sense to get her hopes up.

# THIRTEEN

THE WHOLE SKY TURNED TO INDIGO AND THE STARS BLINKED ON, slowly at first, and then all at once, blanketing the sky with pixie dust.

Cam walked around the *U* shape of the bay until she got to the park on the peninsula. She recognized Asher's car in the parking lot and followed the sounds of voices through the ghostly playground, stopping at the edge of a three-story cliff. Below her, a twenty-foot-wide channel of waves bounced wildly off the rocks on either shore. The current seemed angry and trapped, not knowing which way to get out. On the other side of the channel stood the lighthouse, like an enormous birthday candle shoved carelessly into the giant island cake.

"Campbell! Over here! So glad you could make it!" Asher called, cupping his hands around his mouth so she could hear him over the waves. He waved at her from the island

down below, where he was manning the landing of the zip line.

"Yeah, thanks for inviting me," Cam said sarcastically, but she knew he couldn't hear her.

Standing next to her at the top of the zip line was a broad-chested guy with curly brown hair. He wore a striped, preppy orange and gray sweater with holes in the cuffs and elbows. These people could have stepped right out of a Land's End catalog. She bet they had names like catalog colors too, like Logan or Sage or Persimmon or Russet.

"What's your name?" she asked the boy.

"Royal," he said.

*See*, thought Cam.

Royal handed her a set of rusty, upside-down bicycle handlebars with pink streamers coming out of the ends. The handlebars were attached to a pulley, which was threaded through with some taut nylon rope. The rope was tied at one end to a tree branch on the mainland, and on the other, to a lamppost on the island down below.

Next to the "zip line" was a little funicular cart contraption that the sensible lighthouse keeper used. It, too, hung on a pulley, but in the cart, you could pull yourself slowly, hand over hand, along a thick wire.

"Why can't I use that?" Cam screamed down to Asher.

"We're not supposed to touch it," he replied.

"We're not supposed to be here at all, are we?"

"This is more fun. Come on. Try it," he coaxed.

"You just sort of lean back and then lift up your feet," Royal said helpfully.

In his right hand, Royal held on to another, thinner, slacker rope attached to the handlebars, so that he could haul them back to the launching pad for the next customer.

Cam got set up. "Wait. Safety first," said Royal. He gave her a bright orange life vest.

"What's this for?"

"In case you fall in."

"Won't I be dead if I fall in?"

"Not necessarily. Here."

"Why is it wet?" Cam asked. Had someone else already fallen in?

"You'll be fine. Really," said Royal.

Cam was beginning to sweat in spite of having to wear the freezing cold life vest. It was so strange how her body still went through the motions of being afraid, when really, why should it? If she was going to die soon anyway, it shouldn't matter if it was by jumping off a cliff or lying in some horrible hospital bed.

*Here goes*, Cam thought, and she leaned back and lifted her feet.

The wind rushed and whistled by her ears so she couldn't hear anything else. It felt more like falling than flying. She felt completely out of control. Her whole body was rubbery from fear, in a good way. Asher caught her at the other end, his big hands wrapping around either side of her life vest.

Her hand slipped down to cover his. She felt his knuckles like knots in a tree branch, covered in the same soft downy hair he had on his legs. He was strong and gentle, and for just a millisecond Cam felt safe. A feeling she hadn't had in a long time.

"See what I mean about the damsel-in-distress thing?" said Cam. "I think it's a problem for you. You're like a help-a-holic," she said, catching her breath as he hoisted her to shore and made sure she got her footing.

"You loved it, didn't you?"

"It was all right," said Cam. She didn't want to seem overly excited.

Suddenly she asked, "Hey, how do we get back?" The zip line obviously went only one way.

"Sometimes we use the cart," said Asher. "Or kayaks."

*Kayaks?* thought Cam. The few parties she'd been to in Florida consisted of lounging around the pool in bikinis while the boys played some stupid drinking game and prowled around hoping for a nipple slip. These Maine kids were ambitious.

"The party's over there," said Asher. "Just follow the sounds of drumming."

Normally walking into a party alone would have freaked Cam out, but she was riding high from her trip on the zip line. She climbed over some huge boulders and looked over to the beach where kids, mostly boys, were seated in a circle playing different percussion instruments, while others, mostly girls, danced barefoot in twirling circles in the sand. In the center was a fire. Cam wouldn't call it a bonfire exactly, but it was a fire. Above them, to the left, loomed the lighthouse painted with broad red and white stripes.

She looked around for the keg, but there didn't seem to be one. Everyone must have reached an altered state from the drumming and dancing, because she didn't see any drinking. It reminded Cam of the time her mom found some absurd post on a parenting blog that warned of girls getting secretly drunk by soaking their tampons in vodka.

"Campbell, do you do this?" she'd asked.

"Yes, Mom, I am constantly *tamped* with vodka," Cam had said, proud of herself for suddenly discovering the etymology of *tampon*.

She hadn't had the energy to tell her mom that parents' imaginations were so much worse than anything teenagers could dream up by themselves. No one she knew was weird enough to soak her tampon in vodka. Unless that was how these twirling girls were rolling.

Cam found a through-line around the boulders and hopped down to the beach. It was warmer near the fire. She sat on a rock and watched for a while. She let herself drift into the rhythms of the drums, closed her eyes, and rocked back and forth.

After a minute, she was startled by someone's rough, spindly fingers slipping into her hand and yanking her off the rock.

"You can dance," said a girl with long blonde hair that hung in dirty, wavy strands to her waist. She wore a cream-colored maxidress that was embedded with dirt at the hem and soaked with seawater to her knees. Around one ankle she wore a macramé anklet, something Cam would normally not tolerate. This girl, though, seemed to embody "flower child" from the inside out, willowy and graceful, as if her parents were actually flowers.

Cam said nothing but joined the girl dancing near the fire.

"What's your name?" Cam asked.

"What?"

"*Como se llamas?*"

"Oh. Sunny!" she said, and she smiled dreamily, as if the sound of her own name filled her with bliss. She went back to dancing with her eyes closed.

Cam should have guessed from the little sun tattoo on her other, un-macraméd ankle. "Sunny" was perfect. And could also be a Land's End color.

Cam stepped inside the music and let it close around her like a bubble. Inside the music there was no cancer. No awkwardness. No pain. No abandonment. No Flamingo List. Inside the music, even inside these primitive rhythms, Cam felt free.

Sunny seemed to approve of Cam's dancing, every once in a while opening her eyes to check Cam out and then nodding her a little "Right on."

After a short while, she was surprised to feel the familiar burning sensation of her disease. She hadn't felt it since they'd arrived in Maine. It was hard to describe, but it was as if each of her cells began to individually smolder with sickness. She didn't know if the toxicity she felt was from the cancer or from the chemicals and radiation used to treat it, but there were times when she just felt poisoned, green, acidic. So different from this pure, organic girl spinning beside her.

She tapped Sunny on the shoulder and asked, "Is there any water?" Then she tilted an imaginary cup to her mouth in case Sunny couldn't hear her.

"Over here," said Sunny, and she led Cam to a cooler on the other side of the fire. The water cooler, a big orange jug, like the one athletes used to dump Gatorade onto their coaches, sat behind a wall of rocks. Cam looked around the cooler for cups, but she didn't see any.

"Oh. Like this," said Sunny, and she squatted down and opened her mouth beneath the spigot like a baby bird. "Reduce, reuse, recycle," she said. "No use wasting cups." She wiped her mouth with the back of her wrist.

Cam filled her mouth as well and swallowed what tasted like water from a mountain stream tinged with a little bit of sugar. In one gulp she began to feel purified, that burning, toxic feeling slowly washing away.

"Good, isn't it?" Sunny asked. "It's holy water. We steal it from the baptismal font at the Catholic church. It just tastes better."

"Won't God be upset that you stole his water?" asked Cam.

"I don't presume to know what God thinks," said Sunny. "I like to think she'd want us to have it."

The holy water reminded Cam of the makeshift christening Lily had performed for her on the dock that night. She wished she wasn't reminded of how she threw away her only remaining friendship because she had to be *right* about Ryan. If Cam finally learned one lesson before she died, it would be that being *kind* was sometimes more important than being *right*. All Cam had had to say that night was "I'm happy for you." Four simple words.

"Whoa. Samoa. What are you thinking about? Your whole aura just changed from gold to black."

"Nothing," said Cam. "My name is Campbell, by the way. And how did you know—"

"My little sister hangs with yours, so she told me where you were from. It's rad. I've never met an island girl before."

"Aloha." Cam smirked.

"Right on," Sunny said. "Well, Campbell, you should think good things, and good things will come your way. "

She followed Sunny back to the dancing. Royal and Asher must have finished their zip line duties because they were climbing over the rocks to finally join the party. Cam nudged Sunny with her elbow and pointed her head toward Asher.

"What's his story?" she asked.

"Asher?" Sunny grinned. "Asher doesn't have a story. Ashicus has a *mythology*. And he's totally taken." She giggled as Royal grabbed her hand. Cam watched as he gently pulled her toward the edge of the water, where they walked along the shore talking.

Asher had picked up a drum from one of the drummers who had rotated out and was playing it with a huge smile on his face. Cam continued to dance. She didn't mind dancing by herself as long as she kept her eyes closed. She danced, shifting her bare feet around in the sand, and tried to forget about Asher. Maybe Lily was right. Maybe Cam should experience some things. It was too late to find true love, but it wasn't too late for sex.

And just as Cam thought the word *sex*, a boy she couldn't see slid his arm around her waist and his tongue into her ear.

The boy, Alec, with a *c* and not an *x*, was not named after a T-shirt color.

Cam tried to be cool. She lifted her arms and placed them gently around his neck while he looped his around her waist. She looked up into his eyes, which were brown, heavy-lidded, and half shut—very French, like his name; then she tilted her head downward and leaned it against his chest. He was tall. And thin. And taut. Like a tennis player. He probably was a tennis player. Even on the beach, he wore his blisteringly white shoes. She let him kiss her gently on the forehead before he led her away over the rocks to a place where someone had beached their small catamaran. His palms were a little sweaty. *More in anticipation*, Cam thought, *than in fear*. Cam's hands were icy with dread.

"Ahh," he said in a French accent, gutturally swallowing the final sounds of all of his words. "A bed." It turned out he really was French.

They sat on the black trampoline "bed" of the sailboat, which was laced up the center like a big corset. He promptly rolled on top of her.

"Wait," Cam said, pushing him off of her. "Shouldn't we get to know each other?"

He pointed to himself and said, "Alec."

Cam said, "Cam," and then he rolled on top of her again, kissing her neck and working his hand up her shirt.

Cam got so nervous, she could not stop talking.

"Are those drumsticks in your pocket or are you just happy to see me?" she asked. "Does no mean no in France or does no sometimes mean *oui*? Because in Maine I think no pretty much means no. Although it is a little backward up here, so they may not know that no means no. . . ."

"Are you saying no?" asked Alec.

"No," said Cam.

"Shhh," said Alec as he traced her lips with his index finger and then kissed her squarely on the mouth. His tongue was a little too probing at first, and his teeth, because they jutted out a bit, kept clicking into hers and biting her a little. His fingers slid under the waistband of her jeans and tried to wedge themselves beneath the elastic of her underwear.

"Yes!" Cam said, trying to sit up.

"This feels good, yes?" asked Alec.

"No. I mean yes, I am saying no."

He looked into her eyes with confidence, as if he could decipher her thoughts better than she could and would be the final arbiter of the situation. "No. You are not saying no," he said, and he kissed her more softly this time, looping his tongue around hers. He had an amazing tongue, which compensated for the bad teeth. He kissed her ear, her neck, the soft skin on the inside of her elbow, the center of her palm. Cam relaxed enough for it to feel good, and then it did not feel good, and then it was over.

He was slumped on top of her when they both heard a girl's voice call, "Alec!" from the other side of the rocks. He pulled his pants up quickly as Cam rolled herself off of the catamaran and hid behind one of its pontoons.

"I'm sorry," he whispered. "I must go." And Cam watched from underneath the boat as his white sneakers sloughed through the sand in the direction of the girl's voice.

It was impossible to make a graceful exit when you were trapped on an island. Cam tried to sneak off and use the funicular by herself, but Asher followed her.

"Cam," she heard him call.

Cam ignored him and climbed into the rusty old cart. She slammed the door with a clang and pulled on the rope. It screeched loudly, and she only moved about one foot across the wire. She pulled and pulled, fueled by her embarrassment. A couple of people had gathered out of curiosity and watched her moving herself solo across the wire. Eventually she tired herself out, and she fought back tears. She sat slumped in the cart as the wind swung it back and forth with loud creaks.

"Cam!" screamed Asher. "Campbell, look down."

"Aren't you supposed to tell me not to look down?"

"No. Look down."

Cam stood up slowly so as not to rock the little gondola. When she looked over the side, she noticed that there was no water left between the mainland and the "island" of the lighthouse. The little channel had dried up, leaving just a rocky beach.

"It's low tide, Cam. You can walk across."

Asher pushed a button, and the wire she was hanging from began moving by itself like a ski lift, back to the island. Cam got out and crossed the channel on foot. She didn't even remember the walk home.

After a very long shower, Cam bundled up in her mother's robe and sat back on her bed in the widow's walk. She pulled out the Flamingo List and hovered a black Sharpie above it: *Lose my virginity at a keg party*. Check. The actual presence of a keg seemed irrelevant. *Have my heart broken by an asshole*. Check.

She could have died without experiencing that. But the first time was supposed to be terrible anyway, right? Too bad her first time was going to be her last.

She wished she could forget this night ever happened. That was what a healthy person would do. Healthy people are gifted with selective memory. Cam pathologically remembered *everything*. Details stuck inside her brain like spitballs to a chalkboard. Which was fine if you were taking the SATs, but horrible when you were trying to forget Alec's teeth, or the catalog kids staring up at you from the beach as you swung there on the lighthouse lift.

It was horrible when you needed to forget how your dad looked on his deathbed, bald and shriveled to the size of a child, when his breath, finally, after weeks of holding on, grumbled to a noiseless stop. When you needed to forget that your organs might fail one by one or you might drown of pneumonia in your own bed. Maybe her heart would stop first.

# FOURTEEN

"GET UP. GET UP, CAMPBELL." HER MOM'S VOICE ESCALATED FROM AN angry whisper to a full-on yell as she threw the covers off of Cam. "We don't do this in our family, do you hear me?!"

Cam was still in bed trying to sleep off last night's debacle. Images bubbled up through her consciousness like some kind of bad memory stew: the vertiginous funicular . . . the incredulous stares from the catalog kids . . . Alec's taut hamstrings . . . his fingers unbuttoning her jeans.

"What time is it?" Cam threw her arm over her face to shield her eyes from the bright sunlight streaming into the widow's walk. If she looked out the windows without sitting up, it seemed as if she were floating in the middle of the bay. All she could see was blue. Different undulating shades of blue depending on their form and function. If she stayed here much longer, she was sure she could come up with more than a hundred words for blue, just like Eskimos had a hundred words for snow.

"You mean what day is it. You slept all the way through Saturday."

"Whoa. Cool."

"Campbell," Alicia said, gritting her teeth, "you don't have time to stay up here, reading *The Bell Jar* or whatever it is you do," she said as she kicked some things around the room. "Other girls can wallow in their misery. You. You do not have the luxury to wallow."

"Isn't wallowing part of adolescence? I should experience the full range of adolescent behavior before I die. I thought this town was supposed to save me, anyway."

"Campbell," said her mom as she sat down on Cam's mattress.

"What?"

"I've never known anyone who was saved who did not first save herself," she said.

"Whoa. Did Jesus say that? That would be good on a mug. Or a needlepoint pillow. We can market that."

"You are leaving this house today, do you hear me?"

"Yes, ma'am."

Her mom threw a pillow at her before climbing back down the stairs.

Cam wished she could admit to her mom that she *had* left the house, and that she'd made a "wicked" fool of herself, as they said up here, but how do you admit to your mother that you just lost your virginity for the hell of it to a rude French exchange student on a beached catamaran?

It was better to just leave the house, Cam decided. Tweety was sluggish and looking a little peaked. She could take him to the vet. That was something she could do.

As she got dressed, she noticed the photograph she had stolen from Lily's house balanced precariously on the corner windowsill. The sun shone behind it, and it seemed to glow with its own internal radiance. Cam looked at the wan faces, clonking bald heads, and white-toothed smiles. Strange, but because of Lily, St. Jude's was one of the happiest times of her life.

Lily was the only person who *got* her. Her dad got her a little bit, but he was gone. Her mother used to try to get her, but then that got too exhausting, and she gave up. Perry was too young to get anyone. But Lily *got* her. They just had to look at each other in the right way, and they would explode into that paralyzing kind of open-mouthed laughter without sound. Without Lily, Cam was utterly alone.

Lily would know what to say about last night. Cam was *dying* to tell her that she had crossed two things off of the Flamingo List. But news from Cam's list did not exactly contain the "positive" vibe that would heal the friendship. Cam cringed as Lily's last words rang in her ears. *I need to be surrounded by positive energy. I need you to leave me alone.*

Wordlessly she packed the photo up in an envelope without a return address. She would mail it back to Lily today.

"Mom, I'm taking Tweety to the vet," she yelled when she got to the bottom of the stairs. "Do they have a vet here, or do the animals miraculously heal themselves?"

"Don't get smart. I think I saw something on Cedar Street," her mom called from the dining room. She was trying to work the ancient sewing machine she'd found in the basement and didn't even look up.

Cam unhooked Tweety's cage from its stand in the living room and found her car keys in the pocket of her hoodie.

"Wait! Take me to the beeeea—" she heard Perry whining as she shut the big front door with the dragonfly knocker behind her.

Cam was irritated. Literally. It was hot, she could not find the vet's office, and something was burning *down there*, which was probably normal after what *down there* had been through Friday night, but still a little disconcerting. After her third circle through town, she remembered Sunny and her theory of attracting what you think about. *I will find the vet's office*, she thought, and on her next trip around the block, there it was. A red barn with a silo and a mail truck parked out front. A donkey was penned inside of a white corral, and an old white sign read, ELAINE WHITTIER, with five shingles swinging underneath it: DVM, HEAD LIBRARIAN, POSTMASTER, SHERIFF, ANTIQUES DEALER.

"What are you feeding him?" asked Elaine Whittier as she examined Tweety. She was about sixty and had that self-proclaimed-feminist-from-the-seventies look about her. Long gray hair, dangling feather earrings, and a royal blue caftan blouse covering her seemingly requisite middle-aged paunch. To get to the exam room, you had to walk through Elaine's house, which was decorated with a lot of pine: pine woodwork, pine furniture covered with scratchy brown upholstery, pine floors, and pine plaques on the wall, shellacked with corny messages like HOME SWEET HOME.

"Um, I think there has been some extra papaya in his diet lately," Cam said.

"He's massively overweight."

Cam liked this woman. She did not mince words.

"You hear that, Tweets? No more papaya for you." Cam had to speak loudly over the cacophony of animal sounds. Elaine didn't seem very discriminatory when it came to treating animals. Aside from the standard cats and dogs, the cages lining the periphery of the examination room were filled with hermit crabs, tarantulas, iguanas, ferrets, and— "Is that a muskrat?" Cam asked when she saw the slick black rodent with enormous bony feet.

"He's one of God's creatures." Elaine lifted Tweety's wing and felt around for his glands underneath it. "What brings you to Promise?"

"I'm sick," said Cam. She was inspired by the vet's

demeanor to be direct, but it was strange to hear herself say those two tiny words. It was a relief, actually, to say it out loud to a stranger. She was sick.

"That's too bad," said Elaine. Cam liked that response. No questions. No denial. No "I'm sure you'll get better soon." Just: "That's too bad." It was. It was just too bad.

"So what do you do?" the doctor asked as she cupped Tweety gently in both hands and placed him back in his cage.

"Do?"

"Aside from be sick. What do you do?"

"I'm putting all my energy into that right now," joked Cam.

Elaine smirked. She had the same parentheses dimple on the left side of her smile that Asher did. "A woman has to wear many hats. It's in our nature. We're natural multitaskers. Here. Can you hold Bart for a second?" She plopped the soft, heavy belly of a St. Bernard puppy into Cam's hands. The warm folds of his extra skin draped around Cam's fingers. She held him up so she could look into his droopy brown eyes.

"I could work here, I guess," mumbled Cam. The puppy licked the side of her face just once, as if that was all he could muster.

"What?" asked the vet as she plucked the side of a syringe to get the air bubbles out of it. "Keep holding him." Elaine lifted some of the skin off of Bart's neck and stuck him with the syringe. Bart snuggled his head into the crook of Cam's, arm, and she hugged him close.

"I said, I wouldn't mind working here, if you needed the help."

"You seem to tolerate needles, which means you'd be level-headed in an emergency," Elaine noted. "And you seem to love animals. Those are the only job requirements. Oh, but don't get too attached. Especially to Bart. He's the runt of a big litter, and he may not make it."

"Detached is my middle name," said Cam, which was true in most cases, but she knew she'd already fallen deeply and seriously in love with Bart. Come on. Soft. Puppy. Belly. He was irresistible.

"Great! I have to do the mail route right now. If I'm five minutes late, Mr. Griffith has a panic attack. He never gets anything but the circular from the supermarket, but he really looks forward to it. Can you watch Bart for me?"

"You deliver mail, too?"

"Ayuh. Many hats, remember. Anyway, I'll be surprised if our friend here makes it through the night. If he's not improving tomorrow, I might ease his pain."

"Ease his pain, what do you mean, ease his pain?"

"Put him down, Campbell. He's really suffering."

"He'll make it," said Cam. "He and I have a little pact." Which wasn't exactly true, but she was going to make one with him right now.

Before Elaine left, Cam retrieved her biker bag from the front hall, grabbed the envelope, and handed it to her. "Will you mail this for me?" she asked. Her breath caught for a second as she handed the last remaining evidence of her friendship with Lily to Elaine. But she forced herself to suck in some more air and blow it out in a steady stream.

This is what it felt like to have a broken heart. It felt less like a cracking down the middle and more like she had swallowed it whole and it sat bruised and bleeding in the pit of her stomach.

Cam returned to the examination room and picked up the puppy, who was wrapped in baby blankets and lying on a doggie bed, motionless except for his belabored, snuffly inhales and exhales.

She sat down on the cold tiles of the exam room floor and let Bart rest on her lap, stroking the place where his snout and forehead came together. She and her mom had spent countless nights like this, reclining on the bathroom tiles, which cooled Cam's fever as she waited to throw up again.

Her mom would stroke her forehead, and after vomiting for the seventeenth or eighteenth time—dry heaving drops of bile into the toilet—Cam would say, "I want to die, Mommy. Just let me die."

And her mom would say, "I'll make you a deal, Campbell

Maria. You do not die, and tomorrow, we will have a special day."

"Tell me what we're going to do tomorrow when this is over," Cam would whisper.

Then her mom would make a list itemizing the world's best day. It was always different and always vivid, something Cam could imagine and look forward to.

"Tomorrow we will fly in a hot air balloon over the Everglades," she would say.

"Oh, that's a good one," Cam would sigh.

"No, we really will. We're going to get into the basket of a rainbow-colored balloon with a park ranger–slash–balloon aviator. And you will feel superior badgering him with questions he can't answer about Everglades conservation while he floats us out over the surface of the water and tries to point out the pretty flowers."

"Excellent."

"And then we'll have lunch and bubble tea."

"Don't say lunch," Cam would say before heaving again over the toilet.

"Oh, I'm sorry, baby," Cam's mom would say and then place a cold washcloth on Cam's forehead and the back of her neck. "So after that, on our perfect day, we'll go to one movie and then sneak into a second show to get a freebie double feature. And then we'll come home and sleep dreamlessly all the way through the night."

"Now you're exaggerating." Cam hadn't slept through the night since the cancer had started.

World's Best Day actually materialized a lot in the beginning. Cam's mom would scramble, rearranging her schedule so she could take Cam on a hot air balloon ride or whatever it was she had described the night before. But as Cam got sicker and her episodes more frequent, Cam had to let her mother off the hook. She couldn't keep taking off of work for World's Best Day.

"Okay, pup," Cam said, adjusting the puppy and removing some of his blankets. He was getting a little too warm. "You just need something to look forward to. Are you listening? Tomorrow is going to be the world's best day, so you have to hang on because you won't want to miss it."

Then Cam described the myriad sights and especially smells of a puppy's perfect day. A walk through wet grass, lunch at the back door of the butcher shop, some back-scratching against a tree, a game of fetch, a nap in the sun, chewing on a slipper, some tug-of-war, and a ride in the car with your head out the window.

It seemed to work a little. Bart seemed to be resting more comfortably when Elaine got home around four, with her ponytail stuck through the back of her postal cap. But Elaine said he was still very unstable. Cam made her promise that she wouldn't do anything rash, at least without calling Cam first.

"It's not rash, Campbell. It's medicine."

"Just please don't do it," Cam begged, and as she drove home with Tweety, she didn't pray, exactly. She wouldn't call it praying. But she sent energy to Bart. She used the visualization techniques that Lily taught her to imagine a future that contained a healthy, muscular, full-grown Bart. While she was at it, she visualized a healthy Cam and then, quite by accident, a healthy Asher lying shirtless in the sun.

# FIFTEEN

BEFORE GOING BACK TO THE HOUSE, CAMPBELL PARKED CUMULUS WITH
Tweety inside and took a walk past downtown Promise's
happy brick storefronts streaming with wind socks and balloons. She bought a coffee at the café and then stole three
lobster magnets, a bag of moose-shaped pasta, maple syrup,
and a pair of stripy hand-knit slipper-socks from the gift
shop.

The thrill of stealing distracted her from Bart and the
memory of the Alec Debacle, but she felt this new thing—
guilt?—over stealing, not from "the Man" or "the Mouse" but
from some little old lady who probably spent her evenings
knitting slipper-socks in front of *The Price Is Right*.

Cam had never stolen from Main Street before. Except
for the fake one in Disney, they didn't have Main Streets in
Florida, and the experience of it—the quaint, mom-and-pop,
entrepreneurial, from-days-gone-by, up-by-your-bootstraps

industriousness of it—was giving her a conscience. It was harder to steal when you could imagine from whom you were stealing.

It wasn't *that* hard, though, because she was just about to slip an irresistible lobster claw–shaped oven mitt into her biker bag, when she heard someone yell, "Samoa!" from out on the sidewalk.

"That's not exactly PC," said Cam as Sunny walked in with her catalog boyfriend in tow.

"It's a post-PC world now, Samoa. We're not pointing out your difference; we're celebrating it."

"Hmmm," said Cam, trying to figure out whether that made any sense at all.

"We're going down to the flamingos. Want to come?" Sunny grabbed Cam's hand and spun underneath her arm. "They'll make you feel at home."

"Is there some kind of traveling bird-circus in town?"

"No, they just arrived by themselves. A whole flock," said Royal.

"Hundreds of them," said Sunny. "They're feeding down at the pond behind the elementary school." She pulled Cam out the door, swirling and skipping down Main Street, still barefoot and dirty and wearing Friday night's dress.

Cam let Sunny drive since she was bold enough to ask and she knew where to go. Royal sat in the backseat with Tweety, and Cam gripped the door handle on the passenger side. She was not used to surrendering control of Cumulus.

They drove along the coast toward the lighthouse. To their right, the pounding surf reminded Cam that they were at the end of the Earth, an eerie feeling for someone raised in the middle of a swamp. The horizon was frightening. It was no wonder the pre-Columbians thought they would fall off of it.

"Grab the wheel for me?" Sunny said as she wriggled out of her fleece-lined sweatshirt.

*Gladly*, thought Cam.

"Have you seen those yet?" Sunny asked, driving with her knees as she put her hair in a ponytail. Cam tried to keep one eye on the road as she glanced quickly to where Sunny was pointing: a grassy hill, embedded with large, gray, lichen-covered rocks. Three or four black-and-white cows stood grazing on purple flowers.

"Are those dandelions?" Cam asked.

"Uh-huh. They grow purple here for some reason. Even when they turn to fluff. We have a festival in spring when all the little kids in town get together to make a wish in the town square and blow fistfuls of dandelion fluff into the air at once."

They were quiet for a while. Sunny now had two hands on the wheel, so Cam let herself look around. Almost every home seemed to be selling something in its front yard. Antique shutters, weathervanes, sleds, chairs, bear sculptures carved from the burls of trees with a chainsaw, washers and dryers. She even saw one sign that read, FOR SALE: USED HOT TUBS.

"I like my hot tub straight from the factory," mumbled Cam.

"What?" Royal asked.

"Nothing."

They turned back toward the coast. Cam let herself be mesmerized by the spots of sun glittering off of the waves, when Sunny said, "Look at these bozos!"

Alec with a *c* was hitchhiking along Route 1, looking very European in his gray skinny jeans and oversize black turtleneck sweater. His black greasy hair swung loosely across his forehead. Cam couldn't help getting excited, in spite of how bad he must have smelled in that sweater in this heat.

*Man, that biological imperative is strong*, thought Cam. She should not have been excited to see him; she was supposed to have had nameless-faceless-lose-my-virginity-before-I-die sex. Not fluttery-jittery-I-can't-wait-to-see-him-again sex. And she really should not have been dejected when she saw the beautiful, porcelain-skinned redhead, who must have been the voice from the other night, jump out from behind him and wave the car down. Cam's whole body felt heavy, as if there were mercury flowing through her veins. She felt like a polluted tuna.

Before Cam could say anything, Sunny pulled over. She rolled down the window and asked, "Going to the flamingos?"

Alec climbed into the backseat, and Royal handed Tweety's cage to Cam.

"It's very dangerous to pick up hitchhikers," Cam mumbled under her breath.

"Hi, Autumn and Alec," Sunny said. "Do you know Campbell?" Cam's heart kicked at her chest. She wiped her palms on her shorts and tried to look Alec bravely in the eye.

"No," said Alec flatly. He looked out the window, leaning his head against it, letting his knees splay wide apart. Autumn, another catalog kid, stuck a limp hand out to Cam and giggled, "*Enchantée*," before sinking down next to him and whispering something rudely into his ear.

*Detached*, thought Cam. *Detachment. I am detached*, she chanted to herself. She tried this mantra on the entire drive to the flamingos, but the lump in her throat kept growing and eventually gave way, allowing one tear to slip from the corner of her eye. She never thought she'd feel like this, but she was beginning to miss home.

The five of them unfolded their limbs, climbed out of Cumulus, and took big steps through the ragweed in the field behind the school. Autumn put a daisy in her hair and Royal chewed on a piece of hay. *They could be in a music video right now*, thought Cam. They were so obnoxiously young and beautiful, and—aside from her own petty concerns about having just lost her virginity to the asshole who stood right next to her making out with his *girlfriend*—they were carefree.

She tried to stay a few steps behind the couples, acknowledging her fifth-wheel status, but Sunny ran back, linked arms with her, and kept her with the group. "Wait till you see this, Samoa," she said.

And what she saw when they got to the top of the rise actually made her forget Alec for a second.

It was like flamingo lava—liquid pink—flowing toward them down the hill in the shape of a huge, bright, orangey-pink cornucopia. The whole thing seemed like one enormous amoebic organism blanketing the gentle hillside. Like some giant inside the Earth had blown a huge, bubble-gum bubble that popped all over the swampy mud. As they walked closer, they began to hear the distinct calls of individual birds and see the thousands of reedy legs and knobby knees that made up the inner workings of the flock.

"Isn't pink the most peaceful color in the universe?" asked Sunny as they looked out on the enormous cloud of pink feathers. The five of them sat on the top tier of an old wooden fence and watched as the birds sifted through the silt for the blue-green algae and shrimp that were their only food.

Cam was glad the question did not require an answer. Pink. Pink was the color of chicken pox, pimples, bloodshot eyes, Pepto-Bismol, a syringe full of bone marrow, her eye-dropper of liquid morphine, Alec's tongue. A lot of horrible things were pink. And the flamingos, while fabulously, fiery pink, were not peaceful at all. They constantly pecked and nagged at each other like the senior citizens of their Florida homeland.

Cam sat in between the two couples on the fence. Alec was to her right. He gave her a sly glance and then purpose-fully let his little finger graze hers before pulling it away and pretending to ignore her again at the sound of Autumn's giggle. Cam hated him.

And yet she desperately needed him to want her. She finally understood the Adolescent Postcoital Syndrome: Couple has sex. Girl gets uncharacteristically clingy. Boy feels suffocated. Boy pushes girl away for good. Cam wanted to be cooler than that. She did not want to succumb to the clinginess. The desperation. It was just that even though she had given it to him, she felt like Alec had stolen something from her, and she didn't want him to get away with it.

She jumped down and took a walk along the perimeter of the birds.

Some of the happy citizenry of Promise had meandered over to the school to calmly take a look at them, too, but no one was photographing the flamingos or making a big "to-do," as Cam's grandmother would say. A Little League game continued, uninterrupted, on the baseball diamond in the far corner of the field. Instead of flocking toward the flamingos, the kids who were playing on the school's playground ran screaming to the ice cream truck that had pulled up in the school parking lot. No one had even notified the media, which was a little surprising to Cam.

Not that she thought this was a miracle. Far from it. The real miracle was how an entire *bird* could grow to this size and resplendence from eating mostly microscopic organisms. That was a miracle. The fact that they flew here was a migration. The birds were simply in search of volcanic mud.

Cam watched the birds for another minute, beginning to tire of their honking and nagging and pecking, when two birds moved to the right to reveal a tall mound of mud topped by a chubby bird the size and shape of an oven stuffer-roaster. It was covered lightly with fuzzy gray fluff the color of dryer lint. A baby flamingo! It was so ugly, it was cute.

"Hi, Buddy," Cam said. She turned to point him out to the happy couples.

Unfortunately, though, they had started up a game. They would kiss whenever two flamingos came face-to-face, their curved pink necks creating each half of a flamingo-necked heart. It was cute, really. But it was also Cam's cue to leave.

# SIXTEEN

CAM CAME HOME EXHAUSTED, READY TO HOLE UP IN HER ROOM AND watch a movie. But she couldn't get past the front porch.

"Where have you been? I was about to call the police!" Alicia said. She and Perry sat on Adirondack chairs, sipping pink lemonade, as Asher painted the rungs of the porch's railing a glossy black.

Asher was starting to make a little more sense to Cam. He was a lone wolf at the top of the food chain. And when you're at the top of the food chain, you don't want your prey to lay itself down in front of you like that Barbie doll on the bench that Cam had seen through her telescope. You crave something more complicated. You want to engage in the hunt. Something surreptitious, covert, clandestine. And yet something safe. Something that would guarantee your ultimate bachelorhood and the solitude of your lair. *He must be involved with an older woman*, thought Cam. But after today, she felt too tired to care.

"I can't win. You force me to get out of here and now I'm in trouble for not coming home? Excuse me, I need to put Tweety inside. He's had a very long day." She tried to push past them all, feeling Asher's eyes on her, but her mom stopped her.

"Campbell, you're covered in dog hair."

"I got a job at the vet."

"That's great. Really. But please go wash off in the outside shower."

"Now?"

"Cam," her mom said, and then Perry started sneezing on cue. Even Asher started wiping his eyes on the back of his sleeve. "I'm allergic to dogs, too," he admitted.

"Oh, God." Cam yielded. She handed Tweety's cage to her mom and said, "He's morbidly obese, by the way. You need to stop feeding him the papaya."

"Go!" her mother said, throwing her a beach towel from the porch.

The shower assailed her with its sharp, freezing drops. Only hardy, robust New Englanders would think of installing an outdoor shower. Didn't her family realize that she had zero body fat? She shivered as she soaped up with a cracked and drying bar of Irish Spring, probably decades old. She was trying to ignore the spiderwebs in the corners of the shower when she heard the sudden scratchy sound of her towel scraping against the top of the wooden stall. Cam knew what was coming next, but before she could react, Perry plucked each of her articles of clothing off of the shower stall.

Cam peeked over the stall while Perry proceeded to fling the clothes piece by piece from the cliff to the beach below. Cam stood naked in the shower except for her Chuck Taylors. She wasn't about to take those off.

"*Perry!*" Cam screamed. "Dammit, Perry, I'm freezing." Cam hopped around, trying to stay warm, and turned the red knob of the shower to full steam. She screamed again for Perry.

"Need some help?" Asher asked from outside the stall. "Here, you can take my shirt."

"Here we go again. Asher to the rescue. This is so *It's a*—"

"—*Wonderful Life*," Asher finished. "When they were walking home from the pool and she loses her robe behind the bush. I was just going to say that."

"You could learn a lot from that movie, actually, about what happens to nice guys," Cam said through her chattering teeth. It was the movie about the angel who prevents some sad family man from jumping off a bridge on Christmas Eve. Her mother made her watch it every year. Cam hopped from foot to foot and rubbed her hands up and down her arms to get warm. The sky was eerily dark, like someone had spilled black ink over the stars, and the crickets, usually so vocal, were strangely silent.

"What are you saying? Is it possible that you could have missed the entire point of that movie?"

Cam paused and listened for a second to the waves crashing to the shore in the distance. "What? He didn't go to college, even after he got the suitcase. He missed the honeymoon. He was left at home, and everyone took advantage of him."

"And he had a wonderful life. It's the title of the film."

"It was all propaganda to make you feel like your miserable life is worthwhile," Cam said, staring at the knots in the wood in front of her.

"You don't deserve my shirt," Asher said, but she could see beneath the stall that his feet stood motionless.

"But you're going to give it to me anyway." Cam stuck her hand up and over the stall.

"How do you know?"

"I just do."

"Here," he said, handing it to her.

The shirt was long enough, but it was white, so it was soaking through in strategic places where she actually hadn't lost all of her body fat. She kept her arms crossed in front of her chest and stepped out of the stall. The shirtless, six-packed Asher still stood there, and Cam was taken aback by what football and a little handiwork could do for a body. They shared a speechless moment, and then Cam said, "I can take it from here."

"Oh. Right. Sorry. Nice shoes, by the way," Asher said, and he turned to walk across the lawn. Cam snuck a peek at the view from behind, which wasn't too bad either.

In the house, Alicia and Perry were playing Scrabble at the dining room table. The room was lit by an enormous moose-antler chandelier, which was in such bad taste, it was almost hip. Cam wondered what PETA would have to say about that. "Did they at least eat the moose?" Cam wondered out loud.

"What?" her mom asked.

"Never mind. That was cute, Perry. Thanks for stealing my towel," Cam said as she stood behind Perry's chair, examining her Scrabble tiles.

"Don't mention it," Perry said, still concentrating on the game.

Cam grabbed Alicia's jacket from the back of her chair, wrapped it around herself, and stepped into Perry's pink Uggs. She snagged a carrot stick before heading toward the stairs, where she could finally hole up and get warm.

"Ask her?" Perry said after placing *xen* next to her mother's *O*.

"Good one," Cam said when she saw the board. "Ask me what?"

"Perry wants to know if you heard about the flamingos."

Alicia was wearing her reading glasses, and she looked down her nose through them as she rearranged her tiles.

"Yeah. Down by the school. I saw them."

"You saw them? So now don't you believe this town is special?" Perry asked, her blue eyes round and insistent.

"Why?" Cam asked.

"Why? Because a whole *flock* of flamingos has come to roost here. In Maine, which is not their normal habitat," said Alicia.

"And?"

"And that's crazy and miraculous and may be a sign that we're in the right place, since flamingos are often found in Florida," her mom continued.

"That is so illogical. The flamingos have nothing to do with us. It's a crazy global-warming fallout fiasco, like the bats disappearing from the caves in Pennsylvania or the bees getting lost because of cell phone interference. . . ."

"Cam . . ." Alicia said.

"Or the iguanas freezing to death because the weather's been so erratic in Florida or the polar bears drowning. The flamingos ran out of food somewhere and went out in search of more. End of story."

Cam heard her phone buzzing from the porch, where she had heaped her shorts. She took the phone out of her pocket and read the text from Elaine. *I'm putting him down in the morning,* it read. *Get here early if you'd like to say good-bye.*

Cam walked back into the house feeling defeated and a little betrayed. Why couldn't Elaine just leave Bart alone? Weren't these people all about letting nature take its course?

"Will you bring me over to the flamingos tomorrow, Cam?" Perry asked. "I want to take some pictures."

"Nah. I already saw them, and I have someplace else I need to be," Cam said.

Perry stiffened a bit in her chair. She slid one of her Scrabble tiles in a figure eight on the table, then used her thumb and forefinger to flick it onto the floor. "This was such a waste of time," she said.

"What was a waste of time?" Cam asked, shivering.

"Coming here. You haven't changed a bit."

"What do you want from me?" Cam asked them. "I have to work tomorrow."

"I just thought—" Perry started.

"What?"

"That you might start believing."

"In what? Magic? Hocus-pocus? Sleight of hand?" Cam said, waving her fingers through the air like a magician. She pretended to pull a Scrabble tile out of Perry's ear.

"I don't know. I just kind of wanted this to work," Perry said. The tension behind her eyes let loose a little, and Cam could see her fighting back tears.

"It's amazing that flamingos landed here, okay. But that doesn't have anything to do with me. I just can't make that leap. People die. Puppies die. My father died. Flamingos or no flamingos, I am going to die. Sooner rather than later."

"But you're getting better. Don't you see that? You haven't really been sick since we got here. You've actually been eating and everything," Perry said. "This town has to be magic if you're eating peanut butter sandwiches." Perry's face was flushed. Her eyebrows lifted in hopeful arcs.

Cam had had a lot more energy since they arrived in Maine, it was true, but she had chalked it up to the fresh air and the fact that it might be a stage of dying. People often go through a wellness phase, a remission, biologically constructed so that they can say good-bye, plan their funeral, get all their ducks in a row. . . .

"I'm sorry, Perry, but I have more energy because my death is imminent. Not farther off."

"She's hopeless," Alicia said, slumping back into her chair.

"I am hope-resistant," Cam said. She used the toe of the pink Ugg boot to untangle some of the graying fringe on the Persian rug beneath the dining table.

"You could at least let *us* believe," said Perry.

"I'm not telling you you can't believe."

Her sister folded the game board in half. The letters cascaded back into the box with a series of sad clicks. "You know it's not easy to be me, right?" Perry replied.

*Funny*, thought Cam, *I had always believed it was.* Easy to be Perry. What on earth could be easier than being Perry?

Curiosity got the best of her and she let herself ask, "Really?"

"I make a lot of sacrifices for you." Perry's voice quavered. "Like being here. Do you think I want to spend my entire summer away from my friends? No one ever has time to think of what I want or what I need because your needs are so tremendous. You have tremendous needs. And that's fine. Really. I'm used to being an afterthought. But the least you can do is let us believe that this might work. I do a lot for you, Cam," said Perry, and one tear finally broke loose and slid down her face.

Cam paused, feeling choked up herself as she thought of all the times Perry had to stay home alone with a baby-sitter while Alicia traveled with Cam to a new hospital for a new trial. Or the times Perry was dragged along to doctor's appointments when she could have been at playdates or cheerleading or something. She would have been a good cheerleader.

"I'm sorry," Cam said. "You can believe what you want."

Upstairs, the Flamingo List still sat unfolded on top of her suitcase, corners up, like a shallow bowl. She grabbed a marker and crossed out *Kill my little sister's dreams* and, while she was at it, *Wallow in misery, mope, pout, and sleep through Saturday.*

All in a day's work.

# SEVENTEEN

CAM SPED IN CUMULUS ALONG THE WINDING BEACH ROAD, PAST THE field of purple dandelions, toward the vet's. It was eleven o'clock. She couldn't believe how late she'd slept. She rolled down the window and let the brisk and briny sea air whip against her face to wake her up.

She had texted Elaine twice so far this morning and had gotten no response. She parked Cumulus next to the mail truck, waved to the donkey, James Madison, and ran inside. She prayed that she wasn't too late.

As she approached the door, she heard some barking. It could be any number of the dogs at Elaine's, she reminded herself, keeping her heart in check. But it sounded like the sharp-pitched yelp of a puppy.

"Bart!" Campbell cried when she opened the door. There he was, wagging his tail uncontrollably.

And then he peed.

"Someone's happy to see you," said Elaine. She wiped up Bart's mess and attempted to clean his feet as he wiggled happily in her arms. "Where are you staying, anyway?"

"In that big house. On top of the hill."

"Avalon?" Elaine asked. "Oh, you're the girl Asher told me about. He didn't say you were sick."

"He doesn't know. You know Asher?"

"He's my nephew."

"He's nice," Cam said. She didn't know what else to say about him. Actually, she felt strangely shy talking about him at all. "So what happened with Bart?" She took him from Elaine and let him cover her face with wet kisses.

"I don't know. Just one of those things. He decided to live," Elaine said. She cupped Bart's snout in her hand and gave it a squeeze. "Didn't you, boy?"

"Don't you think it's more scientific than that?" Cam asked. She was so ecstatic about Bart, she didn't even mind walking into the ugly country living room and sitting on a scratchy chair with him.

"Not really. Some things can't be explained."

"There's an explanation for everything."

"Really?" Elaine asked, an amused look on her face.

"Yes. Even those flamingos by the school. They were just looking for food."

"Shouldn't have found it there, though. The Maine shrimp stop running in March." Elaine sat down in the ugly chair opposite Cam and took out her needlepoint. "I'm a little worried about them, actually. If their pond freezes, they'll have to skedaddle. I hope they're not frogs in a pot."

"Frogs in a pot?"

"If you put a frog in some warm water and slowly turn up the heat," Elaine said, wetting her embroidery floss between her lips so she could thread it through a needle, "he'll stay there until he boils. Kind of like people. We're too lazy to change, so we'll just keep doing what we're doing until it's too late." Elaine put her reading glasses on and then took them off, struggling to see the needle's eye. "Ugh! Can you do this?" she asked, handing Cam the needle and thread.

"Ew. You just had that in your mouth," said Cam.

"Oh geez, never mind. Done." She pulled the orange floss through the tiny glint of metal.

Each pane of the bay window of the living room was obstructed by a bright handmade suncatcher hanging from a suction cup. Cam brought Bart to the window so she could find a way to peek around them and look outside. It was a little windy and gray this morning. The bay looked like crinkled aluminum foil. Cam found Main Street in the distance and followed it to its far end, scanning the woods for the dirt road that had brought them here. Arriving at the Dunkin' Donuts seemed like a year ago.

"Do you believe what some people say about this town?" she asked.

"What? That it's enchanted?"

"Yeah," said Cam. She sat back down. Bart walked in a circle on her lap before curling up and falling asleep.

"Everyone has her own theory about why weird things happen here. There's the sacred Indian burial ground theory, the meteorite theory, the alien visitation theory, and the Bermuda Triangle theory. I like the Salem witch trial theory." Elaine rested her large hands over her belly. "It wasn't really a 'witch trial' because those happened much earlier. But people think the ghost of Olivia Hutchins protects the town because she found shelter here. She was sentenced to prison for adultery and witchcraft in Salem in the late 1800s. Her only real crime was marrying the deranged mayor of Salem. One day when he found his wife in a close conversation with the town's handsome butcher, he flew into a jealous rage. He argued that his red-haired wife was a reincarnated witch, and the jury—still sensitive to the taboo of witchcraft—found a way to convict her. Olivia spent three years in prison for petty thievery before mysteriously escapaing and finding her way here. She lived at the house. Avalon. She's Asher's great-great-great-great-grandmother."

"Asher believes it, doesn't he?" Cam suddenly remembered his reaction to her skepticism about the sunset and the whales. And then there was *It's A Wonderful Life.*

"Oh, Asher. Asher is a strange case, that one. Let me get a cup of coffee, and I'll tell you the story of Asher."

"That's okay. I don't need to know," Cam called into the kitchen. Part of her was secretly dying to know. The part of her that scooched herself to the actual edge of her seat.

"No, it's a good story," Elaine said as she settled back into her chair with her coffee mug. "Hey," she said, "aren't you a hula dancer? I'll tell the story, and you can hula it."

"I can't just 'hula it.' It's not like sign language."

"So once upon a time, long, long ago . . . Go ahead—hula it. What's long, long ago?"

Cam stood up, placing the sleeping Bart back down on the chair, and tried to keep herself from smiling. She'd been wanting to dance since she'd seen her mother teaching hula to the senior citizens in their living room the other day. "I need some music at least."

Elaine turned on the radio softly, and some Pearl Jam came on.

"So long, long ago, Asher's and my great-great, lots of greats, one less great for me, grandfather founded this town."

Cam moved her hips first and then her arms over many mountains to indicate long, long ago, and then signed *man* and *town* with little roofs made from the triangles of her thumbs and index fingers put together.

"He was a wise and benevolent man. He made honest treaties with the Indians, and he lived among them. I think we even have some Indian blood in us. He sheltered a woman running from the law, and then he married her."

Cam changed the sway of her hips and indicated *wise* and *benevolent* by touching her thumbs to the center of her forehead and then moving her hands from her chest out into the world. She did *woman, running,* and then the signs for *love* and *safety.*

"Her name was Olivia Hutchins, and later, as if to prove she did not have an adulterous bone in her body, when Asher's great-great-great-great-grandfather was lost at sea, she waited in the widow's walk for five years for him to return. She never lost hope. And then she died."

Cam danced *dangerous sea.* She danced *woman.* It was difficult to dance *waiting,* so she took a long pause.

"Many strange things have happened since then," Elaine continued. "There was ladybug tide, when millions of ladybugs washed onto shore. They had to scoop them up with steam shovels. Or the time that girl walked away from that airplane crash. Or when my broken foot healed overnight . . ."

Cam was improvising now, making up hand movements for *ladybugs* and *steam shovels* and *airplane.*

"People started to believe the town was enchanted. Or haunted by the ghost of Olivia. Everyone, especially our family, seemed lucky. And then one day Asher's young parents decided to go on a vacation for their anniversary. And somehow, for some reason, their luck ran out. On their way to Hawaii, they were sucked out of the side of an airplane."

Cam did the steps for *travel* and then *danger.*

"My father, Asher's grandfather, was devastated and went on a walkabout, from which he never returned. And my mother died of a broken heart."

Cam turned around in a circle, still moving her hips but holding her head down, her arms crossed sadly across her chest. *Sorrow.*

"Asher thinks they died because they left this magical place. Part of him is afraid to leave. This town has a hold on him. It's time for him to get on with the rest of his life and instead, I think he'll stay here forever."

Cam finished with the hand motions for *town* and *forever.* And when she stopped, she felt heavy with sadness. She had put Asher's story into her body and it weighed on her like a lead suit.

Elaine startled her with a loud, "That was amazing!"

"Thanks."

Cam turned the stereo off and went to pet Bart. She was a little embarrassed, and she needed to change the subject.

"But the magic," Cam said. "The purple dandelions, a freak flamingo visit. It's all just coincidence." Bart was still curled up on the chair. He looked like a furry letter *Q.* Cam felt his nose. Yesterday it was dry and leathery, and now it was cold and wet.

"Some people say you should pay attention to coincidence," Elaine said. She tied off her orange thread, put her needlepoint down, and stood up. "It can show you your path. Besides, these coincidences are enough to keep people believing. To give them some hope."

"Believing in what, flamingos? Hoping for what?" Bart stirred and then lifted his head, looking at her sleepily.

"Hope, my friend, is its own reward," Elaine said as she walked down the hallway to put her coffee cup in the sink.

"Hope, Dr. Whittier, is a tease," Cam called after her.

Bart jumped his front paws up to her knees and scratched at her jeans, reminding her that she had a promise of her own to keep. She called into the other room, "Mind if I borrow Bart? I promised him the ultimate puppy day."

"Sure, just don't tire him out."

"Okay, buddy. Let's go for a ride."

Cam might not have believed in hope, but she believed in keeping her promises.

# EIGHTEEN

CAM LET BART SIT ON HER LAP WHILE SHE DROVE ALONG THE OCEAN, hugging its deep blue curves before turning up the big hill to Avalon. Bart kept his little snout out the window the whole time, his tongue wagging behind him in the wind. He was a happy pup.

She played a little tug-of-war with him on the front lawn, fed him the special lamb-and-rice food she had brought with her from the vet's office, and then she let him fall asleep in a sunny spot on the porch. She wandered around back to where her mother was on her knees in the dirt. Big bags of topsoil and fertilizer and trowels and seedlings were scattered around her.

"What's all this?"

"I'm planting a garden. I saw you with the puppy. He's adorable, but don't let him in the house." Her mom looked beautiful. She wore a wide-brimmed straw sunhat with a red

scarf tied around it, a white peasant blouse, and a red skirt that circled around her. She stood up and wiped her forehead with the back of her brown-gloved hand.

"You look like the lady on the raisin box."

"Is that good?"

"You're just all, like, harvesty. Like you're going to stomp on some grapes later."

"Maybe I will." Alicia held her arm up, her wrist cocked to the left, and hopped her knees up in the air.

"Since when are you into gardening?" Cam asked.

"One of those things I've always wanted to do and never had the time," Alicia said as she threw her tools one by one back into the tool bucket.

"Do you know what you're doing?"

"You're supposed to say, 'It won't come up.'"

"What?"

"You had a favorite book as a toddler called *The Carrot Seed*. Do you remember it?" her mom asked, taking off her gloves and putting her arm around Cam's shoulders.

"No."

"A little boy planted a seed, and each of his family members stopped by to tell him, 'It won't come up.' You used to giggle and recite, 'It won't come up,' whenever I turned the page."

"How did it end?" Cam said.

"Campbell. It was a children's book. How do you think?"

"Joking, Mom, God. I miss the old sarcastic you. I should get Bart back to the vet's."

On the drive back, with Bart once again seated on her lap, she thought about the argument with Perry last night. About her mom planting a garden. About how desperately they wanted to *believe*. She was tiring of her role as the naysayer. She pictured herself as a three-year-old saying, 'It won't come up.' She was turning out to be predictable. Cam hated predictable.

She thought about all the things her mom had done for her to create a happy childhood—to perpetuate the innocence for as long as she possibly could. The cookies for Santa, the notes from the tooth fairy, the fabulous birthday parties, all creating the illusion of comfort and safety and magic, when none of that actually existed. Maybe it was Cam's turn to perpetuate some innocence.

She did not believe in the hokey story of how the town got its magic. She did not believe in the "magic" itself. She herself could not hope.

But she could give the gift of hope to her mother and sister. She could help them believe. That was easy.

She just needed to steal some tomato plants.

She found some on the side of the road in a garden that seemed to belong to no one, stretching for acres in all directions and blooming with produce. She climbed over the fence and stepped into it. Vines grew laced and tangled around one another and brushed against her legs as she walked. She swatted at imaginary bugs.

She found three tomato, two zucchini, two eggplant, and an enormous sunflower plant. She used her mother's trowel to dig them up from the roots, extricating them without letting the heavy fruit drop from the vines. Then she placed the plants gently in her trunk and covered them with a wet towel to keep them fresh.

Something about locking them in the trunk felt sinister. As if she were some mafia killer transporting a debtor to the docks for execution.

"I'm sorry," she said to the fearful face of the sunflower. "It's only temporary." And then she slammed the trunk.

At midnight, Cam slipped out into her mother's garden to replant her haul. Even with the half moon bulging toward her with its pregnant yellow belly, night was deeper here, without streetlamps or nearby houses to leaven the darkness. Night even had a specific smell to it in Maine. A fresh, wet, dewy smell that jumped out at her as she pierced the earth with the sharp tip of her shovel. She was thankful the earthworms were asleep.

She was able to get the first two tomato plants to stand

up using the stake her mom had placed next to the seedling. The long green vines wound around the stake like a ladder of DNA. She began the last plant, sticking the trowel into the earth with a satisfying scrape.

"What are you doing?" said a voice from way too close behind her.

She screamed, turned, and threw the trowel. It bit into the side of Asher's forehead before falling to the ground with a thud.

"Ow. Jesus." His hands flew to his face.

"Oh my God! Shit! Are you okay?"

"Yeah. Ow. I think so." Asher said, drawing his fingers away. They were streaked with blood.

"Oh. You're bleeding. I'm so sorry. Here," she said and handed him a towel. "You really need to stop sneaking up on me like that!"

"I thought you heard me coming," said Asher, looking at the bloody towel.

"Direct pressure. Direct pressure. Hold it on there. No, I didn't hear you. You're surefooted, like your deer-hunting ancestors." Cam thought she had remembered Elaine saying something about them having Native American roots.

"What?"

"Never mind."

"Why are you night-gardening?" he asked. Cam now saw his resemblance to Elaine. It was glaring, actually, and she was surprised she hadn't noticed it earlier. They shared the same distinct high cheekbones, square chins, and of course the parentheses dimples around their smiles when something—usually Cam—amused them. She wasn't sure she enjoyed being such a source of amusement.

"What are you doing prowling around here at midnight?" she asked.

"I asked you first."

"My mom likes to believe in all this magical town business, so I'm helping her along. Creating a miracle. I'm a miracle worker."

"Oooooh, that's a bad idea," Asher said, still holding the towel to his head. His shirt was hiked up above his belly button.

*No tocar. No tocar,* Cam said to herself, remembering the time she went to the museum with her Spanish class and they were told not to touch. "Why?"

"It just is. You can't force your will with the universe. You just have to trust how things unfold," he said. "This could blow up in your face." His uninjured eye was disappointed in her. "It's already blown up in my face, for example. Think of what else could happen."

"Yeah, well, some of us don't have time to wait for the universe to unfold itself. Are you going to be okay? You should probably go clean that up," Cam said as she packed up her stuff and stood back to admire her "garden." She couldn't believe she had gotten the sunflower to stand up. "Looks good, doesn't it?" She threw some drier dirt around the plants to cover her tracks.

"It looks good, but I'm telling you, I have a bad feeling about this," he said.

"What harm can possibly come from this? I'm doing a good deed for once. It's not like I'm putting a kink into the space-time continuum. It's good karma."

"It's lying."

"You say tomayto, and I say tomahto," Cam said.

Finally, he smiled. His front teeth overlapped just a tiny bit.

She reached up and slowly peeled the towel away from Asher's brow. "You might need some help bandaging that," she said as she accidentally brushed her chest against his shoulder. "Looks like it's buried in your eyebrow, so you won't see a scar or anything. Sorry about that."

"I'm sorry I startled you," he said. Cam thought she noticed his gaze soften and his pupils dilate. But then she realized it was just a big cloud drifting in front of the moon, changing the light.

"I have a first aid kit in the car. . . . " Cam offered.

"No, I think there's some in the carriage house. Come on. I want to show you something," he said as he walked back toward the woods, away from the house.

"I thought it was this way." Cam pointed toward the front yard.

"Come here," he said, and he led her to a woodshed. He moved some firewood out of the way to reveal a staircase going down into the earth.

"What is that, some kind of root cellar? Creepy."

"Sort of. Come on." He started to descend the staircase, a trickle of blood creeping down the side of his face.

"This is the part of the horror film where you yell at the girl on the screen, 'Don't *go*. You idiot! Don't go! Why are they always so stupid?'" Cam *told* her mom he could be a serial killer.

"It's completely safe."

"Right. Cue slasher music. Oh, that's funny. Slasher rhymes with Asher. That could be your new name. If I survive this, that is." Cam followed Asher down the stairs and into the smell of dirt. The walls around the staircase were just the earthen sides of a hole in the ground, but when she got to the bottom of the stairs, Asher had turned on a light to reveal a bright, capacious hallway, whose white-tiled walls reminded her of the Lincoln Tunnel in New York City.

"What's all this?"

"A secret passageway. This house used to be part of the Underground Railroad, so there are secret tunnels and hiding places everywhere."

"So that explains how you sneak around. See, there's an explanation for everything. Was your family always so virtuous?"

"No. During Prohibition, my great-grandfather got rich using the tunnels to traffic alcohol. He made a fortune. Come on. I'll show you where it comes out."

There was a huge sliding exit at the beach disguised as the face of a rock wall. Growing up at Disney must have inured her to imitation landscapes.

Another tunnel opened up into the floor of the carriage house, and a third came up behind a rotating bookcase in the basement of the main house. They exited through this one, Asher spinning the bookshelf. They stepped into what Cam had dubbed Homer's room.

Asher moved over to his tank and stared at him for a bit. "You should let him go, I think. If you're not going to eat him, he should be free to explore the bottom of the ocean."

He laid his hand on the tank, and Cam could finally read the rubber bracelet around his wrist. FREEDOM, it said.

"Freedom," she said to him now. "You know, you can't really have freedom if you're just waiting around for the universe to unfold. If you're at the mercy of the universe, you aren't really free." Homer stopped trying to climb the glass walls of the tank and retreated to his plastic SpongeBob pineapple house.

"That's an interesting perspective. But if you're trying to control the universe, you're not really free either."

"Yes, I am. I'm free. I have free will. I can control the universe." Cam held up her arm, pretending to make a muscle.

The term *free will* reminded her of the philosophy book in her high school library that had been called *Free Will* until someone had scrawled a *y* at the end of it with a black Sharpie.

"Well, thank you for showing me the bat cave. It's perfect for making my next miracle," said Cam.

"Not another one."

"Yes, indeedy. The next one is a doozy."

# NINETEEN

"CAM! LOOK AT THIS. YOU HAVE GOT TO BELIEVE NOW!"

Cam had been so soundly asleep she had forgotten where she was. She tried to put it all together. She knew whose voice was calling her, but she thought she was still in Florida, and she couldn't understand why it was so bright in her room. For a second she thought she had died.

"Cam!" Perry jumped on top of the bed and shook her awake, and Cam thought she was getting CPR. Maybe she *had* died. And then, slowly, with much work and concentration, she put it all together. Maine. The garden. Perry.

"Okay. Okay, Peri-stalsis. I'm up," she groaned. "What?"

"Don't call me that." The word had something to do with the movement of the intestines.

"You're the one who changed your name, Peri-menopause."

"Stop."

"Well, what? What is so important that you need to jump on my bed? Is it Christmas? The Easter Bunny? What?"

"It's Mom's garden. You need to come see it."

"Fine, fine. I'll come see the garden. Can I have a cup of coffee first?"

"No. Right now."

"Oh, God," said Cam as Perry dragged her down the stairs and out into the backyard. Cam was wearing boxer shorts and a gray tank top, and her hair was sticking up in all different directions. A crease from her pillowcase stretched across her left cheek.

She didn't know why, because she had been practicing her hope-averseness for a long time, but she noticed that she had a hope. She hoped that Asher was still asleep, so he wouldn't see her like this. She must have begun caring overnight what he thought about her. An interesting development that, like her acceptance to Harvard, would go with her to her early grave.

Alicia was sprinkling the garden with a hose, and Cam shaded her eyes from the sun. Did it ever rain here? She stood back and admired her handiwork in the daylight. The sun reflected off of the heavy round tomatoes and the shiny aubergine eggplants. The zucchinis seemed to have grown two inches since last night.

"Can you believe this, Cam? I just planted these yesterday."

"Well, you did use Miracle-Gro. That stuff really works, I guess."

"Cam."

"Okay, okay. That is seriously amazing."

"It is," said Alicia. "I'm going to make a pie and enter it into the pie contest today."

Cam had forgotten that it was the Fourth of July. She had promised her mother she would go with her to the town celebration.

"What kind of pie?" Cam asked, surveying the garden for any kind of pie ingredients. She hadn't stolen any rhubarb.

"Pizza."

"Mom, you can't enter a pizza in the pie-making contest."

"Who says?"

"I don't think they will recognize it as pie," Cam said. "Honestly, I don't think they will recognize it as food if it doesn't have lobster on it."

"Well, we have one of those. I can make a lobster pizza."

"Don't even think about it," Cam said. "Homer is not food." Maybe Asher was right. She should set him free. Let him see the world.

"Get dressed, Cam," said Perry. "The parade starts in an hour."

"You'll have to take her to the parade, so I can make my pie."

"It's pizza."

"Yes. Pizza pie. Tomato pie. That's what they call it in Brooklyn."

According to Cam's iPhone, they were exactly 478 miles from Brooklyn. This was extremely obvious as she and Perry walked down to Main Street and the heart of Promise's Fourth of July jamboree. Cam had never been to Brooklyn, but she guessed that they didn't have jamborees there. Or quilt shows in churches or lemonade stands run by Brownie troops or sack races or bouncy houses or stilt walkers dressed up like Uncle Sam. They definitely did not have prizes for the largest strawberry or a little kids' bicycle parade complete with red-white-and-blue streamered handle bars and ribbons in the spokes.

When they got to the lobster pound, Perry squealed and pulled her toward someone dressed in knickers and a curly white wig. Asher was supposed to be one of the Founding Fathers, but Cam couldn't tell which one.

"Who are you?" Cam asked.

"John Hancock." He carried an enormous quill for signing the Declaration of Independence. He waved it at her now with a flourish.

Just then, the high school marching band rounded the corner playing a John Philip Sousa march, and Asher–John Hancock swept them all to the curb so they wouldn't get run over. Out in front of the band was a blonde girl in white go-go boots and a sparkly red leotard. Her hair was up and she wore a tall white hat that shaded her eyes. But Cam recognized something about her. "Is that—"

"Sunny."

"Whoa," said Cam. She had not pegged Sunny as a joiner. And definitely not as a twirler.

"Her mom makes her do it," said Asher. "Apparently she's pretty good, and she can get a scholarship."

"For twirling that thing around."

"Ayuh."

"Huh."

"Yep."

"Whoa."

"I know."

"Speaking of scholarships, Slasher: Doesn't the quarterback of the state champion team usually get one of those? You get one of those, and then you marry the head cheerleader, go to business school, have three kids and a dog, become VP, CEO, chairman of the board, get a house in Malibu." She counted the list off on her fingers. "That's the trajectory of a champion quarterback, Asher. It's written in the Stars 'n' Stripes."

"Ayuh."

"So."

"So, you girls want to do the scavenger hunt?" he asked,

changing the subject. "I'm in charge, and it's pretty fun." Asher handed Perry a list of things to find.

They decided to split up. On the top of Cam's list was a green balloon. She scanned the streets for green, but the only things that weren't red, white, and blue were the flamingos. A few had wandered away from the flock and strutted down Main Street like aliens from another planet.

As Cam was looking down at her scavenger list, Alec with a *c* snuck up behind her and slid a hand around her waist. She bristled (in disgust or arousal, she wasn't sure—she was confused when it came to Alec), but all the hair on her body suddenly stood on end. "Oh, so you know me today?"

"I am sorry," he said. "Autumn, she is very, how you say? Jealous."

"Right. Well, I am very, how you say? Revolted. Revolted by you, so you may remove your hand."

"Campbell, come on. Let's go get a cup of coffee. Autumn is busy. Sunny makes her wave flags around with the band."

"No, Alec. I will not have coffee with you, thank you very much. I'm in search of a green balloon."

As Cam walked away, she started to feel dizzy. Her palms were sweaty. She was having trouble catching her breath. Would they know who to call if she died there on the spot? Would she never get to say good-bye?

Maybe it was how she woke up this morning, but she was thinking about death a lot today. She thought about how it would happen. . . . Her lungs slowly filling up with fluid, drowning in her own bed, suddenly finding herself without breath, and then without sight or hearing, and then eventually without even the capacity to dream. Without love. That was the saddest and scariest part about it. To be suddenly, eternally without love.

Cam tried to stop these thoughts because they were not helping the situation. She began to hyperventilate, and then she fell over, and once again, everything went dark.

"It was a panic attack, Campbell," Alicia told her.

"Huh?"

"I don't want you thinking this was some bad episode. You simply had a panic attack. Your numbers are all fine. The doctor can prescribe some medication. A little Ativan. Something to take the edge off. And you'll be good as new."

"Did your pizza win?" Cam asked groggily, taking in the sterile doctor's office around them.

"I didn't have time to enter it, but we can eat it when we get home."

Perry was sitting on a chair by the window, busy with the keypad of her phone. Next to the chair was a paper bag overflowing with the random stuff from her half of the scavenger-hunt list. A clothespin, a sun visor, a plastic baseball bat . . .

"I did it again, didn't I, Perry?"

"What?" she asked, her thumbs still wildly texting.

"Ruined something you were looking forward to."

"That's okay."

"No. It's not. Can we at least go home and eat the pizza?"

"Sure. There's plenty of it. I had so many tomatoes. You can invite some friends," Alicia said.

"Ha!" said Perry without looking up from her phone. "Like she has any of those."

As if on cue, Asher, Sunny, Royal, and Autumn sans Alec walked into the doctor's office.

"We just wanted to see how you were doing," Asher said.

"Well, that *is* a miracle," said Perry. She took out her notebook and said out loud as she wrote, "Number forty: Campbell . . . has . . . friends."

"Thanks a lot, Perry," Campbell said.

Perry just gave her a little wink.

"Let's get out of here," Alicia announced. "Pizza, anyone?"

"Perry, you should write this down in your notebook."

The pizza was magical. The dough had a chewy, bendy, bouncy quality, and the cheese pulled away from your mouth in thin strings. Which was perfect. Biting into pizza should be a silent operation. Noiseless. There was nothing worse than a crunchy pizza with cheese that slid off in one piece.

And the sauce. The sauce was an inspiration. Not too sweet or salty or tangy, but a blend of those flavors that perfectly glued the cheese to the bubbling dough underneath. Alicia walked around serving endless trays of it to their guests.

Everyone they knew was there. Her mom's hula friends, Perry's tweeny friends, Cam's catalog kids, who had thankfully shaken their patriotic alter egos and returned to their pretending-to-be-effortless style. Even Elaine was there with Smitty, the cook from the lobster pound. It was a wonderful, spontaneous gathering, the kind that used to happen to Cam's family before everything changed.

They sat around a long table that Asher had set up in the front yard overlooking the bay. They waited for the orcas to make their ritual leaps out of the ocean, and then they waited again for darkness to fall and for the fireworks to begin. Someone was launching them from behind the lighthouse, and they had the perfect vantage point from the lawn of Avalon by the Sea.

Cam watched as Perry and her friends honed their flirting skills on Asher. He was the perfect hot-but-innocuous person to practice on, and he was extremely patient with them, lighting their sparklers again and again, as they pretended to be too frightened to do it themselves.

Cam hadn't gotten the gene that allowed you to flirt. She was convinced it was genetic. You either had the capacity for coyness, or you simply could not pretend to be stupid. Which was what guys really wanted. They wanted you to prove to them how much smarter they really were, and Cam's ego was too big for that. Which, if you thought about it, was just stupid. If Cam were smart, she would pretend to be stupid, so that she would end up less alone.

She was glad Perry could do it. It made her worry less about her.

Asher had hooked up the outdoor speakers, and her mom put on the sound track from "The Spirit of Aloha." Cam was dying to dance but was suddenly terrified to do it in front of Asher. Maybe she did have some coyness in her.

"Come on!" said her mom. "Campbell, this is your number."

"Oh, God." Cam finally hoisted her pizza-stuffed self off the bench. "Just for a minute," she said. But when she lost herself in the music, one minute became a half an hour, and she'd forgotten all about who might be watching. She did the entire volcano goddess hula, which describes the origins of the dance. Pele the volcano goddess needed to escape her sister, the sea. The sea kept dousing her flames, so Pele traveled to the top of the highest hill and found a home where she could truly express herself. Then she danced in celebration.

When Cam was through, she sat down to take a rest. She watched Perry as she very animatedly told her unicorn theory to a bunch of people who'd gathered around her, eating their s'mores.

Cam had heard Perry tell this unicorn story a million times. Her theory started with the idea that there are too many references to dragons for them to have been a complete myth. The idea of dragons could not possibly be entirely fictitious. Someone must have seen some kind of flying lizard who breathed fire.

"There needed to be an origin," she said now. Her audience was rapt. "And the original dragon was probably—like the Loch Ness Monster, who, by the way, is also not a myth—a dinosaur. At some point a very, very long time ago, dinosaurs must have walked the earth with humans. Not a lot of them, mind you, but a few stragglers who had woken up after the Ice Age like iguanas can sometimes do after a long cold winter when you think they are dead. Cold-blooded things can wake up when they get warm. So a few of these dinosaurs—or pterosaurs, actually, because they could fly—must have woken up and existed, and man must have seen one, or there would never have been stories about dragons.

"If you have to believe that there were dragons, then you have to believe in unicorns because people were telling stories about them around the same time."

Cam wondered, between her and her sister, who was Pele and who was the sea. She didn't have to think too long about it. Her sister had an imaginative, erupting spirit, and

Cam continued to douse it with her wet-rag cynicism.

"That was something else," Asher said, straddling the bench next to Cam at the picnic table.

She started to say that yes, Perry would someday make a great unicornologist, when Asher interrupted, "The hula stuff. Pretty amazing. You're really good."

Cam wanted to say something sarcastic, but just then the first rocket went off, announcing the start of Promise's Fourth of July fireworks spectacular, which, when you're used to Disney fireworks every night of your life, was pretty darn pathetic. Pathetic in a way that made Cam start to like it here.

Cam felt happier. Maybe it was the pizza in her stomach, but she felt content. She felt brave enough to text Lily for the first time since they'd arrived.

*Today was a good day*, she wrote. She hoped it was positive enough to warrant a response.

# TWENTY

**"HELP ME GET HIM INTO THE U-HAUL."**

"You know he's a donkey, right?" Asher said. "And a spoiled donkey. He's not just going to do what I say."

"Sure he will. Come on, James Madison," said Cam as she clicked her tongue and pulled him with the lead.

James Madison pulled back. He shook his head, and then he actually sat down, which Cam did not expect.

"Isn't she going to realize he's a donkey and not a white horse? He doesn't exactly have a mythical, magical physique."

"James Madison!" Cam gasped. "Are you going to take that? Stand up and show him your physique."

James Madison just sat there and brayed. It almost sounded as if he were saying "U-Haul."

"Right, James Madison, U-Haulll. Get into the U-Haulll," Cam said in donkey language.

"Are there any air holes in that thing?" Asher asked as the donkey finally stood up and began taking tentative steps out of his corral and into the driveway.

"It's only five minutes to the house," Cam said, pulling again at the lead.

"This just feels like a lie, that's all. And we're also stealing, which is not exactly comfortable for me."

"You've never stolen anything?" Cam asked. "Everyone steals something. Even if it's an ice pop from the freezer when you're six."

"Not that I know of."

"God. That's cute. We're borrowing, Slasher. We will bring him back. That's the definition of borrowing. Taking something and then returning it," Cam sighed, dropping the lead and taking a break from trying to pull the burro. She picked it up and pulled again. "Like a library book," she continued. "Elaine's a librarian. She understands borrowing."

"Borrowers have permission, number one, and you have never seen Elaine when she is angry," Asher said. He picked up a thin stick and tapped James Madison on the bottom. The donkey took a few steps forward.

"She can't be worse than my mom," Cam said as they approached the Vagina Train. There wasn't a place near here to return the U-Haul, so they had paid the rent on it and were going to return it when they got back to Florida. Returning the U-Haul on time was the kind of detail that just fell away when you were worried about dying.

James Madison only fell out once.

It was when they took the big curve in front of the lobster pound a little too quickly. They heard his hooves sliding around and then something like an elephant tap-dancing on a garbage can. Then it got quiet, and the drag on Cumulus got suddenly lighter. And when Cam checked the rear view, James Madison was standing motionless in the middle of the road.

"Don't panic," she told Asher, and she herself popped one of those Ativans that the doctor had given her after her panic attack. They were tiny and dissolved into chalky silt beneath your tongue. She was allowed to take them whenever she felt jittery because what difference did it make at this point if she developed a tranquilizer addiction?

They backed the U-Haul up a bit so that it was directly in front of the donkey. Cam decided to ride him into the trailer. She mounted James Madison and bent down close to his ear, whispering to him to calmly get back into the U-Haul. The donkey straightened, as if listening, and walked forward into the belly of the truck. Cam knocked on the wall of the trailer to signal Asher to take off. She stayed with the donkey inside the tiny dark space until they got back to the house.

"I think you can take it from here, A. W.," Asher said.

The only downside to the whole operation was that Asher now got to call her the "Ass Whisperer," which she deserved, she guessed, after enlisting him in an afternoon of donkey-napping.

They had successfully transferred James Madison from the U-Haul, through the carriage house, and into the secret tunnels of the Underground Railroad. The donkey stood in one of the bunkers, tied to a cot as he feasted on some hay and a carrot. Cam attempted to attach a tinfoil-covered waffle cone to his forelock with some bobby pins. But the magical horn kept flopping to one side.

"Rats," she said. "I don't think I can get this on right." She was feeling drowsy from the Ativan and getting frustrated. Her moods were swinging all over the place. She was so gung-ho a minute ago, and now she just wanted to give up on this crazy idea.

"Maybe some duct tape," Asher offered. "I think I have some upstairs."

Cam followed Asher back up the ramp and through the sliding bookcase into the carriage house. He was neat for a guy, but not pathologically neat. He had hung his barn jacket on the back of the kitchen chair instead of hanging it right away in the closet, like Mr. Rogers. But he hadn't just thrown it on the couch.

The décor was very masculine, with leather furniture and Oriental rugs. A billiards table sat in the far corner. He slept in a vaulted loft space above the kitchen. As he fumbled through some kitchen drawers for the duct tape, Cam looked around. Sepia-toned photos of Asher's industrious ancestors hung on the wall behind the desk. The bearded men wore hats and suspenders and the proper ladies wore corsets and buns. Another photo was of a beautiful woman with long, curly hair to her waist. She was not corseted like the others. Her dress was a loose calico, and she sat, profile to the camera, looking down at her hands, a little like Whistler's mother. Someone had written *Olivia, 1896* in the bottom right-hand corner.

There was a tinge of shame in the way she wouldn't look into the camera, yet she was dignified, too, in the straight way she held her spine. Cam knew at once that this was the woman who had spent many years in the widow's walk.

Then she saw the photo of Asher with his mom. It was so brightly colored compared to the muted tones of the older photos that it was hard to miss. He wore an orange hooded sweatshirt, and his little brown-eyed face, already with the dimple, was looking through the rungs of a blue ladder as his mom held him from behind to help him get to the top of the slide. She was a very beautiful version of Elaine, with golden hair and Asher's glinting brown eyes. They looked happy. Glowing. Never guessing that the day would come when they would be forever apart.

"Where is your grandfather?" Cam asked.

"Dead," he said.

"But I thought you said—"

"I need to assume he is dead."

"Why couldn't Miracle Town save him?"

"Because he left, and he never came back. It happened to my mom and dad, too. They died on their way to Hawaii."

"I know."

Cam felt his burden all over again, the same leaden suit she had worn when she danced his life at Elaine's house. He was the keeper of the house, the keeper of the memories, and, aside from Elaine, the sole survivor. No wonder he didn't want to take some scholarship. Leaving this town for him would be another kind of death. Not the kind Cam was facing, but a death nonetheless.

"You have some serious abandonment issues, Slasher," she said.

"You think?"

"I do. Years of therapy." Cam winked.

"And what about you? What brings you to Miracle Town?"

"I'm dying," Cam said.

Asher stood leaning on the counter with his right hand. He kept his head down for a minute, and Cam stared at the veins bulging from his forearm. He sighed and shook his head. Living here, he had obviously heard this story before. Cam wasn't the first pilgrim to come here seeking a miracle.

"That's bad news for me and my abandonment issues, Ass Whisperer."

"You've got to stop calling me that."

"I will. I just need to work it out of my system."

"Speaking of the ass," Cam said, changing the subject, "did you find the duct tape yet? I want to perform this miracle right at dusk, so she can see him but not too clearly." She could hear James Madison rustling around downstairs, probably getting restless and claustrophobic.

"Here you go."

"Aren't you going to help me?" Cam asked.

"I have to shower. I have, um, someplace to be, and I don't want to smell like ass."

Cam lost her breath for a second and waited for it to come back. The way he said it, Cam knew he was going to meet a girl.

It was difficult not to rush people through their dinners. Cam tried to slow herself down by chewing each mouthful twenty times. But mac 'n' cheese doesn't take much chewing, so she tried other things, like putting her fork down and taking a sip of water after every bite. When it looked like her mom and sister were done, she cleared the table and made a stack of dishes next to the sink. She checked the window while she was there to make sure James Madison hadn't strayed.

He was still there, about thirty yards away, tied to a tree.

Cam had covered him in flour to make him white. He was looking pretty good if Cam did say so herself. She had molded the tinfoil of the horn into a swirly shape, attached it with the duct tape, and painted it white and gold. From a distance, James Madison looked like a squat unicorn.

"Whoa, Perry. You better get busy. That's a lot of dishes," she said.

"What is going on, Martha Stewart?" her mom asked. "Why are you suddenly so invested in home economics?"

"No reason. It's a feng shui thing. I'm worried about the flow. Nothing worse than dirty dishes to clog up the flow of your space. Come on. I'll dry."

"Mom, those drugs are changing her," Perry said. "I think someone should be monitoring her, like, levels."

It wasn't the drugs, though. Cam felt a cleanness inside her—a pureness of purpose. Something she hadn't felt since before the cancer attacked and the doctors counterattacked with their battery of chemicals. For so long she had been afraid to let anything matter. It was too dangerous. But this could matter. It would matter if Perry was happy.

Twenty minutes later, Perry had gotten through all the dishes and had begun on the pots without even noticing the obvious *unicorn* standing in the *woods* directly in front of her *face*!

"Look," Cam finally had to say. "What is that?" God, did she have to do everything herself?

"I don't know," said Perry, leaning her face closer to the window. Just then, James Madison made a little horsey move with his head and neck and pawed at the ground with one hoof. Cam would definitely reward him with extra sugar cubes for that display. *Good boy*, she thought.

"Is that a horn?" said Perry. "Mom!?"

"Oh, my God," Cam said. "Go get your camera! Where is it?"

Cam had made sure to hide Perry's camera and phone between the cushions of the couch in the living room. While Perry searched for the camera, she ran outside toward the trees. She would have just enough time to take James Madison back into the tunnel, cross under the house, and bring him out onto the beach. Perry would never think to look for him there right away, so Cam could lead the donkey out onto the jetty. It made for a magical image, and he would be far enough away to still look like a unicorn.

James Madison was getting used to being led around. She practically got him to trot through the tunnel this time. The donkey seemed to appreciate having something to do besides stand around in the corral. "See how fun this can be if you work with me, ass," Cam said.

She left him balancing on the rocks at the end of the jetty, leaving him with two small apples and a sugar cube.

Before running back inside, she took a moment to appreciate James Madison. He was quite the Method actor. He

stood with his nose in the air and his golden horn sparkling in the sun. He gazed out to sea, as if searching for his
lost ancestors. He looked both proud and mournful, the last
of his kind on a magical quest. The water splashed gently
around his hooves, and the colors of the sunset provided
the perfect background. The scene looked straight out of
the cheesy posters in Perry's bedroom. It was only missing
a rainbow.

"I think I see him on the beach!" Cam yelled when she
got back to the house.

Perry ran out to the lawn, camera in hand. By then the
sun had sunk low enough in the sky that any photo she
took would capture a shadowy silhouette. She clicked a few
times. "I can't believe this! I told you it was true. This place
is incredible."

Cam stared at the tide, watching it rise and begin to splash
over the donkey's ankles. Her sister was smiling as she happily clicked away. Cam found herself smiling, too.

"Whoa!" Perry cried.

Cam turned to see the water splashing around James
Madison's knees. He shifted his feet a couple of times and
rose up majestically onto his back legs. Then he circled his
front hooves in the air, neighed, and leapt with a giant splash
into the dark waters of the bay.

# TWENTY-ONE

CAM DARTED TOWARD THE BEACH JUST AS ASHER STEPPED OUT OF HIS house, wearing an untucked white button-down, rolled-up khakis, and thick leather sandals. He smelled like fresh limes.

"Asher, help!" she cried as she climbed down the steep, twisting path to the beach.

"Help. Don't help. You give me mixed messages." Asher sighed as he stuck his keys into his pocket and followed Cam to the edge of the lawn.

"Look!" Cam insisted, pointing out toward the bay. James Madison was floundering in the water, slowly making his way toward shore. The horn, thanks to the miracle of duct tape, had not fallen off. It stuck straight up and bobbed up and down like a buoy as James Madison struggled to keep his head above water.

"Oh, my God. Can donkeys swim?" Asher asked.

"How do I know?"

"You're the Ass Whisperer."

"Stop. That is getting so old already," Cam said, out of breath. Asher fell in behind her as they scrambled down the cliff. She almost lost her footing and slid a little bit on some gravelly sand before taking a final leap to the flat rocky ground of the beach.

She ran into the water until she was waist-deep and dove headfirst into the middle of an oncoming wave. The cold was paralyzing. She let the heavy wave slosh over her, and then the undertow pulled her out to sea, dangerously close to the rocks of the jetty.

She swam a few strokes before she reached James Madison and took him by the lead.

"Stay way out in front of his hooves or he'll kick you!" Asher yelled as he waded in up to his knees.

Cam gently tugged forward on the lead as she guided the donkey toward land, the cold water causing her legs to ache. He got his footing, and she walked him to the beach, where he shook himself out like a wet dog. His horn hung limply from his forehead and dangled in front of his left eye.

"Wow, that was kind of sexy," said Asher. "Like Bray Watch."

"You . . . are . . . hilarious," Cam said, panting.

"Uh-oh," Asher said.

Cam followed his gaze up to the edge of the lawn. Perry and Alicia were climbing down to the beach.

"I won't say I told you so," Asher said. "I'll give you guys a minute. Open sesame." The face of the cliff slid open, and he disappeared into the earth. "Good luck," she heard him say before the rock slid closed again.

"Thanks, that's so generous of you." Cam wrapped her arms around her body and tried to stop shivering.

"Campbell, what is going on?" asked Alicia as she got to the beach. She covered Cam with a towel, rubbing up and down on the sides of her arms to warm her up, like she did when Cam was little and had just gotten out of the bath.

"Um, nothing." James Madison threw his nose in the air and hee-hawed. The horn flopped limply from side to side. The flour was glomming together from the salt water, exposing his dark fur in patches. "I wasn't sure that unicorns could swim, so I wanted to just, you know, save him or something."

"That's a donkey," her mom said flatly.

Perry stood with her arms folded across her waist. She made circles in the sand with the toe of her sneaker.

"It is?! Really? How weird. You know what? Maybe it's magic. I know. The water. The water turned the *unicorn* . . . into a donkey!! Can you believe that? Perry? Isn't that amazing?"

Perry walked away toward the cliff and pulled her phone from her pocket. "Never mind," she said. "There's no unicorn. Just my sister being stupid."

"I just—"

"You just what, Campbell?" Alicia asked.

"Well," said Cam, "you guys got so excited by the prospect of miracles that I was just trying to make you happy. Help you believe . . . in them, I guess."

"But you don't believe in them yourself because that would be beneath you, right?" Alicia's gaze was cold and hard.

"No. Not beneath me, exactly . . ."

"Well, that was very nice of you. Thanks." Her mom had that dismissive tone, that "I give up" look in her eye. The one that could still make Cam feel desperately abandoned and alone, even though she was practically an adult.

"Maybe we should get you to that shrink." The doctors had given Alicia the number of a shrink after the panic attack incident. She shook her head. "You just don't seem to be giving anything a chance."

"Me, see a shrink?" Cam said. "You guys are the ones who, just a second ago, believed in unicorns and magic tomato plants."

"You did the tomatoes, too?" said Alicia.

"I thought you'd already caught on to that," Cam said sheepishly. She pulled the towel tighter around herself. The sun sank toward the horizon. It was getting colder, and the tide kept coming in. The foamy edges of the waves slid their way beneath her soaking sneakers.

"Cam . . ."

"What?"

"I was hoping . . . Never mind."

"What?" asked Cam.

"I was hoping that, if nothing else, this trip could teach you to surrender control. To trust how the universe unfolds."

"People keep talking about this unfolding. I can't *trust the unfolding*, okay? If there is some higher power making origami out of the universe, it hates my guts. I was a fat kid whose parents got divorced, whose father died, and then who got cancer herself. So no. I don't trust how things are going to unfold."

"That's too bad," said Alicia. She threw a final look at James Madison, who was pawing the rocky beach, still soaked through from his swim. "You better get that donkey home before he freezes to death."

"I was just trying to help," said Cam.

"Some kind of help . . ." Alicia began. It was a line from Cam's favorite kids' song on the album *Free to Be You and Me*. "Some kind of help is the kind of help that you can do without," it went.

Alicia wrapped her arm around Perry's shoulder. They hiked slowly together back up the steep path to the lawn, leaving Cam alone, shivering, on the beach.

In spite of being covered with three blankets, an Oriental rug, earmuffs, and a scarf, James Madison was still shaking when Cam got him to Elaine's. Cam debated leaving him in his corral and taking off. But her conscience got the better of her, and she walked inside.

"Um, Elaine?" she said. The wood-paneled mudroom was cluttered with boots and lumberjack flannels hanging on hooks.

"Hey, Campbell." Elaine was reading in her big chair in the living room. She put down her romance novel and removed her glasses, letting them hang from their cord and drop onto her bosom. That word always cracked Cam up, but it was the perfect way to describe Elaine's matronly chest.

"That's the last thing I'd expect to see you reading."

"Yeah, well, we all have our vices," Elaine said.

"Speaking of vices . . . " Cam began.

"Yes."

"I sort of borrowed something from you today."

"That's okay, as long as you return it. What was it?"

"James Madison," Cam admitted.

"The donkey?"

"Yeah. And he's, um, had a rough day."

"What do you mean?"

"Well, he ended up going for a little swim, and he seems pretty cold."

"Why did you take my donkey for a . . . Never mind. Where is he?"

Cam retrieved the donkey and brought him into the exam room.

"We need to get him warm," Elaine said, rushing to change his blankets. "There are some space heaters in the garage, Campbell. Run and get me some of those."

"Should we blow-dry him?"

"That might work, too. There's a blow-dryer under the sink in the bathroom."

They set up the space heaters, and Cam held the blow-dryer over the donkey's mane, sweeping it back and forth along his neck, while Elaine took his temperature and checked his eyes. She was trying to determine whether James Madison was suffering from hypothermia, which donkeys are more susceptible to than horses.

"I'm disappointed in you, Campbell."

"I'm sorry," Cam said loudly, so that Elaine could hear her over the blow-dryer.

"You know, veterinarians take the same oath as doctors."

"*Primum non nocere*. First do no harm." Cam knew all about it. When treating cancer, it's the first thing they throw out the window. They go after the tumor with bold disregard for the rest of your cells that are humming along innocently, minding their own business, trying to keep you alive. Often it's the treatment that kills you before the disease would. If nothing else came out of this trip, Cam was at least glad she wasn't spending her summer being poisoned by well-meaning oncologists.

"It's a simple rule," said Elaine as she parted James Madison's lips so she could look at his gums.

"I didn't know I'd be harming him. Things just got out of hand," Cam said. She turned off the blow-dryer and covered the donkey's back with a dry wool blanket.

"Well, it showed some pretty poor judgment. I should fire you."

James Madison nudged Elaine with his nose and rubbed his face against her side, leaning in for a hug.

"It's okay, boy. You're going to be okay. What is this sticky paste all over his fur?" Elaine asked.

"Flour," Cam blurted. There was no sense beating around the bush.

"Flour," Elaine stated, as if nothing could surprise her anymore.

"Yeah."

"You dredged my donkey in *flour*? You know what? I don't even want to know."

"I was going to use spray paint," Cam said, "but I thought this would be more organic."

Elaine sighed and then leaned back on one foot. She held the blow-dryer toward the sky. "I think I've got it from here."

Cam slunk back to her car, wondering if she'd been fired. She was not accustomed to such colossal failure. *I'm Harvard material, after all*, she thought, trying to cheer herself up. But she still felt humiliated.

She knew she shouldn't because she'd be gone soon

enough, but she imagined herself disappearing. First her feet, then her legs, her torso, shoulders, arms, neck, and head. She imagined everything was gone, except for her clothes, which magically backed out of the parking lot by themselves.

# TWENTY-TWO

CAM BROUGHT THE U-HAUL TO AVALON BY THE SEA AND UNHITCHED IT from Cumulus. Then she climbed back in her car and breathed in the sweet heaviness of the plumeria oil that reminded her of home. She didn't dare go back into the house. She was welcome nowhere. Talk about backfire. She had tried to make people happy for once, and instead everyone hated her.

She took out her phone and dialed her father's phone number. He was the one she called when she felt lonely.

"Aloha," she heard her father's showbiz voice boom. "I'm not here, but feel free to leave . . ."

Cam had secretly continued to pay the bill on her father's cell phone, so she could call it occasionally and hear his voice. She only called it when she knew she needed to cry. And she cried now, wishing he had never died and wondering if this was happening to her, if the cancer was happening to her, because her father couldn't bear to see her living on Earth without him. He could be very possessive.

When her tears had stopped and she could see again through the windshield, she drove north toward the town elementary school. She hadn't heard much about the flamingos since the Fourth of July, and she wondered if they were still there. She wanted to check on Buddy, the baby, to see if he'd gotten any pink feathers yet or if his legs had begun to grow.

Buddy was there, perched on the muddy stump his mom had made for him so he wouldn't wallow in the acidic mud that would burn his skin.

Cam watched from the old broken-down wooden fence. "Hi, Buddy," she said. She thought he actually acknowledged her with a little flap of his oven-stuffer wings.

She watched the flock for a while. A lot of them slept on one leg with their heads tucked all the way into their tail feathers, their legs invisible in the dark. Dormant pink clouds that seemed to hang suspended in midair. Maybe that's what Cam needed. Sleep. She would go home, and everything would be fine in the morning.

When she rounded the corner to the side parking lot, a Jeep sat there idling, the bass of the stereo vibrating the steel sides of the car. Inside, a thirty-year-old woman with a highlighted bob and bloodred fingernails stared at a man as she ran the fingers of her left hand through his hair. Familiar, golden-from-the-sun hair. Her skinny, Pilates-toned arm was draped between the seats, and her right hand was somewhere in his lap.

*Oh, Asher*, thought Cam. Why did she always have to be right? Why were people so predictable?

Asher turned his head and looked at Cam through the window. Their eyes met for a second before he closed his eyelids in slow motion, pretending she didn't exist. It was as if Cam were already dead.

Back in her car, Cam held her iPhone, willing her fingers to dial Lily. She needed someone to acknowledge her existence. The call went straight to voice mail. She texted and waited ten minutes for a response. Finally, she decided to call the house phone. That was really admitting defeat, if Cam was willing to go through Lily's parents to get to her.

Kathy answered on the sixth ring.

"Hello," she said hazily.

"Hi, um, I'm sorry to call so late."

"Cayum?"

"Yeah. It's me. I was wondering if I could speak to Lily." Cam closed her eyes and leaned her forehead into her hand. She was trying to permanently erase the image of Asher and that woman from her memory. She brought a photo of it into her mind and then imagined making it disappear using broad swipes of some Photoshop eraser tool.

"Oh, God." Kathy's voice caught for a moment, and then she heard her suck in a deep breath.

"Hello?" Cam asked. When she opened her eyes, she could see the dark bay to her left. The yellow beam of the lighthouse made intermittent sweeps out over the ocean as if searching for fugitives. To her right, most of the flamingos still slept, pink powder puffs suspended in midair, like long-legged marionettes waiting for someone to pull the strings.

"Campbell, baby."

"Yes."

"Hon, we meant to call you."

"Why?"

"Lily passed, baby. Three days ago."

Cam was silent. A ghostly moth fluttered in the accusing beam of her headlights. A flamingo talked in his sleep.

"Campbell? Hon?" said Kathy. Cam had forgotten she was on the phone. "I'm sorry I didn't call you. It's just that it's so hard. It's like you relive it every time you have to tell another person."

Cam said nothing.

"Where are you, honey? Are you at home? Is your mother with you?"

"I think it's a transitive verb, *pass*," Cam finally said. "It requires an object. You can pass a test. Pass a football. Pass gas. You yourself cannot just pass."

"Campbell, can I talk to your mom?"

"She's not here, I don't think." Cam dropped the phone onto the passenger seat. She was drifting. Shutting off. She felt her body float away, and she became ether. She was nothing. Just an idea.

She was through. With all of it.

# TWENTY-THREE

CAM HAD ENOUGH RIPTIDE RUSH GATORADE LEFT IN THE CAR TO SWAL-low the seventeen tiny pills in two big gulps. Just for insurance, and because she needed to take her car with her into oblivion, she was going to drive off a cliff.

The only cliff she remembered was the one they zip-lined from to get to the lighthouse. It would be perfect. Cinematic. Like *Thelma and Louise*. There was even a full moon. She just had to start driving before the drugs set in and she lost all control.

Already her arms felt heavy as she lifted her seemingly enormous hands onto the steering wheel. The ends of her fingers were tingling, and her teeth were numb. She somehow managed to coordinate her movements enough to back out of the parking lot and swerve down the coastal road toward Archibald Light.

She fought to stay awake by focusing on the lighthouse's

rotating beam, straightening up a bit every time it swung back into her face. The ambient light from the full moon illuminated the roads, and she rolled down the window, allowing a cool breeze in through the windows. If only the two headlights—was she imagining those?—following close behind would turn off their high beams. She tried to shake them by making a quick left turn without signaling, but the bright, blinding lights trailed her still. "Sssilly headlights," she slurred, feeling tired. So tired. She sped up.

The road dead-ended in the playground parking lot. She drove onto the grass, crushing the stupid purple dandelions beneath her tires as she passed the swings and traversed the lawn to the top of the hill, where she stopped, several yards from the cliff's edge.

She could hear the waves crashing on the rocks below her. She closed her eyes and put both hands on the wheel. "I love you, Cumulus," she said. "Now don't get any Herbie Lovebug ideas and try to save me." Then she lowered her foot on the gas pedal. "Good boy," she said as Cumulus lurched forward, picking up speed like a jet about to take off.

Cam heard the whoosh of the wind and then nothing at all for ten seconds and then an earsplitting pop, which must have been the sound of all of her bones breaking at once. She heard a hiss, which might have been the life seeping out of her, or perhaps it was the sound of the waves.

Even from behind her closed eyelids, she could still sense

the beam from the lighthouse swinging intermittently over her face. She waited for it to stop and reveal the famous tunnel and bright light of the beyond.

Then she heard someone calling her name.

Cam awoke in a pool of her own purple Gatorade vomit. "Who's the genius who induced vomiting?"

"That would be me. I saw the empty pill bottle." Asher's voice echoed toward her as if from very far away.

"Asher to the rescue," Cam said groggily. "Did you at least turn my head to the side?"

"Of course. That's First Aid 101."

"Where's the bimbo?" she asked, suddenly remembering how she'd last seen him.

"She's home," he said. He lifted her tiny, limp wrist to take her pulse. His fingers gently grazed and then pressed on the vein.

Cam pulled her hand away.

"I just need to feel your pulse."

"No. I can take it myself," Cam said, trying in vain to lift her right arm off the ground.

"Relax, I can do it." His fingers brushed the inside of her wrist, and she felt a tingling through her arm.

Cam rested her head on the cool, wet grass, defeated, and stared up into the dark night sky. She closed her eyes, and when she opened them again she saw it. A brilliant rainbow stretched slowly across the black night sky. She blinked, but it was still there when she opened her eyes. The colors glowed radiantly for an entire minute before fading to muted pastels.

"Do you see that?" she asked Asher.

"What?"

She was glad he didn't see it and immediately lump the rainbow in with the orcas and the purple dandelions and the magic sunsets. This was her experience. And it was personal. A message from Lily.

"Never mind. What happened?" Aside from feeling heavy and sluggish, she felt fine. No crushed bones. The life had not seeped out of her limbs.

"You drove into a bouncy house."

"A bouncy house?"

"Yep. From the Fourth of July."

"Saved by a bouncy house."

"And your seat belt. You must have some hope left, or else you wouldn't have buckled up."

"Hope is its own reward."

"What?"

"Nothing. It's just something someone told me once."

"The ambulance should be here any minute."

"Do we really need one of those?" Cam could hear the waves again, sloshing against the shore. Crickets were chirping. The night rainbow had disappeared. Everything was coming back into focus.

"You should probably have your stomach pumped."

"I don't want my pomach stumped. I mean, pomach stumped. I mean. You know what I mean," Cam said, waving her hand weakly in the air. "Uh-oh," she said, and she sat up and retched, hurling one more time onto the grass. "I guess I've ruined Riptide Rush for everyone."

"Yeah. And it was the best flavor, too."

"Sorry about that."

Cam was finally able to sit up enough so that she could survey the damage. The bouncy castle had been orange, red, and yellow. One tiny striped turret of it was still inflated, and it waved back and forth in the breeze. The rest of it was flattened, as if someone had dropped an enormous water balloon from an airplane. Cumulus sat in the middle of the entire mess, his pale Vapor paint glinting in the moonlight.

"Thank God no one was bouncing."

"You can say that again, Ass Whisperer."

"Thank God no one was bouncing," Cam said, and she started to drift off to sleep.

The hospital in Promise was the size and shape of an elementary school. A small square building with gold linoleum tile, sea foam green–painted cinderblock walls, and old-fashioned nurses who still wore white dresses, white shoes, and winged white paper caps. Cam thought she had woken up in 1965.

Her mom and Perry sat in puce-colored vinyl chairs in her private room. They had brought Pilly, the little airplane pillow wrapped in a satin pillowcase that her nana had made for Cam when she was a baby. Cam rubbed the cold corner of it between her fingers, and she was instantly calm.

"I'm fine now that I have Pilly. Can we get out of here?" Her swallowing muscles were sore from the tube jammed down her throat last night.

"I think we should talk about that, actually." A small, dark-haired man sat in a chair to the right of the bed holding a yellow legal pad. He had a full-on GI Joe beard that desperately needed a trim, and he fiddled nervously with his pen. Cam hadn't even noticed him.

"Oh, come on," said Cam. "Didn't anyone warn this bozo?"

Alicia and Perry just shrugged and went back to texting (Perry) and knitting (Alicia). "You need to talk to him, or they won't let you out of here," her mom said without looking up.

"Is that true?" Cam asked the shrink. "And please don't answer my question with a question."

The shrink was about to speak and then closed his mouth, dumbfounded.

"Amazing. Do you want to know what happened to my last shrink, or do you just want to sign those papers and make it easy?"

She and Lily shared the same shrink when they were at St. Jude's. He was a nerdy, nervous guy named Roger, who, as they found out by Googling him, had been the 1986 national Rubik's cube champion. They would torture the poor man by using their sessions to explain the intimate details of their pretend sex dreams. They were discovered finally when Lily got carried away and incorporated a Rubik's cube into one of her dreams, which was too much of a coincidence, even for Roger.

"Are you threatening me?" New Shrink asked.

"How does that make you feel?" asked Cam dispassionately as she glanced up at the TV, pointed the remote at it, and changed the channel. *Wheel of Fortune* came on, and it was a before-and-after puzzle. "Rubik's cubic zirconia," said Cam. And she was right.

"You're acting out," he said.

"Do you believe coincidence is truly coincidence, or do you think we should pay special attention to it?"

"What do you believe?"

"How did I know you were going to say that? Mom? Can you please rescue me from this as—I mean, nice man?" You had to remember who had the power in these situations.

"I'm enjoying watching you suffer, Campbell."

"Why?"

"Why? You need to ask, why? Campbell Maria Cooper . . ." Her mom's voice cracked, and she shook her head.

"What?" Cam asked. "Please don't cry." It was impossible for Cam not to cry when her mom did, because of that oldest-child, emotional-umbilical-cord thing.

"Campbell. I have never, ever, ever in my life, *for one moment* given up on you."

"That's true," said Cam.

"No matter what."

"I know."

"It's like you are my heart, beating outside of my body."

"What does that make me, your liver?" Perry mumbled.

"No, you're my heart, too. My other heart."

"Whatever," said Perry.

Alicia set down her knitting and stood up. "Cam, last night you gave up. On me. On all of us. On everything. And you broke my heart. I couldn't believe you could do that to us."

"I wasn't doing it *to* anybody, Mom. I was just doing it. I just had to do something. I'm sorry." After a moment of heavy silence, she said, "I wore my seat belt."

"Oh, wonderful. Thank you, Campbell. Doctor Zimquist, I think we've got it from here. She wore her seat belt. So it's fine." Her mom laughed through her tears and gave Cam a hug.

"Lily—" Cam blurted as she leaned her head into her mother's hug and burst into tears.

"I know, honey. I know," said her mom.

Perry came to the bed and joined in the group hug.

After a moment Alicia looked up. "Dr. Zimquist," she said, "I think this is what you call in the business a breakthrough. We get to them pretty quickly because we have no time for years of therapy. Can you draw up the papers, please?"

# TWENTY-FOUR

IT HAD BEEN TWO DAYS SINCE SHE'D HAD HER STOMACH PUMPED, AND the whole experience had set her back a little. Cam had gotten used to a certain rounding and browning since she'd arrived in Promise. She had begun filling out. The angles of her joints had become less distinct, and her skin had returned to its natural pigment. But since the episode, she'd become cold, pale, and frail.

Sitting on her bed in the widow's walk, covered with seven blankets, Cam watched *The Sound of Music* on her laptop. People who knew her (*Lily and . . . Lily*, that list went) were surprised that this was one of her favorites.

Of course there were movies she liked better: *Chinatown*, *Ghost World*, *Best in Show*, *Midnight Cowboy*, *Citizen Kane*, *Eternal Sunshine of the Spotless Mind* . . . There were even some movie musicals she preferred, *American in Paris*, for example. Or even *Dirty Dancing* (Patrick Swayze, may he rest in peace).

*The Sound of Music*, though, was her grounding film. The one she came back to whenever she needed to shut out the world, slow things down, and start over. It had to do with how the sadness percolated beneath the hopeful melodies. It seemed real to Cam that no matter what, there was still sadness.

Even the happy moment at the end, as they're crossing the Alps to freedom—when Christopher Plummer hoists Gretl onto his back. Even that moment is suffused with the sadness of them leaving their homeland forever.

Cam had watched it 257 times.

She pulled her seventh blanket tighter under her chin and pulled her sleeves down to cover her hands. *Maybe hope and sadness can coexist*, she thought. That felt like a significant idea. Maybe Cam could hope without denying that huge part of herself that needed to be sad. She didn't have to sacrifice one for the other. Maybe all people were both hopeful *and* sad in every moment of their lives.

Julie Andrews started up the "Lonely Goatherd" puppet show and won the captain over with her flushed and sweaty innocence. He was just about to take the guitar from Liesl and sing "Edelweiss." It was Lily's favorite part—aside from Baroness Schraeder's restrained, tearful good-bye on the balcony, of course. She and Lily both loved Baroness Schraeder. It was the name of Lily's imaginary punk band.

The thought of Lily being gone forever destroyed Cam. It

was as if Cam's soul, if you believed in things like souls, had been vacuumed out of her body.

She hadn't even gotten to say good-bye.

Cam thought again of the night rainbow. She tried to stop herself from thinking that the rainbow was a sign—a final message from Lily, letting her know that everything would be all right. Part of her knew it must have been a hallucination from the drugs. But it seemed so real. And it was exactly how Lily had described it a year ago when she talked about what she would see when she died. That flash of color, that blinding lightness, against a midnight sky.

Captain von Trapp refused to hang the swastika in the front hall. "How silly of me; I meant to *accuse* you," he said to the creepy Nazi sympathizer. Another of Lily's favorite lines.

It was strange, but Lily felt so close. Closer than she had when she was still on the planet. Cam could practically feel her snuggled up next to her in this bed. And it made her feel safe . . . dare she say, hopeful? And less afraid.

Julie Andrews was teaching Kurt the Austrian folk dance when the Captain cut in.

Maybe if you thought about them, people never really disappeared. It sounded so corny, but there was a scientific explanation for it, too. If you believed that thoughts were energy and energy is matter ($E=mc^2$) and matter never disappears, then a person can never truly leave you unless you stop thinking about them. Everything you shared with a person is still there swirling around in the universe. Love, Cam had to admit, might be real. And love endures. Relationships endure. Because thoughts are energy, energy is matter, and matter never disappears.

Cam needed some fresh air.

She stepped out onto her balcony and looked through her telescope. It was almost 11 A.M., so she panned right until she could focus on the gray dock behind the lobster pound where the burly, amber-haired cook, Smitty, was about to take his daily swim. Every day he emerged from the back door of the restaurant in his navy blue swim trunks and held his big furry belly in his hands as he walked to the end of the dock. He dove in, swam to a buoy out in the bay, and swam back. When he hauled himself back out of the water, the belly was essentially gone. He didn't have washboard abs or anything, but he was changed somehow by the water.

She searched for the cemetery. She panned over to the hillside graveyard and scanned the dark gray gravestones that stuck out of the earth like petrified tongues. *Zenobia Drake McClellan 1895–1995*; *Allastair Dubois 1907–2007*; *Amanda Hawthorne 1887–1987*. Almost every one of the beloved sisters, brothers, mothers, and fathers in the Promise cemetery, with the notable exception of *Lisa and Thomas*

*Whittier 1955–1994*, had lived exactly one hundred years.

Maybe this place was a little bizarre. She wouldn't go so far as to say "enchanted," no. But it was definitely bizarre.

"Mail call!" Perry screamed. She had been given strict instructions to leave Cam alone, so instead of clambering up the stairs as usual, she threw a big package up through the hole of the spiral staircase. It landed with a thud on the top stair.

Cam stared at the plain manila bubble envelope. She didn't recognize the handwriting on the outside. *See*, she thought, *bizarre*. No one was supposed to know where to find her. No one had this address. She tore into the envelope.

A familiar white frame fell out onto the bed. It was the picture of Cam and Lily at St. Jude's. They had been sitting on Lily's bed playing Risk, conquering the world from their hospital room. Alicia asked to take their picture and they bent over the board to hug each other. Clear bags of menacing-looking fluids hung from the IV poles behind them, and their arms were bruised with "tracks" from being poked so many times. Still they smiled. Without their hair, they looked almost like sisters.

Lily had BeDazzled the entire frame with sparkly, silver hearts. She knew how much Cam hated sparkle of any kind, which is exactly why she had done it. Cam smiled. It was the kind of thing you do for someone you love.

Cam ran her finger over the lumpy hearts, stuck to the

frame with a glue gun. She exhaled, and it felt like she'd been holding her breath for a very long time.

The next thing she opened was a comic book. Not just any comic book. *Chemosabe and Cueball Take Manhattan*, completely finished by a real comic book illustrator and produced with a glossy Marvel cover.

Cam shook the bubble envelope once more and a final slip of paper fell onto the bed. She immediately recognized the Hello Kitty skull-and-crossbones envelope. Lily's personal stationery. Just seeing Lily's handwriting, which was shakier than usual, on the outside of the envelope was almost too much to bear.

Cam could not open it. She would save that for another time. For now, she lay back on the bed, sinking deep into the comforter, surrounded by her miracle mail.

Cam brought her big yellow Homer bucket to the beach. It was an industrial-size tub that used to be filled with spackle, the kind of bucket some city kids used as drums. She flipped it over and sat on it, pressing the rim deep into the sand. She crossed her legs and stuck her hands in the pockets of her hoodie, pulling it tight around her to shield her from the stiff ocean breeze.

She was getting used to the sand and salt. She liked what it did for her hair, which seemed so thick and glossy now that she'd stopped buzzing it. It had grown quickly, incredibly quickly, reaching just past her chin. Her skin was clean and dry. Not clogged up with the gunk that stuck inside your pores when you lived in the murky humidity of a swamp. Living here meant living in a constant state of exfoliation.

Cam pulled the Flamingo List out of her hoodie pocket. After Lily's death, it seemed appropriate to take inventory of what she'd accomplished in her young, possibly very short, life.

She unfolded it and read her relaxed-at-summer-camp handwriting. The paper flapped lightly in the breeze.

* *Lose my virginity at a keg party.* Check.
* *Have my heart broken by an asshole.* Check.
* *Wallow in misery, mope, pout, and sleep through Saturday.* Check.
* *Have an awkward moment with my best friend's boyfriend.* Check.
* *Get fired from a summer job.* Double check.
* *Go cow-tipping.* Close enough to donkey-napping.
* *Kill my little sister's dreams.* Check.
* *Dabble in some innocent stalking behavior.* Check.
* *Experiment with petty shoplifting.* Check.

Cam almost laughed out loud. Without even trying, just as Lily's book had said, she had accomplished every pathetic thing on the list.

She didn't know whether to be amused or ashamed. If she had known her list was going to work, maybe she would have aimed a little higher. What would have happened if she had written *Eliminate world hunger* or *Reverse climate change?* She had achieved her goal of becoming a normal, miserable teenager, key word being *miserable*. She was glad Lily had never seen her list.

"Hey."

Cam jumped. "Oh, my God, someone should put a bell on your collar."

"I'm sorry. What are you doing?" Asher was wearing rolled-up khakis and a navy blue plaid shirt over a white T-shirt.

"Just sitting here."

"What's that?" he asked, pointing to the list.

"This is nothing. Just my life's work." Cam stuffed the list back into her pocket. She could feel her face begin to burn with embarrassment. She hadn't yet had the chance to thank him for saving her life.

"About the other night—" he began.

"Yes. Thank you for that. Thank you so much," Cam said, for once without sarcasm. A huge sailboat drifted across the bay in front of them. She stared at its white topsail stretched tight against the wind. She couldn't quite look at him yet.

"Don't mention it," he said. "All in a day's work."

"For who, a superhero? You're not officially one of those, are you? I mean, the daring rescues, the bat cave. I should have put it all together." Cam looked down and started boring a channel into the sand with the heel of her foot.

"You scared me, Cam," Asher said. A lobster boat had chugged across the bay, churning up a wake that reached the shore now. The taller waves fell and splashed loudly against the beach for a minute, and then it quieted down again.

"You didn't actually have to, like, do . . ." Cam started. She really didn't want to finish her sentence.

"Mouth-to-mouth?"

"Yeah."

"No."

"Oh, thank God. That would have been gross."

Asher smiled. He took a deep breath and asked, "You didn't do it because . . ."

"Because of what?"

"Because of what you saw in the parking lot?"

Cam guffawed. She wasn't sure if she'd ever actually guffawed before, but she did now. "No. I don't care what you do in your spare time, Batman. Don't flatter yourself."

"Because that is just a weird situation. . . ."

"Really. I don't want to know. Nothing you could ever do would make me drive off a cliff."

"I'm not cliffworthy?" he teased as he picked up a smooth rock, but there was a seriousness in his eyes. He got it to skip five times across the surface of the water. Not up to his usual seven.

"My best friend died of the same disease I have," Cam said soberly, watching the stone disappear below the water's surface.

There was a pause as they both listened to the crashing waves. "I'm sorry, Cam," he said, and she finally let herself look him in the eye.

"Still not cliffworthy," she said.

"Nothing is," Asher agreed.

"I'm so sorry you had to witness that," she said, standing up and pulling her bucket seat out of the sand.

"Water under the bridge."

"Speaking of water," Cam said. "I need to bring some to Homer."

She let him carry the bucket this time. He hiked up with the seawater, trying not to let too much of it slosh on to the grass. When they got to the tank, Homer tapped on the glass and clawed desperately upward, as if trying to escape.

"We should release him."

"Yeah. We should," Asher said distractedly. "He's lonely here."

They brought Homer to the beach in his big yellow pail and walked him out to the end of the jetty. The sun was hot, but the breeze was gentle and cool. The waves slamming into the jetty gave off a salty mist that began to soak through their shirts. Cam's sneakers slipped on the wet rocks, but Asher reached out a hand to steady her.

When they made it to the end—the famous spot where James Madison had taken his unicornly plunge—they took Homer out of his pail and held him up in the air, letting him take in the view.

"We should tag him with your Freedom bracelet," said Cam, her eyes landing on the plastic band at Asher's wrist, "so that fishermen will always set him free."

"Good idea." Asher double looped the plastic bracelet around Homer's joint. He held the lobster up so Cam could give him a little kiss before they threw him far out into the bay.

"Freedom!" they both screamed, and it reminded them of the movie *Braveheart* and Mel Gibson before he got so drunk and crazy. They watched Homer spiral through the air like a lobster Frisbee until he smacked onto the surface. Cam thought she saw him float there for a moment before he was swallowed up by the waves.

She couldn't help noticing that, even though she'd caught her balance a while ago, Asher kept hold of her hand.

# TWENTY-FIVE

## THERE HAD BEEN A SHIFT.

Instead of going about his daily handyman routine or searching out Perry for a game of chess, Asher's first order of business this morning was to yell up Cam's stairs, asking her if she wanted to go for a ride.

"Where?" she asked.

"Just around," he answered. "I don't think you ever got the Promise grand tour."

He couldn't see her, so Cam did a little silent happy dance before calling downstairs, "I don't know. I have a lot to do today." She didn't want to seem too eager.

"Okay. I'll see you later then." She heard some footsteps walking away.

"Wait!" Cam said, and she practically threw herself down the stairs. When she got halfway down, she could see that he hadn't moved. He stood motionless, looking up at her with his arms crossed in front of his chest and his half smile curling up the left side of his face.

"I called your bluff," he said.

"I see that," she answered. "I'll be down in five minutes."

"Right on."

Asher had seven locales he wanted to show Cam, including the magical Indian burial ground, the East Coast's only living redwood tree, and Promise's very own Stonehenge, where three enormous boulders balanced impossibly, precariously on top of one another. They combed through the comic books in the town's old bookstore. At the junk shop/antique dealer, he bought her an old lobster trap, painted flamingo pink.

"So the woman in the car," Cam finally had the courage to say when they were on their way to lunch.

"I thought you didn't care about what I did in my free time," Asher said. He was behind the wheel of the Jeep, driving a twisting beach road through a saltwater bog that smelled like wild sage and oregano.

"That was yesterday. This is today."

"It was nothing."

"Oh," said Cam. "It kind of seemed like something."

"It's over, Cam," he said, swallowing hard and setting his eyes in a serious gaze.

"Good to know," she said.

The road dead-ended at another rocky peninsula. A tiny clam shack and some picnic tables balanced on a piece of slate jutting out over the ocean. Cam ate fish 'n' chips, and Asher ate raw clams. They sat opposite each other, both pretending that their feet were not touching underneath the table.

"You've never had clams before, have you, Ass Whisperer?"

"I've never been hungry enough to think that that was a good idea."

"They're good," he said, squeezing a lemon on one before tilting his head back and sucking down the glistening, peach-colored mass.

"I'll take your word for it," Cam said.

"Come on," coaxed Asher. "Just one."

"Oh, God," Cam said. "Fine. Just one."

"I'll pick out a small one for you," he said, selecting the perfect one and then squeezing lemon juice onto it. "Here you go."

She held the edge of the shell. It was genius, really. Food that came with its own plate. She closed her eyes, tilted her head back, and chewed what there was to chew. It was good. Cold. Wet. Briny. And a little sweet.

On the way home, he kept his right hand on top of hers. She felt it then—that chilling zing all the way up her arm, the one she'd felt when he tried to take her pulse the other night. The exact feeling that Lily had described, when you know that somebody loves you.

At home Cam wanted to put her lobster trap in the basement, so Asher followed her there. She found a perfect shelf for it next to Homer's old lobster tank. When she turned around, Asher stood about an inch away from her.

"You're in my personal space," she joked.

"It's intentional." He put his hands on either side of her waist. The air around them got heavier somehow as he bent his head down toward hers. He kissed her forehead first, and then tilted her chin up so he could look into her eyes.

"I'm going to kiss you now," he said.

"Do you always announce it like that?"

"You just seemed like the type that might get spooked."

"I'm cool," Cam said lifting her finger and tracing it softly over his lips. "In fact, if you don't do it right now, I'm going to kiss you first."

He paused for a second with his lips just a centimeter from hers, teasing her as he breathed in her breath. Finally he let his lips graze hers lightly, then more insistently, before drawing her into a deeper kiss. Cam realized, as she was in the throes of it, that there was an art to it. A back-and-forth. A dance. She'd been practicing this all her life.

Asher backed her up, and she fell onto the ugly plaid

basement couch. He fell on top of her, and she held his chest away from her at arm's distance.

"I don't know if I should get into a relationship right now," Cam said. "I was just released from the psych ward."

"Who said anything about a relationship?" Asher smirked, before bending down and kissing her on the neck.

"Oh it's going to be like that, is it? Well you can't make me any crazier than I already am. Like I said. Psych ward. Et cetera."

"I like my women a little crazy," he said. He lay down beside her, propped up on his elbow. Their legs were intertwined. "Just don't do anything like that again."

"I promise," Cam said, brushing some hair out of his eyes.

They walked to town, rented *Braveheart* because Cam had been chanting "freedom" all day long, and snuck up into her cupola to watch it together, snuggled in her bed. When the movie was over and the sun had finally set, Cam looked out the window and started counting out loud.

"What are you doing?" Asher asked as he connected the dots of the freckles on her thigh.

"Counting my lucky stars," said Cam. "This day almost never happened."

And in spite of all the work her mother had done in the past to provide them for her, this was the world's best day.

# TWENTY-SIX

"NANA, WHAT ARE YOU DOING HERE? HOW DID YOU FIND THIS PLACE?"

Her grandmother stood at the front door of Avalon by the Sea with a rolly bag and a round yellow leather suitcase. She was wearing her straw sun visor, big green plastic sunglasses with the sides on them, and her red nylon running suit.

"It wasn't easy," Nana said, still shifting around. Her tracksuit made swishing noises every time she moved. "Let an old woman in to use the bathroom, would you?"

"Sure," said Cam, moving aside.

"Nice place," Nana said as she followed Cam to the bathroom. She talked through the door the entire time she was in there. "I heard about the shenanigans," she said. "Campbell, you know I don't tolerate shenanigans, and I know your mother is useless when it comes to shenanigans. So I'm here to set things straight. Plus, I missed you," she said as she opened the door and gave Cam a big hug.

"I'm so glad you're here!"

"Mom," said Alicia as she entered the kitchen. "Aren't you hot in that thing? You should wear some natural fibers. Something that breathes."

"This breathes. They said it has 'wicking properties.' It wicks. My daughter. Two seconds in the house and she's criticizing me."

"Sorry, Mom. You look great!"

"Well."

"Well."

"Campbell. Stop trying to kill yourself. What are you thinking, trying to make your life even shorter? Are you insane?"

"It was just temporary insanity, Nana. I'm fine now."

"She has a boyfriend," whined Perry accusingly as she came in and gave her grandmother a big hug.

"Ah. Alicia, see? Didn't I tell you that's what she needed to begin with? Maybe a little schtupping and it would make the cancer go away. It works with pimples."

"Nana!"

"What? What's his name?"

"I'm Asher," said Asher. He came in from the dining room, where he was fixing the door on the built-in cabinetry. He put his screwdriver in his tool belt and shook Nana's hand. "Pleased to meet you, Mrs. . . ."

"Oh, God, call me Nana." Nana blushed.

"Get used to that, Nana. He has a way of appearing out of thin air."

"Oh my. Asher. Hm. Hm. Hm. Turn around. He's beautiful, Campbell. Are you schtupping my granddaughter?" she asked him.

"No, ma'am."

"Well, I give you my permission."

And just like that, Cam's love life was ruined forever. If and when she ever "schtupped" Asher, she'd have to do everything she could not to think of her grandmother.

"I brought in your mail," Nana said, and she handed Cam two more envelopes of mystery mail. How was this stuff finding its way to her?

"Nana, you go get settled, and I'm going to take a look at this," said Cam, and she went upstairs to her room and tore open the envelope from Harvard.

For all the hype that Harvard gets, it was amazing how low-tech they seemed to be. According to some flimsy pink piece of paper, printed by a dot matrix printer, it was time for her to select her freshman seminar, which was strange. She shouldn't be able to select anything, because she had never officially registered. *Huh*, Cam thought.

She knew she shouldn't, but Cam let herself look at the list of possible classes. If she could take any of these—and she knew that she couldn't—what would it be? She could breeze through Biology and Science of Cancer and Its Treatments.

The Life and Work of George Balanchine appealed to the dancer in her. Why Do Animals Sing? culminated in a student performance of animal sounds at the natural history museum. Were they serious?

She would take The Science of Sailing because she knew nothing about it, and wasn't the point to learn something new? Plus, if she'd be hanging out with rich kids, it was probably good to know something about sailing. Or she'd take The Poems of Walt Whitman because they used the words *prosody* and *bildungsroman* in the course description.

The other envelope was from Make-A-Wish. She swallowed and ran her finger under the flap.

*Congratulations, Campbell!* The letter read. *Make-A-Wish is sending you and up to ten friends to Disney World!*

Cam laughed, and her eyes watered at the same time. *Good one, Lily,* she thought.

"Cam!" Asher yelled from downstairs. She scrambled to hide the mail underneath her bed.

"Just a minute."

"I have to go check the traps."

The traps? "What in God's name do you mean, Daniel Boone? Is it 1765? Are you a fur trader all of a sudden?" she called down the stairs.

"Lobster traps. Do you want to come?"

"Me? Kill lobsters?"

"Only the big ones," Asher called. "The small ones you

throw back. You can think of it as saving baby lobsters."

"Well, when you put it that way," Cam joked.

The boat, named the *Stevie* because Smitty had a thing for Stevie Nicks, was docked behind the lobster pound. It rocked and bounced and squeaked against its bumpers as the waves knocked it around. Inside it was a tangled mess of ropes—"lines," Cam learned to call them—mesh traps, buckets and hooks, and knives and pulleys. Everything looked sharp and dangerous. Like a floating lobster torture chamber.

"I don't know about this," said Cam.

"Come on. You just need to get outfitted. Here," said Asher. He pulled a long wool hat with earflaps over her head and gave her some big rubber boots and huge orange gloves that looked like lobster claws. "Adorable," he said.

"Ew. I don't want to be part of your fisherwoman fetish," said Cam.

"Too late," said Asher. "Get in."

Before they could leave, though, Royal pulled up and maneuvered a different boat to the dock. He was with another robust Maine teen named Grey.

"You're late," Grey said as he wound a line around a metal mooring. "We already took care of it, boss."

"You did?" Asher asked.

"Ayuh," said Royal.

Cam was impressed by how willingly these guys had left their boyhood at the dock and shouldered the responsibility of men. It was refreshing to meet people who actually worked. She would never meet this kind of person at Harvard, she thought. (Not that she was going there.) People who were still connected to the land, the sea, their community. People who felt responsible for something other than their grade point averages. She shed immediately her cutesy little refusal to eat lobsters and vowed to eat one as soon as they got back.

"Lucky us," Asher said. "I guess this is just a pleasure cruise, then."

"All dressed up and no place to go," Cam said, holding up her orange-gloved hands.

"We can catch at least one for you," Asher said.

"Can we eat it, too?"

"As you wish." He winked.

Asher anchored the *Stevie* in the center of a tiny secluded cove of the bay, shielded from the world by steep gray rocks that enveloped them like a fortress. They rocked violently next to a buoy. Asher pulled it from the water, threaded the line through a complex pulley system, and began hauling. He pulled and pulled at the rope.

"Here, you get it the rest of the way."

He handed the line to Cam, and she threw her whole weight into it like a little kid ringing church bells. The trap was heavy with the whole ocean on top of it. When it finally surfaced, Asher grabbed it, opened it up, and began picking out the seaweed. The sun glinted off of his sunglasses and the yellow highlights in his hair. The sight of him literally stopped Cam's breath for an instant. She would never admit that to anyone in a million years. Or the few weeks she had left.

Two lobsters faced each other in the trap, holding their big, awkward claws out as if delicately clasping teacups. "Here, you do the honors. Just grab them by their backs," Asher said.

The first one she pulled out was infested with thousands of tiny black globules stuck to its belly.

"Ew!" Cam almost dropped it.

"Wait, those are eggs," Asher said. "We have to throw her back."

The next lobster's shell was the exact width and circumference of Homer's. Cam pulled it out tail first and flipped it over to check for eggs. It unfurled its tail and snapped it a few times, like a happy Labrador retriever whacking his tail on the floor.

"Easy, boy," she said.

She turned him around to the side and noticed some seaweed wrapped around the joint of his pincer. She used the index finger of her gloved hand and wiped at the algae-covered thing on the lobster's arm. *F . . . R . . . E . . .*

"Um, Asher," she called. He was busy rebaiting the trap with a dead fish. "Asher! You're not going to believe this!"

"It's a lobster, Cam. I see hundreds of them every day."

"Asher . . ." Homer snapped at her again, and Cam dropped him. He landed with a thud on the bottom of the boat.

"Did you get pinched?" Asher asked. She was silent as he bent down to pick him up.

"Homer?" he said.

"Is it possible?" Cam asked.

"And he's already found a lady. Way to go, Homz."

"He can't seem to leave Promise."

"I know the feeling. Here. Give him a kiss and we'll throw him back." They lifted him to the sky once more, and they both yelled, "Freedom!" as Homer swirled through the air and then belly flopped back into the ocean.

Cam took a deep breath. The air had the cool clean-sheet feeling it had had on the day they first arrived in Promise. Asher put his arm around her waist and hooked his thumb into one of her belt loops as they stared out at the blue-gray cove that was Homer's new home. She felt the weight of Asher beside her and noticed a softening in her gut. An unfamiliar warmth inside her that she realized, slowly, was the feeling of contentment.

Cam shook her right hand, shocked that she'd touched Homer again. She remembered what Elaine had said about paying attention to coincidence. Was finding Homer a coincidence? Or was it a sign? Even if it was a sign, a sign of what? That she was on the right path? Path to where? Did it mean she was one step closer to life, or to death?

Cam looked out to sea and decided that it was a coincidence. But she was starting to pay attention.

# TWENTY-SEVEN

CAM SUNNED HERSELF ON THE BOW WHILE ASHER COOKED IN THE TINY galley. The boat had rocked her almost to sleep. Each time she began to feel a little too much sun, a gentle breeze would stream right over her and cool her off. She could have stayed there forever, listening to the music of the gulls and the clanging of the masts of the sailboats in the harbor.

"What do you want to do?" Cam asked Asher when she finally joined him in the galley. He was sitting behind her now, his smooth biceps wrapped around her, trying to help her crack her first ever lobster claw.

"What do you mean, do?" His forearm brushed against hers as he worked on the claw, and all of her hair stood on end.

He pulled the white meat from the claw and fed it to her with his fingers dripping in drawn butter. "I mean, you can do anything. Go anywhere. Be anyone. What are you going to do with all that possibility?" She was in love with how capable Asher was. He could fix things. And he could pilot the boat and catch the lobster, cook it, and feed it to her. He was one of those people who could survive anywhere.

"I don't know. Sometimes I feel like I'll never leave. I'll be doing this forever, and that might be okay." He kissed her neck.

"What about school?" If she could live a normal life, she would go to school forever. She loved school. The new notebooks, the pencils, the pens, the new shoes. The first day of school had always been her favorite holiday. She couldn't imagine giving that up.

"What about it?"

"Don't you want to go?"

"Sometimes it doesn't matter what you want."

"You should go." She turned around, straddled him, and pinned him down on the small cushion behind them.

"Who's going to make me?"

"I am," she said, giving him a buttery kiss.

"Wait, what are *you* going to do in September?'

"Nothing. Probably. But I got into Harvard."

"You brainiac. That's only three hours from here, you know."

"Like you would visit me."

"I might," he joked, and he sat up and flipped her over so that he was on top of her on all fours. His golden five o'clock shadow was beginning to sprout, and Cam noticed for the first time the sexy, über-masculine cleft in his chin.

"*Ou te alofa ia te oe*," she said.

"What does that mean?"

"I'll tell you some other time." She pulled him toward her by the collar of his T-shirt.

They were covered with the one grayish white sheet that happened to be on the boat, and it didn't seem very clean. Cam got up to get dressed.

"Come here," he said after she had tugged on her sweat-shirt. He hugged her and pulled her back down onto the couch-slash-bed-slash-dining-table of the boat's tiny cabin. The boat rocked back and forth, and the water lapped at the sides of it with little tongue-clicking sounds. Cam lay back with her head on his chest. Through the porthole she could see a seagull floating by, right at her eye level. Asher kissed the top of her ear and whispered, "Do you believe in love at first sight?"

"What do you think?"

"Probably not."

"I just recently began to acknowledge the concept of romantic love. I didn't really believe in it," she told him.

"And you do now?" he asked.

"Uh-huh."

"Because of the sex?"

She smiled up at him. "No."

"Because that was just sex," he told her seriously.

"It was?"

"Ha! Campbell. I'm just kidding. Can't you tell it was more than that?" he asked, tickling her ribs. "The moment you walked into that lobster pound and asked to adopt a lobster, I was head over heels."

"You were?" asked Cam. She lay on top of him, propped up on her elbows so she could see his face.

"I was." They kissed again, playfully at first, then more romantically, until Cam found herself undressed all over again.

"I love you," he told her when they were through. He hugged her and kissed the top of her head and said it into her hair again.

Cam had never really anticipated this moment. If she had had to guess what it would feel like, she'd have thought she would feel giddy, excited, joyful, flighty. But instead, she felt instantly grounded, as if she'd finally arrived home after a long journey. *Of course you do*, she wanted to say, because it all just so instantly made sense.

"*Ou te alofa ia te oe*," she whispered again.

Cam got dressed once more and combed her fingers through her shiny, thick black hair. She climbed out of the cabin and sat cross-legged on the bow of the boat. She watched the sun setting as usual behind the lighthouse as Asher battened down the hatches or whatever it was he had to do to prepare for their ride home.

When she sat down, her mind started racing, and she began to Harvard seminar–ize this experience. If she could study the experience in a rousing informal discussion with Harvard freshmen, what would she call it? Male Adolescence and the New England Landscape, Lobstering Economics, The Psychology of Coincidence, Chaos and Contentment . . . Asher came to the top of the boat and sat her on his lap. The Chemistry of Young Love . . .

A piece of white feathery fluff drifted down from the sky, followed by another.

Cam held out her hands to catch some in her palm. It was bitingly cold. "I think it's snowing," she said, but even she didn't quite believe it.

"It's July, Campbell."

"Look!"

He looked up and squinted at the sky. Fluffy flakes the size of sand dollars were falling softly and straight down because there was no wind. They formed a sheer curtain in front of the fiery sunset. Already a half an inch covered the surface of the boat.

Cam scooped some up and made a snowball to throw at Asher. He threw back until they ran out of snow. It was surreal. Cam looked to the shore of the cove, where the snow had collected in downy puffs at the ends of the pine branches. A heron took flight to escape the cold.

"The flamingos!" she cried, suddenly remembering.

"What about them?"

"They'll die if their pond freezes over. We need to get them out of here!"

Cam stood behind Asher with her arm around his waist as he sped the boat, pounding violently over the waves, back to Smitty's dock. The snowflakes, like big butterflies now, splashed her in the face as they went.

He quickly tied up and covered the boat and grabbed some big boots. "We'll need these," he said as they dashed to her car.

Just as Elaine had predicted, the flamingos simply stood there shivering in the snow. Most of them had tucked their heads into their feathers to shield their faces from the wind, like ostriches burying their heads in the sand. The water around their ankles was just beginning to solidify into a thin film of ice.

"Come on!" Asher said, and he started running toward them, flapping his arms and squawking, trying to get them to take flight. Cam was about to follow him, but she couldn't because she was too busy doubling over in laughter.

"Come on!" he yelled. "You're the one who said we should do this."

"I'm sorry. You just look so funny. Okay." Cam took a deep breath. "Here I come." She donned her boots and ran out into the mud, flapping her arms and yelling as well. A few of the birds removed their heads from their feathers, looking at her curiously. They paced nervously, but none of them took off in flight. Cam kept circling the perimeter. "Which way is south?" she yelled to Asher. "We should guide them toward the south."

"How should I know?" He was walking now, trying to shoo the birds with an underhand sweep of both arms.

"Use your nautical instincts," Cam said, and she ran again straight at another clump of them. Her boot stuck in the mud, and she fell flat on her face into the brown sticky muck. Now it was Asher's turn to laugh. She was completely brown, as if someone had dipped her front side in chocolate.

When Cam finally peeled herself out of the mud, she was directly eye level with Buddy, who was still sitting on his stump. *This is why they won't go*, she thought. Buddy's mother was standing directly over him, reaching her long neck down to anxiously peck at him. Trying to get him to fly, perhaps? But he didn't yet have wing feathers.

"I've got him," Cam said to the mother. "Don't worry. I'll take care of him." She tiptoed closer and tried not to startle the mother bird. She had learned from Animal Planet about the protective instincts of mother birds. She also knew that once she touched the baby, the mother would abandon him forever. What she didn't know was whether Elaine had the wherewithal to take care of a baby flamingo, but she would have to take the chance. It helped that she now smelled entirely like flamingo poop.

She snuck up behind Buddy, trying to walk gawkily like a flamingo with her head jutting forward. Then she scooped him up and cradled him in her right arm, defending herself from the mother's wild attack with her left. The mother flapped and kicked and pecked Cam in the head with her beak.

"Asher, help!" she yelled. But he was laughing again, and all he could do was say, "Run!"

Cam ran toward the fence with Buddy tucked under her arm like a football. The mother chased after her, on foot at first, and then she spread her wings. With two flaps, she took flight. A squawking chatter spread through the entire flock, and then they alighted in orderly rows, following the lead of Buddy's mother, an enormous pink cloud of feathers drifting upward through the snow.

It took ten minutes for the entire flock to float overhead. Cam let herself wonder for a second if they had indeed been a sign. What if they had come there for her? Maybe the big universe unfolder in the sky was folding her life into a neat origami swan instead of crumpling it up into a ball and tossing it unfinished into the wastepaper basket like she was a big cosmic mistake. Maybe she would live for just a little bit longer.

She closed her eyes and tried to envision it. The bricks of Harvard Yard, the color of Boston's beloved baked beans. Asher walking around Cambridge in his flip-flops. Studying with her on her narrow dorm room bed. Drinking pints with new friends in ancient low-ceilinged pubs.

She took a deep breath. "We did it," she said.

"We did," Asher agreed. He took her hand in his as the last of the birds faded out in the distance, a pink-and-black undulating quilt of flamingo stitched together by sparkling bits of sky.

# TWENTY-EIGHT

"I BROUGHT YOU A PEACE OFFERING," CAM SAID AS SHE WALKED INTO Elaine's mudroom.

"Cam?" asked Elaine.

"And Asher," Asher called.

Cam was afraid to face Elaine alone. She hadn't spoken to her since the donkey incident, and she wasn't sure if Elaine had cooled off yet. James Madison had thankfully recovered and was standing in his corral, dressed in a navy blue blanket to shield him from the snow.

"Oh, my goodness, Cam, let me get you some clothes. Stay there."

Elaine returned with a huge red PROMISE JAMBOREE 1993 sweatshirt that she said Cam could wear as a dress. "What is that smell? God, maybe you should take it outside."

And just like that, Cam was forced to take another one of those frigid outdoor showers, while Asher broke the news to

Elaine about Buddy. At least it had stopped snowing. It felt good to get clean, and Cam let Buddy join her. He took a birdbath, splashing and shaking his little self in the puddle at her feet. "Oh, Buddy," said Cam. "What are we going to do with you?"

Asher was waiting for her in the mudroom when she came back inside. She wore her sweatshirt dress tied around the middle with his belt.

"You look gorgeous."

"It's nice. It has an eighties *Flashdance* thing going on," she said, and she pulled it down over one shoulder.

"I know. I wasn't joking," he said.

Buddy had already taken to following Cam as if she were his bird mother. She turned to look at him walking down the hallway behind her. He looked really happy, flopping his big webbed feet down one after another like a strange upright duck.

"Elaine, meet Buddy. Buddy, Elaine," Cam said when she entered the kitchen. Elaine was sitting in the built-in pine breakfast nook, blowing on her cup of hot chocolate. She had set two other mugs on the table for Asher and Cam.

"What am I going to do with a Buddy?" Elaine asked.

"I thought you could keep him here until he can fly south," Cam said. "We had to shoo the flamingos. Not like you shoe horses, shoe, I mean like we had to shoo them like you shoo flies, shoo."

"I know what you meant, but unless one of you is willing to eat some shrimp and throw it up for him, I don't know how we're going to feed him."

Cam and Asher were silent.

"Well, I'm thinking we could call the zoo in Portland and find out what they feed their baby flamingos . . . or something," she suggested.

"What happened to flowers or a box of chocolates?" asked Elaine. "You steal my donkey and then to apologize you bring me a flamingo?"

"He's irresistible, though," Asher said, lifting Buddy onto his lap and pretending to squeeze his cheeks. "Look at that face."

"He is the ugliest thing I have ever seen."

"I know," said Asher, "but he's one of God's creatures."

"Oh, my God, fine," said Elaine. "I'll figure it out, Campbell, but you need to help me."

"Is it okay if I start next week?" Cam asked. "This week, I'm taking Asher on a trip."

"No, you're not," said Asher, stiffening in his chair.

"I didn't know Asher went on trips," Elaine said, intrigued.

"We're going to Disney World. You'll like it there," said Cam. "It's another 'Magic Kingdom.'" The idea had been seeded, and now it was growing like a plant in her mind. She wanted to prove to him that he could leave. He could leave, and the world would not fall apart. He needed to know that he didn't have to stay here picking up the pieces like Jimmy Stewart in *It's a Wonderful Life*. She was going to shoo him like she had the flamingos.

"That's nice, but how are you going to get him on a plane?" asked Elaine.

"I don't do planes, Cam Chowda," said Asher.

"We can work on that," said Cam. "What's with the Cam Chowda?"

"Just testing it out."

"I don't like it."

"How 'bout just Clam? Or Clampbell?"

"Absolutely not."

Alicia was not on board with the Disney idea either.

"Absolutely not," she said as she banged a kitchen cabinet shut. "Are you kidding me?"

"It's entirely free. From Make-A-Wish. We can't look a gift horse in the mouth. And you could visit Izanagi."

"Campbell. Look at you. You're living a normal life for once. Your energy is back. Your skin is clearing up. You're eating, working a summer job—dare I say, falling in love? Why would you want to jeopardize that? It's been so nice to see your smile."

"How am I jeopardizing anything? If Promise has done this, it will still work when we get back."

"If you leave, you'll have to start all over when you get back. You'll undo everything. What if you break the spell?" Alicia leaned with one arm on the kitchen counter. With the other hand, she pretended to smoke a plastic drinking straw.

Cam was starting to make her own rules about the magic, or whatever it was. She would go to Disney because the Make-A-Wish letter was a sign. It was showing her what to do next. She wasn't going to get addicted to Promise and let the town develop the crazy grip on her that it had on Asher.

She tried to see her mother's point of view. She knew the story. "My only job is to keep you alive, Campbell," Alicia had said. "That's my primary responsibility as your mother." So far, she had protected Cam from crib death, choking hazards, drowning in the bathtub, strangling in the cords from the blinds, being scalded by water from teakettles, getting hit by a car, drinking bleach, falling out the window, being kidnapped, and diving into shallow water. She thought she was in the clear. The only thing left on her danger radar was a drunk-driving accident on the way home from the prom. She didn't expect to be blindsided by this illness. And she was powerless against it. It was difficult for Alicia, Cam knew. But somehow she also knew that she was going to do this anyway. She wanted to honor Lily's final request and show Asher where she came from.

Upstairs she set up a little henna tattoo parlor, where she planned to paint Asher's entire arm with a Samoan tattoo.

"We're leaving tonight," she told him.

"There is the issue of the plane," he said.

She wanted to ask him, "What are the chances that you *and* your parents would die in separate unrelated airplane incidents? It's practically statistically impossible," but she knew not to reason with him. His fear was irrational, number one, and number two, logic, per se, did not always play itself out in Promise. "That's why we're here," she said, motioning to the tattoo setup. "I'm going to protect you."

She'd found the ink and the brush at the gift shop in town, and she showed him a few of the designs he could choose from. Most of them were complex, diagonal patterns of straight and swirling lines, and they all included large solid patches of black, which proved the mettle of the tattooee because those were the most painful to sit through.

"I'm not really proving my mettle, though, if you're using a paintbrush instead of a shark's tooth," Asher pointed out.

"It's just symbolic, metaphorical. It will give you strength."

"This isn't metaphor. It's replica."

"Brace yourself for more replica to come, Slasher. We're going to Disney World."

Cam played Samoan drumming music and she got busy

painting. "Try to be completely still and silent," she said. "It will help you to get into a trance for the plane."

She started with a curving pattern around his pectoral muscle and then worked her way around the shoulder and bicep. The contours of his body proved to be a very distracting canvas.

"Stay still," she said.

"It tickles, Campbell," he said, and he pulled her in for a kiss. "Hey, what's that?" he asked, pointing to a tiny, perfectly round little blue spot on her forearm.

"It's nothing," she told him. "I probably knocked into something on the boat. Be still," she said, and she painted and painted until the drumming on her iPod had stopped. She wasn't going to worry about a blueberry spot. They had disappeared before. They would probably disappear again.

# TWENTY-NINE

THERE REMAINED THE ISSUE OF PERRY. THEY WERE SNEAKING OUT tonight, but Cam didn't know whether she should take Perry with them. Everyone else on the trip would be older—Cam had invited Sunny, Royal, Autumn, and Grey—and could prove to be bad influences. But she would love to spend some time with Perry back at home. And Perry, originally so comfortable in Maine, was beginning to show some serious signs of homesickness. She had been moping around a little and spending more time in front of the TV. She even asked Nana to share a room with her.

In the end they decided to bring her. They couldn't tell Perry about it beforehand, though, because Cam knew she could not keep a secret. They would have to snatch her from her bedroom in the middle of the night.

Asher called it "Operation Tween Extraction."

The stakes were high. Alicia, a light sleeper, was already

on her guard. And when Alicia was on her guard, she was a vigilant scout. One of the major disappointments of Alicia's parenting life was the fact that Cam never broke curfew. She had been ready for it. The first night Cam took the car out alone, Alicia painted her face black, put branches in her hair, and sat inside a bush, ready to pounce on Cam when she came home a minute after midnight.

Cam never did come home late, though, and upon hearing the snapping of gum coming from the bush, just said, "Hi, Mom," and walked into the house.

"Watch out for trip wires," Cam told Asher as they tiptoed down the hall toward Perry's room.

"Is all of this really necessary?" he asked. She'd made him dress in black and wear a headlamp. He carried a coiled rope around his shoulder and held a roll of duct tape in his hand. He looked ridiculous.

"Affirmative." Cam giggled.

Their other challenge was keeping Perry quiet. Their target was a squealing, screaming, giggling beast. They might need to bind and gag her. Only temporarily, until they got her in the U-Haul.

Nana snored like a bulldog as they cracked open the door. They shuffled into the room in their socks. Cam pointed furiously to the suitcase on the floor and then to the dresser, indicating that Asher should pack up some clothes for Perry. He pointed to himself and shrugged his shoulders, as if to say, "Me?" Cam nodded her head, "Yes, you," and then she got busy.

She rolled Perry over on the trundle bed mattress near the floor, grabbed her hands, and sat her up.

"What?" Perry moaned as her head lolled to the side.

"We're going on a trip," Cam whispered.

Nana rolled over with a snorting growl.

"Where?" Perry asked. Her eyes were still closed.

"Orlando," Cam said. "Just for a couple days."

"Ya—" Perry started to let out a joyful scream, but Cam quickly covered her mouth. Perry mumbled beneath her palm as Cam motioned to Asher to come to the bed and pick her up. Asher hoisted Perry over his shoulder, Cam grabbed a suitcase, and they all crept toward the front door. Perry whisper-screamed in excitement as she pounded Asher on the back with her fists.

Outside they dumped Perry into the U-Haul with Sunny, Royal, Grey, and Autumn. None of them had a big enough car for everyone, so they'd decided to take the Vagina Train. "Thanks for bringing me, you guys!" Perry screamed out loud now.

"Here." Cam tossed in the suitcase.

"What's this?" Perry asked.

"Your clothes," Cam answered, getting impatient. She pulled down the rolling door to the trailer and locked it shut.

"Wait!" Perry whined. She pounded the side of the U-Haul.

"That's not the one I packed," Asher said.

"It's not?" asked Cam.

"Nope."

Cam lifted the back of the U-Haul door to find Perry holding up a pair of Nana's enormous, silky white underpants.

"Whoops," said Cam. "You'll have to make do." And she shut the door, ignoring Perry's continued pounding on the side of the trailer.

"I packed some cute stuff for her, too," Asher said regretfully.

Grey and Royal had to practically carry Asher onto the plane. He made it as far as gate C4 at the Portland airport when he started to turn the gray-green color of faded camouflage pants. Cam was starting to second-guess herself, but she knew if he could get through this, he could do anything. Like Operation Tween Extraction, it was do or die.

The other boys surrounded Asher, held him by the forearms, and helped him walk down the Jetway to the plane.

"Is he drunk?" the attendant asked as they boarded the early morning flight.

"Not yet," said Grey. He was the loose cannon of the group and someone to keep far away from Perry, Cam noted.

"Did you at least bring my notebook?" Perry asked. "I wanted to show Izanagi."

"He's at the top of your list of people you want to see?" Cam asked.

"Close to the top. Why?" Perry asked. She shambled down the gateway, wearing Nana's blue slippers and an enormous slippery pink jacket from one of her grandmother's track-suits.

"No reason. I just thought you'd have other priorities."

Cam could imagine twenty things she'd like to see before even making a call to Izanagi. And that reminded her to call Jackson. She'd love to check in with him to see how his bouncy, trouncy summer was going.

On the plane, Cam wished she had some of that Ativan to give Asher as he sat petrified in his first-class seat, but she'd been permanently banned from tranquilizers.

"Sit on top of him, Cam," said Sunny. "It's called a cow press. The weight and pressure calms autistic kids. It works."

Cam sat on top of Asher, trying to press all of her weight into him. She did feel him relax a bit underneath her body, but when the plane took off and they had to sit side by side, Cam couldn't tell what seemed louder: Asher's heartbeat or Alicia screaming "Cam!" thirty thousand feet below when she woke up and noticed they had gone.

# THIRTY

"COME ON, PERRY AND PERRY," CAM SAID. ASHER WAS SO GIDDY AFTER having survived the plane flight, Cam had begun calling him Perry 2. "Asher, if you skip, I might need to break up with you." He was too cool and stoic to ever really skip, but there was a jaunty little hop to his gait as he walked around the lake.

After huddling around the map, arguing for some twenty minutes about where to go and what to see, the group had finally dispersed. Sunny and Autumn had gone to the water park, Royal and Grey to the sports bar on the boardwalk, and Cam, Asher, and Perry to the World Showcase at Epcot.

"What? I'm happy. You were right, Cam. I needed to do this." On the plane they had discussed Asher's fear of leaving Promise. Some of it had to do with a lifetime of overhearing the townspeople gossip about how the "magic" of Promise was related to his family. He had developed the notion that if he left, the magic would leave with him.

"Promise will always be magic, Asher, especially to you," she had told him. "Because it is your home. The magic thing about home is that it feels good to leave, and it feels even better to come back."

Cam realized how true that was as she walked around Epcot. As much as she liked Maine, this place was her place. The sky was her sky. The flora, even if it was pristinely man-icured and carved into the shapes of circus animals, was her flora. She took a deep breath of the heavy, swampy August humidity and enjoyed how it seemed to ease the pain in her lungs. How had Lily known she would need this?

"Oh God," said Perry. "Did you just tell her she was right? Never tell her she's right. It goes straight to her head. She usually *is* right, but it's better for everyone if you keep her a little off balance. A little insecure."

"Is that how you manage me, Perry?"

"One of the ways," Perry answered.

"Here," Cam said to Asher as they approached their first "country," the pinkish-gold pyramid of the Mexican Pavilion. She handed Asher a pair of black mouse ears on either side of a plastic top hat. They were the groom's ears, reserved for people honeymooning at Disney. Cam had stolen them, and a pair of white bride's ears for herself, from the little office behind the entrance.

"What do I do with these?" he asked, reluctantly begin-ning to remove his Red Sox cap.

"Wear them," she said.

Cam secretly loathed the nerdy couples who honeymooned at Disney World. It was like they were too immature to realize that they were actually "grown-up married" and not just "pretend married," going on a pretend honeymoon to the pretend countries of Epcot. Cam always wondered what happened to them when they got home and had to face the marriage realities of joint bank accounts and layoffs and health insurance and taxes and the fact that she always left the kitchen cupboards open and he would never in his life think about cleaning a toilet.

But it was okay for Cam and Asher to wear the wedding ears because they really were *pretending*.

Plus it got them straight to the front of the line.

"If you guys are married," Perry said, "what does that make me?" She applied some lip gloss to accent her gorgeous outfit. Today she wore one of Nana's short-sleeved polyester shirts as a dress. It had three huge purple diagonal stripes going from the right shoulder to her left knee. She'd belted it with Nana's purple bathrobe tie, and it hung loosely off of one shoulder.

"My illegitimate daughter from my teenage pregnancy," Cam said. Really, Perry looked like some lost dancer from an eighties music video. All she needed were a headband and some leg warmers.

"Of course," said Perry, and they gave each other a little exploding fist bump.

"Cam?" someone behind them said.

Cam turned to see Alexa Stanton herself, the girl on whose lawn Cam had tried to dump Darren the plastic flamingo. Only she was dressed head-to-toe as Cinderella. *So she got the part*, Cam thought. She and Alexa were friends once. In kindergarten, they saw *The Wizard of Oz* together and then spent weeks playing flying monkeys on the playground, trying to process the trauma of it all. Things changed in second grade when someone—probably her mother—told Alexa not to mingle with the entertainers.

Look who was entertaining now. Alexa-rella wore a pale blue ball gown. A yellow-haired wig was plastered over her ears.

She took Cam by the elbow and swept her behind a rack of sombreros. "Cayum, are you may-rried to *him*?" she whispered out of the side of her mouth.

"Why is that so hard to believe?" Cam whispered back.

"No reason," Alexa whispered.

"Well, it was nice catching up with you, Cinderella. Tell the prince I said hello," Cam said.

Alexa composed herself, cleared her throat, and in her best Cinderella voice said, "Yes. I shall send your regards to the prince." She lifted up her skirts and floated away toward the China Pavilion.

While Asher rode the speedway with Grey, Cam and Perry did all the things they used to do together as kids while their parents were performing and they had run of the park. Space Mountain, the Country Bear Jamboree, Pirates of the Caribbean. They bought egg creams at the soda fountain on Main Street and made their way to the Haunted Mansion.

The two sisters sat on the stone wall in front of the spooky old house and waited. They'd asked the rest of the group to meet them here at nine, so they could show everyone how they climbed up the wrought iron latticework of the mansion and watched the fireworks from a secret perch on the roof.

"So maybe you should give me some sisterly advice before school starts up again," said Perry. Her face was flushed from spending the entire hot day trapped in the polyester "dress," which was now splotched with chocolate and ketchup.

"Um. Okay."

"You've never given me any before." Perry stirred her egg cream viciously in between her tiny staccato sips. She always made the drink last longer than Cam's, so she could taunt her with it.

"You never seemed like you needed it," Cam said. "That's the thing about being the youngest—you come out relaxed and cool and knowing exactly how to get what you want."

"That's true. But you can give me some advice, anyway. Just so you feel like you've fulfilled your role as an older sister." Perry held out her glass to measure it against Cam's and make sure she had more egg cream left.

"Well, let's see," Cam said. "How about, 'don't be like me'—that's good advice. Like in high school, you should join something. Not color guard like Autumn and Sunny. God. That doesn't teach you any applicable skills. But something. The tennis team might be cool." Cam thought for a minute. "Be yourself," she continued. "And be kind."

"Kind?"

"Yeah. Being kind is one of the hardest things to be in high school because you're so terrified of being cut down yourself that you're always on your guard. But don't be like that. Be kind and you will be truly different. A standout. Unique and happy."

"That's it? Be kind. All the dangers out there lurking in the mist, and you give me 'be kind'?"

"I think it's good," Cam said confidently with a final slurp of her egg cream. "It's better to be kind than to be right."

"All right," said Perry. "I'll try it."

"Good."

Cam looked up as, suddenly and right on time, the catalog kids ambled toward them giddily from every direction. Sunny and Autumn held bright pink mouse-shaped balloons that bobbed up and down as they skipped in from the east. Grey and Royal—in their preppy striped shirts, boat shoes, and leather choker necklaces—came at them from the west.

"Boo!" Asher startled them from behind.

Cam jumped. "I hate when you do that!" she lied.

"What? It's the Haunted Mansion."

Cam led them to the back of the gothic structure, where they climbed one by one up the sharp black metal vines. They found a flat part of the roof behind the main turret and hid themselves beneath the branches of a spooky weeping willow. Grey started up a game of Would You Rather while they waited for the fireworks to begin.

"Keep it PG, mister. This has to be the Disney version," Cam pleaded, pointing at Perry not so subtly behind her back.

"Okay," Grey said. "Would you rather make out with Jasmine or Cinderella?"

Cam shot him a look.

"What? I said 'make out,'" he said innocently, but Cam shook her head. "Okay, fine. Would you rather 'hold hands'"—he made air quotes—"with Jasmine or Cinderella?"

"Definitely Jasmine." Autumn giggled. She tilted her head forward, hiding her face behind her curtain of thick auburn hair.

"Yup," Royal agreed. "I would love to hold that woman's hand."

"Hey." Sunny slapped him weakly on the thigh.

The August air sat on top of them like an ancient sea that had only somewhat evaporated. It was hot and humid and heavy, and they barely had enough energy to swat away the mosquitoes that swirled around them in the dusk.

"Here ya go," Sunny said, spritzing Cam with her portable Mickey Mouse fan, complete with spray bottle. She put her arm around Cam and laid her head on her shoulder. Her hair smelled like vanilla. "Thanks for bringing us here," she said.

"You're welcome," Cam replied.

"I have one." Autumn was tracing the lines of Grey's palm, pretending to read his future. "Would you rather . . . know your destiny or spend a lifetime figuring it out?"

"That's an easy one," Royal answered. "I feel so bored already knowing. As if my life is already over. As if I'll never again be surprised." Royal was enrolled in premed at UMass and had promised his mother he'd become a doctor.

"I'm full of surprises, though," Sunny exclaimed, lifting her head from Cam's shoulder.

"That's true," Royal admitted. He gave her a hug and said, "Life with you is never boring."

"I don't know," Autumn said. "I wish I knew what I wanted. It would make things so much easier. Sometimes I don't even know if I want chocolate or vanilla."

"I like not knowing," Perry said. "It's exciting. Maybe I'll be a pilot."

With that, the first of the fireworks shot into the black night. It was a golden one. Metallic and bold as if they had just won a prize.

Asher pulled Cam closer. "You are my destiny," he whispered. And then they kissed, oblivious to their friends on the roof.

"Hey, who's the one who said to keep it PG?" Grey laughed.

"It's okay, I've seen them kiss before," Perry said, completely unfazed.

Cam felt like she *had* won a prize. Not only the person sitting next to her, but the friendship of the catalog kids. That was something she didn't even know she'd been craving. Teenagers run in packs. And for too long she'd been trying to go it alone.

When the last pyrotechnic popped and fizzled, leaving smoke snakes hanging tangled in the air, the group climbed back down the latticework. They made their way to the park's exit and Cinderella's castle. Make-A-Wish had arranged for them to stay in the Royal Suite.

The faux opulence was spectacular. Marble columns, vaulted ceilings, canopy beds draped in thick velvets and brocades, a parlor room, a magic fireplace with fiber-optic fireworks display, a sunken Jacuzzi tub with a waterfall faucet surrounded by stained glass windows.

As they approached the castle now, Autumn, Grey, Royal, and Sunny kidnapped Perry. They grabbed her and pulled her toward the monorail to sweep her off to her first under-twenty-one dance club in Downtown Disney.

"Wait," Cam tried to protest, reaching for Perry's hand. "You don't need to take her."

"We've got this," Sunny insisted as she shoved Cam through the heavy door of the private elevator that led to the Royal Suite.

At the top, a carpet of red rose petals covered the floor and formed a candlelit path to the bedroom. Asher waited in his new Mickey Mouse boxer shorts, holding two glasses of sparkling apple cider. Asher, the perfect, did not drink alcohol.

Cam laughed. It was so unbelievably corny. "This isn't really my thing, you know."

"I know, but I figured, when in Rome."

"Are we in Rome?"

"No, I think we're in medieval France."

"Cinderella was French?"

"*Oui*," he said, and he clinked glasses with her, downed his cider, and then threw her, full glass and all, onto the impossibly large bed covered in slippery golden silk sheets.

"I'm a little intimidated," she said as he kissed her ear, her neck, her chest. He lifted her shirt and ran his tongue in soft loops down the center of her stomach.

"Just go with it. You are a princess."

"What does that *mean*, though?" Cam asked. "How—"

"Oh, my God, Campbell. Be quiet!" He laughed.

Later she realized she could be a princess. Not really a

princess, but something other than a cancer patient. She could choose the cancer and the misery or the other, more wonderful parts of her personality. She was a dancer, a scholar, a sister, a veterinary assistant, a girlfriend. She could make the cancer into a much smaller part of her being. For the first time in a long, long time, the cancer was not everything.

# THIRTY-ONE

"DO WE HAVE TIME TO SEE THE WORLD TODAY?" ASHER ASKED AS HE stretched and yawned when they finally got up around noon. The girls had already left for their royal spa treatments, and the guys were on the golf course. They were all going to meet up at five for the "Spirit of Aloha" show at the Polynesian.

"The Small World, maybe," Cam answered, running her fingers down his fabulous front. After the show, they'd get on the next plane to Portland. Alicia had texted Cam about seventy-five times, begging her to come back, and Cam promised her they'd leave tonight. But they couldn't go without seeing the world first.

The wait time at It's a Small World was twenty-five minutes, which actually wasn't bad. As they wound through the snake of a queue, fanning themselves with their maps of the park, Asher peppered her with questions about "Spirit of

Aloha," the bizarre subculture of a subculture in which she was raised.

"It's so weird to me that instead of living your culture, you perform it," he said.

"Well, it's like Sly Stallone described preparing for *Rocky*," Cam explained. "Some people work from the outside in, and others work from the inside out. He had to get Rocky's body and dress like Rocky and talk like Rocky before he could feel who Rocky was. Another actor would feel who Rocky was and then start dressing like him. So some people feel Polynesian, and it moves them to dance. And others, like me, dance to feel more Polynesian. It doesn't matter how you do it—the end result is the same."

"Now I need to see *Rocky* again," Asher said.

"I know. Me too. You didn't hear anything I said, did you?"

"No. I was just thinking about *Rocky*."

They made the queue's last turn. Cam winked at a little boy in front of them who kept swinging on the railings in spite of repeated warnings against it. Finally it was time for them to board the boat. They pushed through the turnstile, stepped onto the moving dock, and slid into an open bench. They were off to travel the world. The sickeningly sweet world. It was as if the whole thing were made of candy. As soon as they entered the tunnel, they were assaulted by bright pink, orange, glistening gold, and drizzling glitter. It was a wonderland of papier-mâché. An über-diorama with life-size moving parts.

As a kid, Cam was enchanted by the idea of children in different countries wearing different clothes and eating different foods and speaking different languages. It really was magical to her. The ride's strange stereotypes of the shirtless African kids playing drums on the back of a giraffe, or the South American women carrying baskets of fruit on their heads, or the French women lifting their skirts to cancan, seemed like a celebration of the world's fabulous colors.

*Stereotypes work for kids*, Cam realized, *because they still have intact that basic understanding that no one could possibly be less human than anyone else.* And this ride brought you back to that notion.

They were in India, and a row of saried women tiptoed their way home from the glowing, white, bulbous Taj Mahal made of sheets. Asher was grinning, completely one with the spectacle. He didn't notice the exit signs above the hidden back doors of the warehouse or the repairman in the corner changing a lightbulb.

"Awakening your wanderlust, Batman?" Cam asked him, sliding her palm into his.

"A bit," he answered. And then, "I did get a scholarship, you know."

"I knew it," Cam said as they moved from the enormous shadow puppets of Indonesia to the geishas of Japan.

"Ayuh. BC."

"Are you going to take it?

"It feels like a life-or-death decision for me."

"It's not. You can always go home again. You should try it."

"It is a small world," Asher said.

"After all," Cam answered.

But as she said it, she had a vision of Asher's life at college. Watching his teammates open their care packages sent from their mamas and how that would reinforce his own loneliness. It was sad. "Elaine will send you care packages," she mumbled.

Then she envisioned the alternative. Asher staying forever in Promise, coaching the high school football team, flirting with the cheerleaders, letting himself drink beer. Just a little at first, and then a six-pack each night as he sat in a recliner, wondering what his life would have been. "You have to leave," she whispered to him. But her voice was drowned out by another rousing chorus of children's voices.

The pace of the drumming was picking up as the guests gathered on the gray faux volcanic stone lanai outside the amphitheater. The tiki torches were lit even though the sun had yet to go down, and little girls in sundresses and white pants were climbing on the fake big-headed Polynesian sculptures. The guests ducked their heads so the performers could drape leis around their necks, and the show had reserved the bright purple ones made of real flowers for Cam and her party. She was grateful that none of the catalog kids blurted out any getting lei'd jokes. It was a serious pet peeve of Cam's. Not because it was disrespectful. Just because it was way too easy.

Izanagi had met them at the hotel. He had his arm around Perry's shoulder as he escorted her from the hotel lobby. He smiled and twirled her around, presenting to everyone the new pink flowered dress he'd bought for her in the gift shop.

"Cam, how could you bring her here with no clothes?" Izanagi asked.

"It was an accident," Cam said. "How are you?"

"I'm fine," he said, kissing her on both cheeks. Then he held his head down as if remembering again his disappointment that Alicia hadn't come with them. He had forgotten to shave or to iron his usually crisply laundered slacks.

They all sat at the center table in the front row. The plaintive and lonely Izanagi perked up a tiny bit once the food came and he was able to fling pieces of pineapple into people's mouths with his knife.

After the first number—a Hawaiian dance in honor of the sun—the MC, Momma Suzi, announced that an old friend had come to visit the show. She asked Cam to come onstage and juggle her fire knife.

"I think we still have it, Campbell. Ah, here it is," she said as John, one of Cam's dad's old friends, carried the knife out to center stage. It was about the size and shape of a rifle.

Fire juggling was one of Cam's more tomboyish pursuits. There were not many girls who really wanted to do it, and she had mostly learned so she could spend time with her father. She wasn't sure what Asher would think. The crowd applauded, and they played her favorite song.

Finally she got up and lit each end of the knife. She began spinning it, vertically at first, with two hands. She threw the knife high into the air, spun around, and caught it behind her back. She swept the fire underneath her legs. She twirled the knife with one hand and then the other. She was in a trance, fully in the moment, when she heard the crowd start laughing, and she saw something big and orange in her peripheral vision.

Tigger was juggling a fire knife.

"Jackson," she yelled. "Isn't that suit flammable?"

Tigger nodded his big chin up and down.

"Then get out of here!"

Tigger nodded again and tossed his fire knife to John, who caught it and doused the flames. Tigger waved to the audience and stepped down off the stage.

Cam twirled one more time and then realized that what she was doing was very similar to Sunny's twirling gig. She looked over at Sunny, who was beaming attentively at the whole production, and got an idea. She doused her flame, breathing in the familiar fumes of the lighter fluid, and gestured offstage for them to throw her another knife. Then she invited Sunny to come up to the stage.

The Florida sun had freckled Sunny's face, and she couldn't hide her big-toothed grin as she climbed onto the stage in her maxidress. Cam gave her one of the knives and then said, "Just do what I do."

She shifted her weight back and forth from one foot to the other and then began tossing the knife between her hands. Sunny followed suit with her own knife, and then Cam began throwing hers higher into the air. Sunny did the same until they were both twirling madly. They ended with a big simultaneous toss-and-catch behind their backs.

The crowd went wild, shocked that a white girl could get all native like that without any preparation. *We are more alike than we are unalike,* Cam quoted to herself from Maya Angelou, *as much as Disney would try to have you believe otherwise.*

Cam and Sunny took a bow, to the standing ovation of Mainers in front of them. Asher beamed at them, and Royal let out a piercing whistle. "Encore, encore!" they cried, but Cam and Sunny were done. They sat back down to enjoy the stomping and slapping dance of the Samoan men and the Hawaiian volcano goddess hula that closed the show.

Jackson left his Tigger costume in the kitchen and joined them with his new girlfriend, a cute little blonde girl named Peg.

"See what I mean?" Cam nudged Jackson and gestured with her chin toward Peg. "It would have been a mistake to try and date me. You look really happy."

"I am," he said. "Asher looks nice, too."

"Ayuh," Cam said, and she laughed because she had said it completely without irony.

After their steaming chocolate lava desserts, the show was over, and Cam said her good-byes to the cast of "Aloha," Jackson, Joe the cook, and Momma Suzi the MC. Izanagi had been lurking around, waiting for his turn. He finally approached her with his head down, fiddling with the jade ring their mother had given him before she left. He didn't yet speak. It was as if he needed to concentrate to keep his composure.

"Bye, Iz, it was so nice to see you," said Cam.

"Yeah, um, yes," he stammered. When he finally looked up, his eyes were droopy and red rimmed as if he hadn't slept since they had left. *Wow*, thought Cam, *my mom really is a wicked heartbreakah.*

"Don't be sad." Perry wrapped her skinny arms around him and said, "We'll go to a Devil Rays game when we get back."

"Okay," Izanagi squealed, and then he let out an audible sob. He continued to sob on Perry's shoulder. Perry, still locked in this embrace, looked up at her sister, incredulous and slightly amused. She mouthed, "What do we do?"

*We can't leave him like this*, thought Cam. There was nothing sadder than a man left alone and adrift.

"Come with us, Iz."

"Really?" He looked up, blew his nose in his handkerchief, and smiled.

"Yeah." Cam smiled. "We have a magic ticket."

# THIRTY-TWO

CAM ASKED THE FLIGHT ATTENDANT FOR SOME WATER AND SOME herbal tea and an aspirin.

"You okay?" Asher asked.

It was nice of him to notice. They were still parked at the gate, and he was already sitting straight-backed and stiff, white-knuckling the armrests, beads of sweat dripping down the side of his face.

"I'm okay. You just take care of yourself." She had a little headache and a sore throat, but she was probably just dehydrated. "Close your eyes," she said to Asher, "and imagine yourself on the ground in Promise."

"That's nice."

"Yeah. Just fast-forward through this whole flight thing and imagine what you'll be doing when it's over."

She talked Asher through an entire summer day in Promise, from his western omelet breakfast at Dad's, his

favorite home-style diner, to hauling traps on the *Stevie*, to his workout, to dinner on the bay at sunset and then sitting down to watch *Rocky* in the living room of the carriage house. At one point, he fell asleep, but when he awoke, she kept telling the story, picking up where she'd left off. She was halfway through the plot of the movie, to the place where Rocky was breaking the ribs of the beef carcasses at the meat packers, when the pilot came on and told the flight attendants to prepare for landing.

"We're already landing?" asked Asher.

"Yup. You made it."

"You're awesome. Thank you."

"No. Thank you. For doing this. You'll see. Promise will still be there when we get back."

Cam looked behind her. Across the aisle, Izanagi sat next to Perry. They were playing some kind of dice game on their tray table, which was supposed to have been stowed away for landing.

Cam realized with sudden clarity that Izanagi wasn't just another of Alicia's flings. Cam hadn't really given him the time of day because she didn't need to. She had had a father and was at an age when she needed a replacement one less and less. She never thought for a fleeting microsecond to make a father figure out of Izanagi. But for Perry he was more than the annoying guy who left too many messages on the voicemail. To Perry, he was a person. A person who helped her with her homework and encouraged her to try out for the track team. To Perry he was exactly what she needed. And it gave Cam an idea.

It made Asher a little nervous when they couldn't find the entrance to Promise right away. They had to circle the Dunkin' Donuts block about three times before they finally found the opening in the bushes that led to the gravel winding path into town.

"See, Ash, still here," said Cam when she saw the lighthouse and the bluff and the quaint little town on the docks. "The sun's still setting behind the lighthouse, the orcas are still leaping from the bay, and the purple dandelions are still purple. Everything's just the way we left it."

"Except for that." Perry pointed to a colorful fifty-foot-high totem pole standing on the front lawn of Avalon by the Sea.

"Ye . . . ahh," said Cam. "But that might have happened anyway."

They drove up to the house in Cumulus, and Cam and Perry went in to tell their mom and Nana that they'd returned. It was Asher's job to clean up Izanagi and sneak him up through the tunnels and into the house.

"I don't know about this," Asher had said when they were still in the car. "I've seen your schemes go south before. Are you sure this will work? What if she says no?"

"She won't," Cam said. "I don't think she will, anyway." This was more than planting tomatoes. This made perfect sense. This filled all the gaps.

"You better hope not," Asher said, pointing to Iz, who was desperately sketching his proposal out on the back of another Dunkin' Donuts bag, "for his sake."

"Hi, Mom!" Cam said as she walked in the front door.

Alicia was washing dishes and ignored them like Cam knew she would as they plopped their bags down in the foyer.

"How's it going?" Perry asked.

Alicia just held up her talk-to-the-hand hand, and Nana sat at the table and shook her head back and forth. She couldn't help herself from tsk-tsking just a little bit and then letting out a big sigh.

"Mom, we have a surprise for you," Cam said.

Alicia turned around and leaned against the sink with her arms folded in front of her. She opened her mouth to speak and then changed her mind. She shook her head and contin-ued with the dishes.

"Come on, Mom," Perry said. She and Cam dragged her downstairs, Nana following close behind, to the rotating bookshelf that led to the secret passageway. Cam pushed on it, and the shelf spun around to reveal Izanagi. He was clean-shaven now, but still unpressed, holding a few purple dandelions as a bouquet. Asher stood behind him. He gave Cam a little wink as he joined her on the house side of the bookcase. Izanagi got down on one knee and said:

"Alicia, you are the love of my life. Will you marry me?"

Alicia stood silently, her head down with her hand in Izanagi's for what seemed like an eternity before she finally whispered *yes*. She whispered it at first and then repeated it more and more loudly until she shouted it out loud. She hugged Izanagi, and they kissed. "I missed you so much," she said to him.

"*That's* what he was writing so furiously on the Dunkin' Donuts bag?" Cam whispered to Asher.

"He was nervous, so we edited it down."

"Good choice," Cam whispered.

"Thanks."

Alicia spun around to face her daughters. "Wait, I should ask the girls' permission. What do you think, Campbell?"

"Mom, it was my idea," Cam said.

"It wasn't your idea?" Alicia asked Izanagi.

"No, it was his idea." Cam jumped in. "I just encouraged him."

Alicia held out a finger to Cam and said, "Don't think this excuses you for what you did. You had me a nervous wreck, Campbell, and you kidnapped Perry."

"And you stole my underwear," Nana added. "What did you want with my underwear?"

"It's a long story," Cam said. "Sorry."

"No matter," said Nana. "We have a wedding to plan. This deserves a toast!"

They broke out the champagne. Her grandmother dropped a sugar cube into each fuzzy glass. They even gave a tiny sip to Perry, who stood between Alicia and Izanagi, giggling. "I think I'm a little drunk," she said.

Cam looked at them from across the room and said distantly to Asher, "Look at what I made."

"What?"

"I made a little family," she said. She looked at the three of them laughing together, and she was overcome at once by sadness, because she felt so left out, and joy, because she knew they would thrive together, with or without her.

# THIRTY-THREE

THE ITALIAN-JAPANESE-POLYNESIAN WEDDING WAS TO TAKE PLACE ON the front lawn beneath a Jewish huppah tied on one side to the fifty-foot Algonquin totem pole. Nana and Izanagi had been tag-teaming in the kitchen all week, preparing the sushi, teriyaki, sausage and peppers, lasagna, and a cannoli canoe, while Cam had the usual job of carving out pineapple boats for the Polynesian rice. Perry was in charge of the music; Asher, lighting, seating, and structures; and presiding over the service was Elaine, who was, not surprisingly, a certified minister and wedding planner.

This wasn't the first party on the lawn of Avalon by the Sea. Almost everyone who got married in Promise got married here, so Asher simply had to roll the chairs and tables out from the secret passageways and set them up on the lawn.

Elaine was outside supervising the setup. She had brought

Buddy and Bart along for a quick romp before taking them back to the kennels. Their strange friendship was a children's book waiting to happen. They were both in their awkward stages and tripping over their too-big feet as they chased each other back and forth. Buddy would peck at Bart, stretching out his newly elongated and pinkening neck, and then run away, spreading his wings and taking big leaps that were beginning to approximate actual flight. Bart would swat at Buddy's beak, rearing up on his hind legs to try to reach him. Then Bart would run away, tripping on the slightly sloping grass and tumbling into a furry heap toward the drop-off.

"Okay, that's enough, you two," Elaine finally said. She rounded them up just as Smitty pulled up with his kissing flamingo ice sculpture.

His temper at the lobster pound made it difficult to see, but Smitty was actually a big teddy bear. He carried his heavy creation over to Asher, smiling and chuckling through his thick hay-colored beard. "Be careful of the necks," he said. They get a little fragile at the top."

"That's incredible, Smitty. Thank you," Cam heard Asher say. She watched the whole scene from the windows of her widow's walk. Her mom came up to join her and spread onto Cam's bed the cranberry chiffon halter dress she had finished hemming.

"Do you ever think about your wedding?" Alicia asked.

"Yes, this is exactly how I envision it," Cam deadpanned.

"With the adolescent flamingo . . . and the totem pole, and, oh, look, the sixty-year-old ladies in muumuus." Alicia had invited all the women from her Hula 101 class.

"Yeah. They're going to do a little number. It's sweet."

"Yep." Cam watched them practicing on the lawn, turning in small, cautious, old-lady steps as if afraid to break a hip.

"How do you envision yours?" Alicia took a hairbrush out of Cam's suitcase and combed through Cam's now shoulder-length black hair.

"Um, I don't."

"Not at all?"

"Nope." It was true. Cam had never once fantasized about her wedding. Before her diagnosis, she dreamt about other things. Making a movie, perhaps. Winning an Oscar. Writing a book. Visiting Egypt. But a wedding seemed insignificant in her scheme of things.

"Even now that you've met Asher?"

"Can't even begin to picture it," said Cam.

"I guess that's good." Alicia ran the brush down the crown of Cam's head. "I think some girls get so caught up in the wedding part that they forget about the marriage part, and they end up bonded for life to the wrong person. It's not the wedding part that matters." Cam watched out the window as Asher happily set up folding chairs and covered tables in gold damask linens. *He would be the right person*, she thought.

"Are you happy?" Cam asked.

"Yes, Campbell. Very. You were right. This is what I needed. Thank you. I'll make it work this time," she said as she finished brushing and turned Cam's head so she could look in her eyes. Cam was happy, too.

"All you can do is the best you can do. And your best is always better than everyone else's. You are an awesome mom," Cam said. She had the intense feeling of missing her mom, even though she was right next to her.

"Well, that's a dream come true," Alicia said and kissed her on the forehead.

"Now it's time for my dream come true. Every daughter dreams of walking her mother down the aisle."

"Awkward?" Alicia asked.

"Yeah. But I'll get through it. I have to face the facts." Cam sighed. "You're not my little girl anymore."

Putting Perry in charge of music was perhaps a miscalculation. Her mom, flanked by Cam in cranberry and Perry in yellow, walked down the aisle to Katy Perry. Alicia looked beautiful in a simple cream eyelet dress. She had violets woven into her hair, and she held a bouquet of tiny yellow and cranberry orchids. Izanagi wore a simple gauzy brown short-sleeved shirt with linen pants and sandals. He was suddenly more handsome than Cam remembered. He was tall and broad-shouldered with a strong chest and flawless nut-brown skin and smiling eyes that glimmered when he saw her mother. Asher stood next to him at the altar and gave Cam a little reassuring wink.

Alicia and Izanagi smiled at each other, and Cam let herself daydream about their future. Snapshots moved through her head. The two of them dropping Perry off at college. Traveling the real, actual world, not the world of Disney make-believe. She saw them hiking with goat herders in the Himalayas of Nepal. She saw them posing on the Great Wall of China. Clanking two enormous beer steins together in Germany. She saw them aging, slowly, happily together in the photo album in her mind.

Then she tried to inject herself into their lives. She concentrated and used her strongest of strong wills to try and force an image of her twenty-one-year-old self sitting on the couch with them at Christmas. She tried to picture Izanagi uncomfortable in a suit at her Harvard graduation. She tried to picture the way her mother would look at her first grandchild as she counted his fingers and toes. The ideas came into her head, but the pictures would not come. The pictures were blank.

She focused instead on the present moment. The present moment was all that mattered, she reminded herself, and what was happening in this moment was good.

Elaine, thankfully, kept it short, not torturing them with any kind of a sermon, but getting right down to the nitty-gritty:

*By the power vested in me by the state of Maine, I now pronounce you partners for life.* Then the party got going. Perry and her friends scampered around the edges of the lawn, giggling, spying, imitating, posturing, pretending they were adults, and trying to steal drinks from the bar. Asher kept giving them virgin piña coladas that they imagined were the real thing.

The catalog kids posed themselves here and there, like gorgeous colorful statues in the temple of preppiedom. Izanagi and Alicia danced almost the entire time, to whatever happened to spew itself from Perry's iPod. When it came time to throw the bouquet, Alicia served it, volleyball style, to Elaine. She snagged it enthusiastically and then danced the rest of the evening cheek-to-cheek with Smitty.

The sun went down behind the lighthouse. The mother orca, whose baby must have grown up and left her, leapt solo out of the bay. Everyone ate and laughed and danced and forgot. They forgot about deadlines and checking accounts and college and job applications and divorces and taxes and the minutiae of living. They all forgot, except Cam, who was in the second-floor bathroom watching with crossed eyes as the mercury in the thermometer inched past 104.

"Cam!" Asher knocked on the door. "Are you okay? You've been in there for a while."

"I'm fine," Cam sang. "Just powdering my nose." She rifled through the medicine cabinet looking for the Advil. She finally found some and swallowed four. The googly-eyed seashell frog from South of the Border was giving her an accusatory stare. "Shut up, I'm fine," she told it.

"Hey," Asher said when she opened the door. "Everyone's going to the lighthouse. Want to go?"

"No. Why don't you go, though? I should stay here with my mom."

"Um, I don't think she's going to miss you." Asher pointed out of the hallway window to the lawn, where Izanagi and Alicia were kissing against a tree.

"Gross," Cam said. There was nothing worse than old people kissing.

"Yeah . . ." said Asher. "So, you want to go?"

"No, no. You go," she said. "I'll stay here and clean up."

"I can help you. Or we can do it in the morning."

"Asher."

"What?"

"Just go, okay. I need some time alone."

"Okay, babe," he said. "That's weird, but okay."

"Okay," Cam said. "Now go."

When he was halfway down the staircase, he paused and looked back up at her.

"Go!" she said.

"Okay."

She waited until he was out of sight to double over from the stabbing pain in the center of her gut.

# THIRTY-FOUR

AFTER A FITFUL NIGHT'S SLEEP FILLED WITH TERRIFYING DREAMS OF earthquakes, volcanoes, and tsunamis, Cam awoke. She looked out the window to find her mother and grandmother sifting like refugees through the scattered detritus of the wedding: ribbons, dead flowers, little piles of rice, the melted puddle of the ice sculpture, plates of half-eaten cake.

Cam's skin was on fire, but she knew if she could get to the Advil she could hide her fever for another day. She took some and then went back to bed and waited for it to kick in. She dug in the pocket of her cargo pants and found the little eyedropper of pink liquid morphine that she hadn't used in weeks. For the hell of it, she squeezed three drops under her tongue. *I will be in a delightful mood today*, she thought. Like a crazy-eyed, homeless, psychotic vet from the Vietnam War, probably, but at least she would feel no pain. She was tempted to take a toke on her inhaler as well, but if her shortness of breath was caused by the tumors pressing against her heart and lungs, an inhaler was not going to help.

"Cam, you okay?" Asher called up to her from the bottom of her staircase.

"Yeah, come on up. There's something I need you to help me with."

Asher circled his way up the stairs. He wore brown plaid Bermudas and a soft brown T-shirt that showed the contours of his chest without being too obnoxiously tight. Asher the perfect.

Cam sat on her mattress leafing frantically through the pile of miracle mail that had found its way to her in Promise. She was looking for the little gray Hello Kitty envelope with Lily's handwriting on it. She had a feeling she should open it now before it was too late. She shook the Harvard admission papers upside down, and finally the envelope dropped, corner-first, onto her bed.

"I need you to open this," she said.

"Are you afraid to get a paper cut?"

"No," Cam said a little irritably. She wasn't in the mood for jokes. "It's from Lily. I need to open it, and I don't want to be alone when I do."

"No sweat. Let's open it." He sat down on the bed behind her, straddling her with his thighs.

She sighed and picked up the envelope.

He kissed her shoulder. "Go ahead, Cam."

The envelope popped right open, the seal moistened from weeks of misty, salty sea air. Cam pulled out a folded-up piece of lined paper. It was Lily's Flamingo List, torn from a spiral notebook more than a year ago. Lily had decorated it with black ink drawings of flamingos around the border, and inside she'd made neat check boxes to the left of every item on the list. Cam ran her finger over the ink as if reading Braille. She wanted to feel more of Lily, how she pressed the letters into the paper.

Most of the items on her list were checked off with a glittery, silver gel-pen check mark. Like:

* *Go to Italy.*
* *Learn to paint.*
* *Skydive.* (*Wow*, thought Cam.)
* *See a Broadway show.*
* *Get Bono's autograph.*

Next to this last one was a note, "enclosed." Cam shook the envelope and a movie ticket fell out onto the bed, an autograph scrawled across the back.

Lily had outlined the empty check boxes with a red Sharpie. With the same Sharpie, she had written, underlined and in caps, *CAMPBELL, DO THESE!!!*

The unchecked items included:

* *Skinny-dip.* (She lived on a lake, thought Cam. You would think she could have made this one happen.)
* *Go surfing.*
* *Eat surf & turf.* (She must have been free-associating.)
* *See a volcano erupting.*
* *Swim with dolphins.*
* *Visit the Taj Mahal.*

The final red box, left conspicuously and heartbreakingly blank, was *Find true love.*

"Shit," Cam said, as her heart bounced off her diaphragm and did a jackknife dive into her stomach. "Oh, Lily." Cam sighed, and she sucked in a deep breath to hold back her tears.

Asher took his carpentry pencil from behind his ear, reached over Cam's shoulder, and checked that one off immediately.

"Asher," Cam said.

"What? It's true," he said.

"I know. But . . ." She felt like she was stealing this one from Lily, and she felt for a second that she didn't deserve it.

"She's happy for you, Cam."

"I know."

Cam grabbed the pencil and checked off the volcano

because she'd been to Hawaii a couple of times for hula seminars. She checked off the surf & turf because eating the lobster was close enough. She'd seen the It's a Small World version of the Taj Mahal at Disney, and that would have to suffice. She checked it off.

"The rest we can do in one day," Asher said.

"We can?"

"We will."

Cam stood on the shore of the beach on the far side of the lighthouse, where she wrestled with a black heap of neoprene.

She could not figure out her wet suit. It was getting even colder in Maine as the summer stretched into August, so thankfully, Asher had built a little fire on the beach. It crackled and hissed a little and fought to stay alive in the sea breeze.

"Put it on like panty hose," Asher called from the shore, where he had dragged her enormous foam training board. "Or just don't wear it. Then you can check off the skinny-dipping and kill two birds."

"I'm not surfing naked, Asher."

"Rats," he said.

When she finally zipped up the suit, Asher made her lie down on the board in the sand and practice snapping up to her feet a couple of times. Finally they got into the water, paddled out a bit and sat straddling their boards, rocking side by side.

"This is the part where sharks mistake us for sea turtles."

"Asher! You know I hate sharks. Dammit!" The sea looked a dark and menacing gray all of a sudden.

"Just joking. We don't have sharks in Maine."

"You don't?"

"No. Wait. What's that?!" he pointed to something close to Cam's leg.

"Asher! Seriously! Stop!" Cam's eyes filled with tears for just a moment. She wasn't feeling well, she was emotional about completing this list for Lily, and she really didn't like sharks.

"Sorry, Cam. Really. I didn't know you'd be so afraid. Come here," he said, and he hugged her right there in the water. Their boards knocked into each other as they bobbed atop the ocean waves, trying not to tip over.

"Okay, lie down on your board. I'll push you into a wave at the right time, and then you just have to stand up."

"'Just stand up,' huh? I think if it were that easy there'd be more people surfing right now." Cam scanned the stretch of sand, sea grass, and rocks in front of her. They were the only people for miles around. The town off to her left seemed small and abandoned, like one of those miniature ceramic towns people put around their Christmas trees.

"You can do it," he said. "Allyoop."

Cam lay down on her board, and Asher held the back of it to steady it for her. He steered her into an oncoming wave right before it was about to curl over and break. Cam pressed herself from her hands to her feet in one smooth motion like she'd seen on TV, and then . . . she did it. She was standing on water. Master of the universe. She could feel the ocean rolling and rumbling beneath her feet. It was thrilling! Who wouldn't want to feel this?

She made it all the way to shore. A little beginner's luck surfing miracle. Asher pumped his arms up and down in celebration as he bobbed on his board. He found a wave and stood up on his own board, cutting back and forth inside it as perfectly as Cam expected he would. He asked her to go back out and try again, but as much as she'd enjoyed riding the wave, she was exhausted. She still had a fever masked only by Advil. Just getting into that wet suit had tired her out.

"You go," she said. "I can watch for a while."

On the beach she peeled herself out of her wet suit, bundled up in her fleece-lined hoodie and her sister's pink boots, and sat near the fire. She took out the notebook Izanagi had given her and unfolded Lily's list. She checked off *Go surfing* and then paged through the book. At some point during her stay in Promise, she had started recording the revelatory notions that her time here had seemed to accommodate.

* *Thoughts are energy, energy is matter, and matter doesn't disappear.*
* *Pay attention to coincidence.*
* *You can choose your identity.*

And a recent one: *Only the present moment matters.*

She sat with the present moment, watching Asher surf with the joy and concentration of a child. Surfing brought about conditions where you had no choice but to live in the present moment. You had to pay attention. Maybe that's why people got so spiritual about it. Cam was glad Lily had it on her list.

# THIRTY-FIVE

AT HOME THEY TOOK HOT SHOWERS. CAM POPPED SOME MORE ADVIL, and they rested before embarking on Asher's plan for the rest of the evening. He said he knew of a special cove in the bay, perfect for "night swimming," which was his euphemism for skinny-dipping.

"Oh, we should totally play that song," said Cam.

"Of course," said Asher. He would take her there in the boat after the sun went down.

The rest of the family was playing bocce on the lawn: Perry and Izanagi versus Nana and Alicia. Cam sat on the picnic table to watch for a while. She was cheering for the old-lady team. She didn't need to, though, because those two were ringers, and they had the situation under control. Asher joined her.

Cam looked over to the beach. The familiar purple and orange stripes behind the lighthouse seemed to hang there forever before they would let darkness fall.

"Can't we go now?" she asked after Asher got back from judging a close call on the bocce court. She was anxious to finish the list.

"No, it has to be dark," he said.

"I don't think anyone will see me."

"That's not why it has to be dark."

"Then why?"

"Patience, Campbell."

The boat's deep-throated engine rumbled through the black dark of the bay. As they got closer to their destination, Asher put on R.E.M., and the wake behind the boat started to glow and sparkle as if someone had put a spotlight underneath the water. He anchored the boat near the moonlit sandbar.

It had to be dark, it turned out, because he had taken her to a bioluminescent cove, where the water glowed magically in fluorescent, neon-colored sparks. Cam had heard of this before. The glowing was caused by ancient single-cell organisms that were neither plant nor animal. They were the beginnings of life. The inhabitants of the original primordial soup. The only place where electricity and water could coexist. It was science and it was magic and it was absolutely unbelievable.

When Cam looked down, she could see trails of glitter through the water. Tiny blue fish darted back and forth through the dinoflagellates, the magical glowing algae.

"Ladies first, madame," Asher said. "Hop in."

Cam skinny-dipped the wimpy way. First she eased into the water with her bathing suit on. The water was warm. She slid around in it, wiggling off her suit and throwing it back up to Asher in the boat. He caught it and stripped down before doing a naked cannonball. The splash lit up the sky like liquid fireworks.

It was shallow enough for Asher to stand, so he held Cam and kissed her as she wrapped her legs around him. The glitterlike pixie dust swirled around them when they moved. It was like swimming inside a star. She used her finger to paint a stripe of glow-in-the-dark water down his nose. He painted her face and her neck and her chest. They kissed and then swam to the sandbar where they made slippery, cosmic, half-here-and-half-in-some-world-beyond love.

"That wasn't on the list," said Cam.

"I was improvising."

"Good work." Cam was sprawled on the beach like a mermaid.

"I want to be with you forever," Asher said as he looked down at her. Her hair, now wavy and long, spun around her head like silky seaweed in the sand.

"This is forever." She stretched her arms up over her head and yawned contentedly.

"Don't get all metaphysical on me, Ass Whisperer." Asher smiled with the gorgeous dimple side of his mouth.

"No. This moment." Cam looped her hands around the back of his neck. "The present moment can be chopped into infinitely smaller present moments. This moment is forever. And it is all that matters."

They both heard a swoosh, which was eerie because they were alone in the dark in the middle of the ocean.

"Look!" he said, and they sat up on the beach.

Two lavender blue dolphins leapt from the sea simultaneously, creating an arc of sparkling gold water in the air behind them.

"They come here all the time," Asher said. "It's like a playground for them."

"Aren't they colorblind?"

"They must be able to see the light, I guess. Is this close enough to swimming with them, or do you want me to go get one for you?"

"I don't think you're going to have to," said Cam. The dolphins jumped again, a little closer to the sandbar and the boat. They were curious about Cam and Asher and wanted to play.

Cam stood and waded in up to her waist, still naked, like Brooke Shields in *The Blue Lagoon*. She watched a fin come closer to her. "Asher!" she said shakily. "You need to stand next to me. This is a little too sharklike."

"They're definitely not sharks, Cam."

Asher stood next to her with his arm around her waist. Cam stuck her hand out, and the dolphin slid up against it like an enormous purring cat at feeding time. Its skin was slippery to the touch.

"Grab onto his fin," Asher said. "He'll give you a ride."

She held on to either side of the fin, and the dolphin, all muscle, all power, took off.

Cam shrieked. "I hope you're watching this, Lily," she said, and she let the dolphin pull her about ten yards before letting go. She didn't want to be dragged into the oblivion of the deep sea.

As she swam back to Asher, she hoped for a sign, some validation that Lily's life was made complete. She had gotten used to everlasting sunsets, nighttime rainbows and flamingos flying through the snow. Some small part of her had changed its mind about the probability of miracles. She had almost come to expect them.

She waited for something, a light in the distance, a tidal wave, something grand and definitive. But there would be no sky-splitting miracles tonight. She thought she felt the soft tickling wisp of a butterfly kiss on her cheek and then a chilling breeze, and she took this to mean that Lily had officially moved on.

Asher's face grew sterner as he drove closer to the dock. Cam tried to tickle him. "I see your lips curling," she said, trying to get him to smile. His mood confused her. He slammed things around as he prepared to dock the boat, and finally she saw it. She looked toward shore, at the big red-and-white SMITTY'S LOBSTER POUND sign, and she saw a thin blonde sitting on top of a stack of lobster traps with her legs crossed, swinging her front leg back and forth, waiting for the boat to return.

"Shit," Asher said.

It was "Marlene," according to the personalized license plate on her Mustang. She was the woman, too old for her mother to have used the Land's End catalog as a baby-naming book, who was with Asher in his Jeep that night.

Asher didn't look at Cam as he deboated with his head down and his hands in his pockets like a guilty little boy about to get scolded. He walked toward Marlene, and Cam's hands went numb. Finally, he turned back to Cam and said, "I'm sorry. Just give me one second, 'kay?"

Cam's skin burned in humiliation, in sadness, in the recognition that there was no righteous place in reality for their love.

She climbed into Cumulus and turned on the heat, trying to melt the chill in her bones. Five minutes later, Marlene was still talking animatedly from the driver's seat of the Mustang while Asher sat silently with his head down. This was going to be a while.

Cam pulled out of the driveway of the marina and willed herself to blend into the mist. Invisible, invincible, and alone.

# THIRTY-SIX

CAM WOKE UP WITH AN EVEN WORSE FEVER. HER THROAT HURT, HER right side ached, and her stomach felt like it was filled with cement. She knew she should probably get to the hospital, but she also knew that if she went in, this time, she would never come out.

She was barely able to get down the stairs and into the kitchen, where Perry sat at the island reading a book.

"I thought you were with Asher," Perry said as Cam opened the fridge and looked around inside for something that wouldn't make her throw up.

"No."

"Why aren't you with Asher?"

"I don't need to be with him 24-7, Perry."

"Are you guys breaking up?"

"God! Perry. No, okay. I'm just having a glass of orange juice, which I can do very well on my own without Asher."

Just then Asher came into the kitchen, grabbed Cam from behind, and dipped her. "No, you can't," he said. "You need me to pour you some orange juice."

"Actually, I don't," she said, completely deadpan.

"Brrrr. That's cold, Cam Chowda," Asher said, looking seriously into her face. He still had her in a dip.

"I told you I didn't like the Cam Chowda thing," she mumbled, and she wriggled free.

Asher righted himself. "I am in the dog house, no? *Le château de bow-wow.*"

"No. You just have to know that I don't need you in the way you love to be needed." Cam opened a cabinet and poured herself a bowl of cereal that she had no intention of eating.

Perry took her book into the living room.

"You seemed to need me yesterday."

"No. I'm not the kind of person who needs people," she said, reaching in the fridge for some milk.

"Campbell," Asher said after taking a deep breath, "I have a past with her, all right? But she was just a temporary fling. A placeholder for the real thing. You are the real thing." He stood, taking hold of her hand and stroking her palm with the tip of his rough index finger.

Cam pulled her hand away. "That's nice. I'm glad I'm the real thing. Isn't that an ad for Coke? "

Asher moved toward her again, but she pushed him away.

"Just be honest with yourself, okay, Asher? Just admit that there's a strong chance that you're going to waste away in this stupid town getting the life sucked out of you by the likes of that woman, who will take whatever you give her and keep asking for more unless you grow some balls and get the courage to create your own life."

"Cam."

"You won't, though, will you? You will never leave your precious big-fish-in-little-pond status. You're a coward. You could be somebody. You could have a future, and you're too afraid to try. What a waste," Cam said as she threw the milk back into the fridge and slammed the door. Her hands were shaking, and she cried, hot, angry, feverish tears.

Asher took a step away from her, like she might take a swing at him. "I like it here, Campbell. I have everything I need. Why would I want to be anywhere else?"

"Because most people want things, Asher," she said to the fridge door. "They want something, and they go after it. It's not okay to wait for your life to happen to you."

"I thought you said I should reside in the present moment."

"That was me. *I* should reside in the present moment. But *you* should plan your future because you effing have one."

"You have one, too. Have you sent those forms back to Harvard?"

Cam turned and looked at him. "We're not talking about me, Asher, but *of course* I did. Come September I leave here, and I never look back. How could you think this was more than a summer fling?"

"I don't know, maybe because you told me you loved me. Or maybe you didn't. You said it in Samoan, so I have no idea what you said."

"I'm sure I'm not the first girl who's told you that."

"At least the other ones meant it."

She leaned down onto the counter with her head down and listened as he walked away and slammed the front door behind him. She knew she had to push him away, but she'd never felt heavier. The force of gravity pulled so strongly on her body, she thought she might get sucked through the floor.

Cam had cried herself to sleep and was woken up by the sound of the wind whistling through the windows of the widow's walk. For the first time since they'd moved to Promise two months ago, clouds gathered in the sky. Gray clouds that seemed to be moving at warp speed, like in one of those nature documentaries where they dramatically speed up the weather. One big raindrop finally splatted against her east-facing window, and it was like the keystone drop that, once loosened, let all the other ones fall behind it. The rain began to pelt the windows like shrapnel.

At first she could hear individual drops, and then the

walls of water slammed against the window with slapping thuds. Cam had seen some impressive storms in Florida—deep, resonating thunderclaps with crackling displays of lightning—but the staggering thing about this storm was its permanence. Storms in Florida were fickle and ephemeral. Utterly temporary. This one had settled in for the long haul. Cam wrapped herself in her blankets and kept watching it, analyzing the shape-shifting shades of gray.

"He's out there, you know," she heard a scratchy old lady's voice say from the corner of the cupola.

Her fever must have been really high because Cam could actually see the shadowy figure of the long-haired woman from Asher's photograph. *Olivia, 1896* was sitting upright in the antique wooden chair where Cam usually piled her laundry. It probably *was* a pile of laundry, Cam reminded herself.

She'd had hallucinatory fevers before. The hallucinations usually went away if you didn't talk back to them, so Cam ignored her.

"You really know how to dole out the 'tough love.' Isn't that what they call it on *Dr. Phil*?" said the shadow.

*It's a pile of laundry*, Cam repeated to herself. *It's just a chair and a lumpy pile of laundry.* She fumbled around the floor next to her bed to find the Advil and swallowed eight at once.

"Pretty selfish of you to go ahead and decide for him how he needs to handle this," said the chair.

"He doesn't need to experience any more loss," Cam couldn't stop herself from saying. "It's better for him to be angry than depressed."

*Rats*, she thought. Now that Cam had spoken to her, the creepy witch would never go away.

"You are such a know-it-all," the widow said. "Maybe he needs to grieve. He needs to say good-bye. Maybe he needs some closure."

Cam hated that word, *closure*. It was even worse than *tough love*. "Where did you get ahold of the self-help books?"

"There is so much you don't know about men."

"Oh, and you know so much. Sitting up here and waiting your whole life for one to come home."

"We weren't put on this earth to go it alone."

"Maybe not, but we all die alone, don't we?"

"What am I, chopped liver?"

"You're here to help me die?" A crack of lightning lit up the cupola, and Cam could see the figure more clearly. She sat with her eyes down, focusing nonchalantly on the needlework in her lap. She wore an ankle-length black skirt and a black cardigan sweater. Her nose was long and sharp. Her face was wrinkled and grizzled now, but her hair was still a beautiful, wavy strawberry blonde.

"Ayuh."

"Now?"

"Soon, child."

"You are a pile of laundry."

"Mmmm."

"Why did they send you? Why didn't they send my father? Or Lily? And if this town is so magic, why can't you just save me? How is it magic to give me something to live for and then just pull it out from under me? That's cruel." *All the bullshit rainbows and flamingos and snowstorms in July can't stop me from dying like some crazy lady, talking to a chair*, Cam thought. How could she have believed that they could?

"He's out there, you know," the widow said again, lifting a creepy, gray, arthritic finger and pointing toward the sea. Cam got up and looked out the window. The sea looked like it was boiling. Hot licks of black lavalike seawater crashed together at odd angles. It was chaos. Cam looked back at the pile of laundry, but the woman had disappeared.

Her gaze shifted to the carriage house, just twenty yards away.

Cam sat on the bed, still watching the storm. "Pretty crazy, isn't it?" she asked as a white zipper of lightning seemed to crack the sky in half.

"Hey, hon, I need to tell you something," Alicia said, handing Cam a steaming milky mug. She had come upstairs with some hot cocoa.

"Yeah?"

"Perry said that you and Asher had an argument."

"So?"

"Well, apparently after that, he left." Alicia sat on the bed and held Cam's hand.

"So?"

"In the boat, hon. He left in the boat, and no one's been able to contact him. He's lost out there in that storm."

Cam looked again at the violent churning of the sea and sky. *He can handle this, right?* she thought at first, imagining the strength of his capable forearms hoisting and steering and managing the swells. *There is nothing he can't do.* Then another clap of thunder rumbled deeply in the distance, rolling toward them menacingly like an oncoming train. It banged with a final, ear-splitting smack.

"I'm going to get him," said Cam. "I'll take the kayak." She hoisted herself off the bed and began rummaging through the laundry—*See, it's only laundry.* Adrenaline had taken over, and she forgot her pain. She pulled on her jeans and a couple of T-shirts and made for the stairs. She could do this. She had taken a few lifesaving courses at the Polynesian's pool where they taught you how to make a life preserver out of your wet jeans by tying the cuffs together in knots and filling them with air.

"Campbell, you cannot go out there."

"Yes, I can," said Cam, but as she reached for the railing

around the stairs she swooned from dizziness and almost fell over.

Her mom grabbed her elbow. "Wait for him here, Campbell. That's all you can do, sweetheart."

Cam threw open the glass door of the cupola and stepped onto the actual widow's walk. The slanting rain soaked her instantly. She screamed "Asher!" into the wind. "Asher, you idiot. Come back!" She had wanted him to leave and enjoy his life without her, not leave the planet.

"He can't hear you, Campbell!" her mom yelled.

She watched the beam of the lighthouse swing around the bay and scanned the water for a boat, but all she could see were dark platinum waves and whitecaps slapping into one another and hurtling toward the shore. "He's got to be right out there. Why can't someone just go look for him?" she cried desperately.

"They can't send anyone out in that storm, Campbell. We just have to wait for things to calm down."

Cam walked back and forth in the rain. "I'm staying out here to look for him."

"Campbell, don't be silly, you can't do anything from there," her mom said.

"No. This is my fault. I'm waiting for him."

"Campbell!" her mom said, exasperated, and then she went inside to find a raincoat and umbrella. She found Asher's yellow slicker sailing suit and forced Cam to come inside, dry off, and then put it on before stepping back out onto the widow's walk. "Why can't you wait inside? That's why they built this thing. For waiting."

"I just have to be out here, okay?" She needed to be feeling what he was feeling, without any impediments between them. She had to be out there, sending him thoughts, because thoughts are energy, energy is matter, and matter never disappears. Her thoughts could keep him close. She knew if she stopped paying attention he would drift away forever. "You don't need to stay with me."

Her mother stayed with her, of course, and the two of them shrank down and huddled against the wall. Alicia tried to shield Cam from the rain with umbrellas, but they kept whipping inside out from the wind. Finally she gave up and put her head down against her knees. Cam thought she heard her mumbling some Hail Marys.

"Is that the right prayer?"

"It's the only one I know. I'm a bad Catholic."

"That's okay," said Cam.

She kept up her vigil, visualizing over and over again Asher steering the boat for home. She imagined it drifting toward the dock, and then she saw him in her mind's eye, hopping off gracefully and tying up the lines like she'd seen him do.

It was still raining when the first white rays of sun tried to shoot their way through the storm clouds. The wind had let up a little, but it blew the rain sideways against Cam's face. The bay was calm now, but black and empty.

Cam tried to stand up but stumbled and fell onto her mom's knees.

"Campbell, my God, you're burning up!" Alicia said.

She helped Cam get inside and take off her clothes and then the convulsing began. The cold, the fever, the pain, and the exhaustion came together and erupted inside of her, and she could not stop herself from shaking. She was shaking so hard that it took Perry, Nana, and Alicia working together to get her into a warm shower and get her dressed. But the shaking continued until the seizure began, and that's when they knew that the little square brick hospital in Promise was not going to do, and they piled in the car headed for Portland.

# THIRTY-SEVEN

STRANGELY ENOUGH, CAM FELT SAFE HERE. BACK IN THE HALLOWED, sterilized halls of Western medicine, her journey had come full circle. The irregular beeping of the monitors soothed her, and she felt cool, clean and hydrated, thanks to the saline solution pumping into her veins at 10 ccs per minute. They must have been pumping something else into her, too, because in spite of having been stabbed through the back of her rib cage with two thick chest tubes, she felt no pain.

She felt nothing at all, really. Was that her foot sticking out of the blanket, with the chipped remainders of black nail polish speckling her toes? It had to be. That was embarrassing. To be caught at death's door without having had a pedicure. She wondered if the undertaker would paint her toenails black. *What do they do with the toes?* she wondered. Probably just cover them up. Just as well.

She heard that familiar hushed, mumbling sound of Alicia in a grave conversation with a doctor, and she knew it would soon begin to escalate. Especially when he told her what Cam already knew. That this was the end.

The hospice nurse had already been in, and Cam had heard her conversation with Perry.

"It will be over very soon, when the fingernails start to turn blue."

"Blue like when your lips turn blue or like when your fingernail falls off blue?" Perry asked.

"Like the lips," said the nurse, and then she left, leaving some information packets about death and dying.

"No. That can't be true!" Cam heard Alicia yell. "You should have seen her two days ago. She was perfectly fine. How can this have happened in two days?"

"I believe she's been fighting this for quite a while. Seven years, it says on the chart," explained the doctor.

"Yes, but that was before," Alicia said.

"Before what?" he asked.

"I don't know," Alicia sighed. "Before we brought her to Maine. She was getting well here."

"People often go through a kind of a wellness period. Or remission before a more serious attack. We don't quite understand it. There's still so much we don't know," he admitted.

"No. There's still so much *you* don't know," Alicia said. "This was something different. She really *was* well. It was not a wellness *period*. I need you to find me someone who knows what they're talking about."

"Respectfully, Ms. Cooper—"

"Now! I want someone else in here, who is not just going to give up on my daughter!"

"Ms. Coop—"

"Mom," Cam moaned without really meaning to. "Give the guy a break, will you? He's just doing his job."

"Cam?"

"It's time for you to say something nice to me. You know, like, 'You were the best daughter, aside from Perry, that I ever could have imagined. I feel so lucky to have known you. Honored to have been your mother.' Something like that. Doesn't the hospice brochure give you some kind of a script if you don't know what to say?"

"I know what to say, Campbell."

"Then you better say it, okay? For your sake, not mine," said Cam. Her mom exhaled, let her arms fall to her sides, and walked over to the bed.

"You cannot conceive of the depths of my sorrow, Campbell Maria Cooper." Alicia brought her fist to her mouth and her other hand to the rail of the bed and took a deep breath before she continued. "I will never be the same when you are gone. Things for me will be dim and gray and flat. But there is one thing that will keep me going, Campbell, and that is a belief in my connection to you. This thing. This crazy enmeshed love feeling that I have for you is real. Like this cup is real. Or this phone is real. And it will not just go away when you do. Okay? Wherever you are going, you will be connected to me by this thing, and you will never, ever be alone, okay? I want you to know that."

"Wow, was that in the brochure?" Cam asked, sniffling.

"No, I made it up," said Alicia, wiping her eyes with a hospital tissue.

"It was good."

"Thanks."

"Thank you for everything you've done. And for bringing me here, Mom." Promise hadn't saved her, but she understood now that it had made her life more complete than if she had lived a hundred years in Orlando. "I love you."

Cam closed her eyes, letting her tears slide across her temples and land on the pillow. Her mom kissed her on the forehead, and then Cam turned her head to the side.

"Cam!"

"I'm not dead, Nana. I'm just resting."

"Oh, thank God," said Nana.

Perry held Cam's hand and said, "You know, I think you gave me the wrong advice."

"I did?"

"Yeah. I think I should try to be more like you. Not less." Perry climbed onto the bed with Cam, so Cam could stroke her wavy blonde hair with her fingers.

"That's nice, Per," she said. "Take care of Mom."

"I will."

Nana was at the foot of the bed, rubbing her hand back and forth on Cam's shins. She hung her head as she prayed silently through her tears. "Don't be sad, Nana," Cam said. "If things go your way, I'll be having breakfast with Jesus or something, right?"

"I don't know about breakfast. Maybe brunch. He likes my sausage and peppers."

"How do you know?"

"It's between me and him," she said. She made the sign of the cross and then said, "*Te amo*, Campbell Maria."

"*Te amo*, Nana."

It was past midnight, and everyone had fallen asleep in the uncomfortable reclining chairs around her bed. Cam was grateful that Izanagi held her mother as they slept together in one chair. They had remembered at the last minute to bring Tweety, and he slept on his little perch inside his cage, making tiny little puffs with his exhales.

The whole stage had been set. It was time for her to leave, but Cam could feel herself holding on. Clinging to something.

She had learned a little about hope this summer, and she was going to hold out hope until her last wish came true.

She knew he would come to say good-bye. She knew he would make it back. And when she opened her eyes, Asher was there.

He was wearing his father's old cable-knit fisherman's sweater, and he leaned on the bed rail as he looked at her. He'd been crying, and his eyes were red rimmed and swollen.

"Are you real?" she asked him. She had been drifting in and out of dreams for a few hours now, and she couldn't be sure if it was him or some cruel apparition concocted by the crazy chemicals of her dying brain.

"Yes," he whispered.

"Prove it," she said. "Pinch me or something."

"Cam, I don't want to pinch you."

"Then kiss me already."

He placed his blistered hand on her forehead and kissed her gently on the lips. His lips and face were rough, and he tasted like the sea.

"I love you," she said. She wanted to get that in before she ran out of time.

"I know," he said, and that was better than him saying it back. She needed to know that he knew.

"The argument—"

"Cam, it's okay."

"I wasn't trying to send you out into the Perfect Storm."

"It *was* the perfect storm. I was trying to leave, and it

kept pushing me back into the harbor. It was like it knew I needed to be here. With you."

"Asher?"

"Yeah?" The tears now flowed freely down his face.

"You were right about something."

"Ass Whisperer, I thought you were always right."

"Usually. But you were right about one thing."

"What's that?"

"The Jimmy Stewart thing."

"It's a wonderful life?"

"Yeah. However it plays itself out."

Cam looked out the window. A handsome, tall orangey-pink flamingo stood alone in a square patch of grass in the courtyard.

"Buddy!" she said delightedly, but she couldn't tell if she thought it or if she actually said it out loud. The courtyard was flooded by a bright white light. Cam felt her entire soul become imbued with love. *How about that*, Cam thought. Death did not mean being without love.

She felt herself drifting. Her gaze followed Buddy as he spread his wings, flapped twice, and then took off, his neck folded in a *Z*, his long pink legs trailing behind him . . . departing.

# ACKNOWLEDGMENTS

THIS BOOK COMES TO YOU ON THE SHOULDERS OF COUNTLESS FRIEND-ships. My heartfelt thanks to new friends who: got me day jobs, shared their offices (and beach houses), watched my child, bought me lunch, and sent me constant loving support. And to old friends who believed in the work a long time ago when believing seemed absurd. You are my heart and my other hearts.

I'm thankful to Cam, who bravely showed me her voice. Thankful to my daughter, Cadence, who makes this mothering gig a wonderfully delightful romp. Thankful to my own mom for showing me the way. And thankful to my gem of a husband, whose kind, brilliantly funny spirit inspired these pages. Many thanks to both his family and mine for cheering me on.

Thanks to the far-out and talented Alexandra Bullen for sharing her success when she didn't have to. And to "Team

Miracles":  the fabulous folks at Razorbill for their keen vision and committed support, and Josh Bank, Joelle Hobeika, and Sara Shandler at Alloy, whose brilliant ideas and persistent, encouraging warmth could melt through the most unyielding of writer's blocks.

Many thanks to you for reading.

*Namaste.*